CANAPÉS FOR THE KITTIES

CANAPÉS FOR
THE KITTIES

Marian Babson

St. Martin's Press ♏ New York

A THOMAS DUNNE BOOK.
An imprint of St. Martin's Press.

CANAPÉS FOR THE KITTIES. Copyright © 1996 by Marian
Babson. All rights reserved. Printed in the United States
of America. No part of this book may be used or
reproduced in any manner whatsoever without written
permission except in the case of brief quotations
embodied in critical articles or reviews. For information,
address St. Martin's Press, 175 Fifth Avenue,
New York, N.Y. 10010.

Library of Congress Cataloging-in-Publication Data

Babson, Marian.
    Canapés for the kitties / Marian Babson.
        p.   cm.
    "A Thomas Dunne book."
    ISBN 0-312-16929-9
    I. Title.
    PS3552.A25C36   1997
    813'.54—dc21   97-16232
                                        CIP

First published in Great Britain by Collins Crime,
an imprint of HarperCollins*Publishers*
as *Miss Petunia's Last Case*

First U.S. Edition: September 1997

10   9   8   7   6   5   4   3   2   1

To
ELIZABETH WALTER
who read them all

CANAPÉS FOR THE KITTIES

1

CHAPTER TWENTY

Miss Petunia Pettifogg adjusted her gold-rimmed pince-nez and surveyed the tea table with deep satisfaction. 'I see that our invaluable Mrs Bloggs has outdone herself again,' she remarked to her sister.

'Jam sponge.' Lily began lifting the little white muslin tents covering the dishes to display the treasures hidden beneath. 'Scones, crumpets, walnut bread . . . woman must have been baking all day.'

Miss Petunia closed her eyes briefly and inhaled the delicious fragrances. All part of the comfort and delight of coming home to their dear Blossom Cottage after a tedious and exhausting day in London trying to convince the singularly obtuse hierarchy at New Scotland Yard that there had, indeed, been yet another murder in the deceptively rural and peaceful village of St Waldemar Boniface.

'Let's eat,' Lily said, tilting the teapot and beginning to pour.

'But . . . where's Marigold?' Miss Petunia looked around for her youngest sister.

'Off on some mysterious errand of her own,' Lily said. 'Don't know how long she'll be. No point waiting for her.'

Even as Lily spoke, they heard the sound of footsteps running down the path to Blossom Cottage and the quick scrape of a key in the lock. Then the front door slammed on loud and obnoxious shouting which came to them, unfortunately, all too clearly.

'Come back out here!' a male voice howled. 'And I'll *do* yer! Come out and I'll show yer what it's for!'

Another door slammed and Marigold was suddenly in the room with them, leaning against the door, her red-gold curls dancing, her bright blue eyes sparkling with the merriment of the chase.

'Oh, dear!' She tossed her head impishly. 'I'm rather afraid poor Colonel Battersby is *overrefreshed* again.'

'You mean the drunken sot is drunk again!' her sister Lily growled tigerishly. 'You must stop encouraging these vulgarians. One day you'll go too far.'

'I was merely following your instructions,' Marigold pouted. 'I was questioning him – very subtly – about the strange disappearance of his sister-in-law, the cyanide in his wife's cocoa, the bonfire which destroyed any evidence that might have been hidden in the compost pile and the reason why there were bloodstains on his knitted silk tie when, for no reason at all, he suddenly got very upset and began shouting at me.'

'So you came home immediately,' Miss Petunia said. 'How very sensible of you.' Outside, the shouting died to sporadic sulky outbursts.

'I most certainly did *not* desert my post that easily,' Marigold said indignantly. 'I went to the bar and bought him another drink. When I came back, he seemed quite reasonable and we had a pleasant little talk. He asked me how much I was insured for. Then, before I could answer, he said no matter how much it was, it wasn't enough.' She frowned thoughtfully. 'I hadn't realized that Colonel Battersby had taken to selling life insurance as a sideline.'

'He's sly, that man,' Lily growled. 'Sly and dangerous. As too many women in this village have found out . . . too late.'

'He's gone very quiet suddenly.' Miss Petunia felt a strange flutter of apprehension.

'Perhaps he's fallen asleep,' Marigold giggled.

'Passed out, you mean,' Lily said, lighting another cigarette.

'Oh, my dear, I wish you wouldn't.' Miss Petunia was moved to make one of her rare protests. 'You don't want to shorten your life.'

'Be quiet!' Lily ordered roughly.

'It's only for your own good, dear.' Miss Petunia was hurt.

'Not that, Pet –' Lily gestured towards the front of the house. 'I mean, listen . . .'

'Yes, I can hear something!' Marigold gasped, her eyes widen-

10

ing. 'It's the car! Of course, I took the keys away from him because he was in no fit condition to drive. That was when he got upset all over again. Then I threw the keys into the bushes when he was gaining on me, in order to distract him. He must have found them and gone back for the car. Oh, I hope he doesn't kill someone!'

'He's racing the motor,' Lily judged. 'He's heading this way –'

There was a tremendous crash at the front door.

'He's ram-raiding us!' Marigold shrieked.

'I'll put a stop to this!' Lily snarled. They all rushed out into the front hall.

The door was half off its hinges; the motor car blocked any hope of getting past it. As they stared aghast, it burst into flames.

'That does it!' Lily roared. 'The man is a menace and must be stopped. Marigold, ring the fire brigade. I'll take care of Colonel Battersby!' She led them into the front parlour and opened the window.

'Battersby, you old fool!' she bellowed. 'You're under arrest! This is a Citizen's Arrest! I demand that you step forward and surrender immed –'

The rock struck her on the temple with great force, hurling her back into the room where she lay motionless.

'Lily! Lily!' Miss Petunia knelt beside her. 'Speak to me!'

'Oh, Petunia –' Marigold put down the telephone, her hands shaking. 'There's no answer. There's not even a dial tone. Colonel Battersby must have cut the wires. The line is dead!'

'So is Lily,' Miss Petunia said grimly.

'What?' Marigold rushed over to stand beside her, looking down at her fallen sister. 'You can't mean it!'

'Thus was Goliath slain!' Miss Petunia rose to her feet, one hand clasping Marigold for support. Suddenly she felt quite giddy. 'Colonel Battersby has gone too far!'

'Oh, Petunia, what are you going to do?'

'Lily shall be avenged! Marigold, run upstairs and get me Daddy's old Service revolver. We have always kept it well cleaned and oiled in his memory. Now we are forced to take the law into our own hands!'

Marigold left the door ajar as she dashed from the room and Miss Petunia became aware of grey tendrils of smoke curling along the floor. As soon as she had dealt with Colonel Battersby, it might be wise to leave the cottage, as it seemed to be alight.

In the distance, she could hear Marigold coughing as she stumbled up the stairs.

'Be careful!' she called out instinctively. Marigold always dashed about so impetuously. Already she must have found the gun, for she was now hurrying back downstairs. The smoke was thicker.

Marigold must have been halfway down the stairs when there was a squeal and a shot rang out. There was the sound of a body – Marigold's body – falling down the stairs.

'Marigold!' Miss Petunia dashed into the front hall to find Marigold, as she had feared, lying at the foot of the stairs. Daddy's gun was still clasped to her bosom, above it a dark-red stain blossomed.

'Oh, Petunia,' Marigold said faintly. 'I tripped.' And said no more.

Tears, as well as smoke, blinding her eyes, Miss Petunia dragged Marigold's body into the parlour to lie beside Lily's. She could not bring herself to remove the gun from Marigold's hands.

She was alone now and must face her fate as best she might. The hallway, she had noticed, was alight at both ends. Colonel Battersby had obviously set another fire by the back door to trap them in the house.

There was only the window for escape. Coughing, she made her way to it. Strange, how difficult it was becoming to walk.

The window was still open, curtains fluttering in the breeze. Was that wise? Wasn't there something about not creating a draught in a house that was on fire? Perhaps she should close the window . . .

No! No! She must get out through the window. Laboriously, she threw one knee up on the sill and –

The rock crashed into her temple. Ah, but her head was harder than Lily's, she congratulated herself, even as she was being borne backwards by the force of the blow.

She fell across Lily and Marigold and rested on them a moment, fighting for breath. The room was completely fogged with smoke now. To think that she had reprimanded dear Lily for lighting a cigarette!

Smoke inhalation! She was being overcome by the smoke. Miss Petunia tried to push herself to her feet, even to her hands and knees, but she felt too giddy. She must try . . . she must fight . . . but . . .

As she collapsed again across her sisters' bodies, the thought came to her that this really was . . . *t*

h

e   *e*   *n*   *d*

Lorinda Lucas slid the last page out of her typewriter with a feeling of peace and accomplishment.

Quickly, she rolled another page into the machine. While the euphoria lasted, she could force herself to put the repellent Petunia, the nauseating Marigold and the appalling Lily through a few more of their paces. Paces which, unfortunately, would leave them triumphantly alive and kicking and ready to trudge through the next book in the series.

She typed steadily for another hour, then pushed her chair away from the desk. She stood and crossed to the dark-red filing cabinet where she hid her guilty secret, the death-dealing chapter, in the increasingly thickening folder marked 'FINAL CHAPTERS'. Soon she would have to begin another file folder – if she kept on like this.

And she probably would. Only to herself could she admit the deep satisfaction it gave her to dispose of the detestable Sibling Spinster Sleuths ('Try saying it quickly three times,' a critic had written. 'A few drinks may help, but you need a few drinks to pick up this sort of book in the first place.') in ever more lurid and gory detail. Other series writers might moan about how sick they were of their creations, but her own safety valve was blowing off steam quite nicely, thank you, as she wrote alternative endings for each book, each story and, sometimes, each idea. Reichenbach Falls had nothing on this!

As she turned away from the filing cabinet, the view from the window caught her eye. A picture-postcard village of quaint cottages, several with thatched roofs, sprawled into the distance along both sides of a winding road. Beyond it, a curving river sparkled in the fading sunlight. On the other side of her house, she knew, the view was of the High Street, which had several shops too many for a real village; the place had ideas above its station and was aspiring to Town status.

Lorinda made a face at the olde-worlde prettiness displayed below her and turned away, conscious of a dissatisfaction that was not solely caused by her professional discontent.

It had seemed like such a good idea at the time.

'I've made the discovery of a lifetime,' Dorian had brayed over the bridge table a year ago. 'Brimful Coffers. Delightful little village. Undiscovered, unspoiled, easy reach of London. Several highly desirable bijou residences going for a song because of the modernization they require. Cheap as they are, the natives can't afford 'em, but they'd just about come out of petty cash for *us* – and we'd always be sure of a fourth for bridge.'

Somehow, it had escaped her attention that she didn't care all that much for bridge. After living here for six months, she wasn't sure that she cared all that much for her colleagues, either.

Dorian King, as befitted the creator of Field Marshal Sir Oliver Aldershot, was a brilliant organizer. One by one, he had driven his chosen colleagues down to the village, introduced them to the local estate agent, accompanied them on their tours through the properties on offer, helpfully pointing out improvements that could be made . . . doing everything, in fact, except forcibly guiding their hands as they signed the contracts to purchase. Nor did he help with any mortgage arrangements, as it became clear to his victims that his idea of petty cash varied considerably from theirs.

Even so, it was, she had to admit, a lovely little cottage, and just what she had thought she wanted. Furthermore, the cats adored the garden and enjoyed exploring their immense new territory, revelling in a freedom that traffic had denied them heretofore. Another positive aspect was that there was no lack of cat-sitters or someone to pop in and feed them when she had to go up to town or off on a research trip. Nor did she mind being called upon in her turn to look after someone else's pet. No, the growing unease went deeper than that, but it was early days yet and no doubt they would all soon settle down satisfactorily.

Flip-flop . . . flip-flop . . . the familiar sound was followed by the thud of soft little paws on the stairs as the cats bounded up and headed unerringly for her study.

Had-I was in the lead, of course, with But-Known right behind her. They made a quick tour of inspection, then sat down side by side and regarded her with bright-eyed improbable innocence. She knew that look.

'*Now* what have you done?' She was instantly suspicious.

Flip-flap . . . flap . . . flap, scrabble . . . '*Aaarreeeooow . . .*'

'Oh, not again!' she scolded.

'*Meerryooowrrr . . .*' The wail of distress soared upwards, filling the air, beginning to border on panic.

'All right, all right, I'm coming,' she called. The cats rose to their feet and followed her down the stairs. 'Let's go and see what the damage is,' she told them.

The huge orange cat was well and truly jammed into the catflap. Head and shoulders protruded, wriggling, with one trapped paw waving under his chin. He looked up piteously at Lorinda and renewed his struggles, but he could move no farther forward, nor could he back out.

'Oh, Pudding,' she said reproachfully. Pudding was not really his name, but it should be. He was sweet and thick. 'Will you never learn?'

'*Aaarrreeeooow,*' he moaned, trying to twist around.

'No, no, don't do that. You'll only make it worse.' She stooped to pet him comfortingly. 'Just be calm and I'll get help.'

Had-I was going to be no help at all. Was she ever? With a disdainful look at the helpless captive, she strolled over to her bowl and ostentatiously began to munch.

'*Meeeyyyaaooo . . .*'

Had-I shot him a smug look and took another morsel, crunching it loudly. She was clearly saying, '*Yum-yum-yummy.*'

'You stop taunting the poor thing!' Lorinda pushed Had-I aside, scooped up a few of the tiny fish-shapes and carried them over to the catflap.

'Here . . .' She popped one into the eager mouth and then another. He was calming down now, with his mouth full and a trusted figure stroking his fevered brow.

'That's better.' Lorinda went to the telephone in the living room and pushed the automatic dialling button for one of the frequently called numbers. Then she held the receiver a safe distance from her ear, waiting for the shot that began the answer tape.

'BANG!! Ya missed me, sucker! You don't get Macho Magee that easy! I'm on the prowl down those mean streets with my trusty Roscoe, looking for trouble. Maybe I'll find it. If you want to find me, leave a message when the screaming dies . . .' A long shrill scream ended the announcement.

'You'd better come over here and pull out your trusty Roscoe,' Lorinda announced briskly. 'He's stuck in the catflap again.'

'They do it deliberately.' There was a click and the querulous voice began complaining. 'I've seen them. Those wretched creatures of yours lead my poor Roscoe on.'

It was too true to argue with. Had-I and But-Known all too clearly thought it was the best joke in town to lure poor Roscoe into their catflap and then laugh at him when he couldn't clear it and jammed halfway through.

'He ought to know better by now,' Lorinda said. 'But he's well stuck in this time and I'm afraid of hurting him.'

'Oh, all right. I'll be right there.' He slammed down the phone and Lorinda went back into the kitchen.

'All right, Roscoe,' she said carefully; she mustn't get caught calling him Pudding. 'Daddy's on the way.'

Still tranquillized by his snack, Roscoe regarded her amiably. But-Known, perhaps with a belated attack of conscience, was busily washing his face, which was also helping to soothe him. He had stopped struggling, but still looked terribly uncomfortable.

Had-I had abandoned her food bowl, finding no fun in it if Lorinda was going to be such a spoilsport as to share the munchies with Roscoe, and was perched on a chair watching the others. Now she lifted her head and turned towards the window, aware of an approaching presence before Lorinda could see or hear it.

It had to be Macho. Taking her cue, Lorinda gently eased the door open, trying not to panic Roscoe.

'Steady on, boy. It's all right. Don't worry.'

Reassurances were useless. Roscoe let out an unearthly shriek at discovering he was moving horizontally through the air at no volition of his own and without human arms around him.

'I'm coming! I'm coming, Roscoe!' The figure at the far end of the garden broke into a shambling run and lurched forward precipitously. 'Hang in there!'

16

Really, there wasn't much else Roscoe could do. He swung, suspended by his ample middle, from the catflap, hind legs scrabbling for purchase and yowled his terror to the skies.

'Here I am! Daddy's here!' Macho Magee dropped to his knees beside his anxious pet and glared up at Lorinda. 'I don't know why you have to have one of those porthole-type catflaps. It's antisocial!'

'It was here when I bought the house.' Lorinda sighed, they had been through this before. 'And my *own* cats,' she pointed out, 'have no trouble with it at all.'

'Nevertheless, the thing is a menace. You should take it out and replace it with a square flap with one end flush with the floor. That's the best kind. It's what I have.'

'It's draughtier,' she said, without adding that she did not particularly wish to allow Roscoe, however sweet he might be, unlimited access to her house. Nor did she think Had-I and But-Known would appreciate an interloper roaming through their territory at will, however well they got on with him.

Roscoe had begun purring trustfully and Macho Magee got to his feet to assess the problem.

'It looks pretty bad this time,' he said fretfully, glaring at Lorinda as though it were her fault. 'We may have to dismantle the flap.'

'No,' Lorinda said.

'Mmmm . . .' He walked around the door, checking both ends of his cat. 'Perhaps, if we grease him . . .'

'We did that last time and he didn't like it.'

'True, and it took him days to get all the butter out of his fur.' Macho took another turn around the door. Roscoe was beginning to look anxious again.

'If you can work that paw loose from under his chin,' Lorinda suggested, 'you ought to be able to back him out then.'

Had-I and But-Known just sat there and looked superior, quite as though they'd had nothing to do with luring Roscoe to his entrapment.

'I don't know . . .' Macho knelt before his cat again and gently took hold of the paw. 'Easy now . . .' he soothed. 'Easy . . . does it . . .'

If his fans could see him now . . . Lorinda thought, not for the first time. She looked down on the polished pink dome of the creator of the eponymous Macho Magee, arguably the hardest-boiled private eye in print; certainly the most politically incorrect. What Macho Magee hadn't blackmailed, stabbed, strangled, set alight or blown away wasn't worth thinking about. He considered any book that didn't attract a minimum of fifty letters of complaint one that hadn't come up to scratch. The man's very name was a challenge. Deliberately so.

It had to be. His real name was Lancelot Dalrymple, a good enough name in ordinary life, but not one to stir the blood or set the cash registers jingling in the private-eye world, although it might do well in the realm of gardening books. A Dalrymple sounded as though he would be more at home mulching roses and bedding begonias rather than every tough blonde who strayed across his path.

'There, we've got it now.' He freed the paw, easing it through to the other side of the porthole. Roscoe immediately lunged forward, trying to get into the room with them.

'No, no, Roscoe.' Macho restrained him. 'Just cup his head in your hands, will you?' he instructed Lorinda. 'I'll go round and pull and you guide his head through. Mind that he doesn't catch his ears.'

Lorinda crouched and encircled Roscoe's head, murmuring softly to soothe him as he began moving backwards, his eyes rolling wildly.

'Nearly there . . .' She protected his ears as his head vanished through the opening and the flap fell back into place.

'That's better. You're all right now.' Roscoe reappeared, cradled in Macho's arms and Lorinda swung the door shut behind them.

'Come and have a drink,' she invited. 'You're through for the day now, aren't you?'

'I might do a bit more later but, basically, yes.' He carried Roscoe into the living room and settled in an armchair. Had-I and But-Known trailed along in his wake, eyeing Roscoe thoughtfully.

The fictional Macho Magee drank nothing but the genuine Mexican tequila with the worm curled at the bottom of the bottle (often the closest he got to ingesting any protein in the course of an entire book). Fortunately, Lancelot Dalrymple was quite content with a dry sherry. Lorinda poured sherries for both of them and set a bowl of mixed nuts within easy reaching distance.

Had-I and But-Known moved forward to investigate the bowl and retreated, flinging Lorinda looks of utter disgust. No cheese! No pâté! What was hospitality in this house coming to? They sat down together and concentrated their attention on Roscoe again.

Roscoe stirred restively in his owner's arms.

'No, no, stay here.' Macho tightened his grip. 'Ignore them. You know they only lead you into trouble. Treacherous jades!'

His language might also surprise his fans, as would the Byronesque ponytail tied with a black velvet ribbon trailing down to his shoulders. Both were probably a legacy of his years as a history teacher and his abiding interest in the subject.

'Book going well?' Ignoring his opinion of her cats (her own opinion of his wasn't all that high), Lorinda sank into the facing armchair and leaned back.

'Oh, well enough.' Now it was Macho who appeared restive. 'I need to get the body count higher, but I should be able to take care of that in the next chapter.'

'I'm sure you'll manage it,' Lorinda agreed absently. She was mentally composing and discarding opening sentences, trying to find a subtle lead-in to the subject she wished to introduce.

'I suppose you've heard the latest?' Macho had no such inhibitions. He leaned forward intently, loosening his hold on Roscoe, who promptly slid to the floor and ambled over to join Had-I and But-Known.

'Which latest?' The way gossip was proliferating in this village, there was a multiple choice.

'They've rented the last of the flats in Coffers Court. And guess who's got it?'

'Mmmm . . .' Macho was looking entirely too gleeful. 'Why do I get the feeling I'm not going to like the answer?'

'Because you're not. Go ahead.' He tugged at his goatee, pulling down his lower lip and disclosing a set of thin gnarled lower teeth. 'Who's the last creature in the world you would care to tiptoe hand-in-hand into the sunset with?'

At the moment, Macho himself was becoming the leading contender in that category. Lorinda regarded him without fondness.

'There are so many,' she murmured. And most of them seemed to be congregating in Brimful Coffers.

19

'The absolute worst,' he insisted. 'Beside whom the Marquis de Sade looks like St Francis of Assisi.'

'No!' Lorinda leaped to her feet. Had-I and But-Known had closed in on either side of Roscoe and were hustling him towards the kitchen. 'Come back here! You're not going to jump him through the catflap again!'

They stopped short and gave her injured looks. How could she think such a thing of them?

'Just a minute, Macho.' She hurried into the kitchen and turned the knob immobilizing the catflap. They could butt their heads against it in vain now.

'Roscoe! Come here, Roscoe!' Macho appeared in the doorway and advanced on his pet.

Roscoe evaded the outstretched arms and strolled over to the bowl of dry cat food and began to help himself. Had-I gave Lorinda a reproving look for spoiling all their fun and sat down and began to wash her face. But-Known went over to stand hopefully in front of the fridge.

'They're all right now,' Lorinda said. 'Come and finish your drink.'

'I don't know.' Macho settled back in his chair and allowed Lorinda to replenish his drink. 'Sometimes I think I should just get myself a tank of goldfish.'

'Not while Roscoe is still around,' Lorinda said.

'No, no. They wouldn't last ten minutes.' Macho was instantly cheered by the thought of his pet's hunting prowess. 'I only hope he never gets a chance at Dorian's tank of tropical fish.'

'Amen, amen,' Lorinda said fervently. The mere thought of Had-I and But-Known getting within paw-dipping distance of Dorian's aquarium was enough to make her feel faint.

'Cold fish,' Macho mused. 'Dorian, I mean. It quite amazed me when he began lobbying for all of us to come and occupy the same village. He's the last person in the world I would have suspected of having any desire for the company of his colleagues – on a long-term basis, that is.'

'Plantagenet!' Lorinda suddenly made the connection with Macho's earlier teasing. 'Plantagenet Sutton! Tell me it isn't true!'

'True enough,' he sighed. 'Pity. Coffers Court must have been quite a respectable place when it was occupied by flint-hearted bank managers foreclosing on widows and orphans.'

'How true,' Lorinda agreed.

The decommissioned bank building had been designed with typical late-Victorian lavishness to resemble a wealthy landowner's town house rather than a commercial establishment. Built of sandstone, now weathered to a rich gold, festooned with window boxes filled with seasonal blooms, it dominated one corner of the village green. Since the architect had been in the forefront of the technology of his time, along with the obligatory marble hall, it boasted a luxurious red-plush-and-mirrored lift with a padded bench curved invitingly around the walls. Thus patrons could be conveyed in solid comfort from the bank manager's office on the top floor to deposit their valuables in the basement vault. The vault had now been divided into a caretaker's flat and a series of boxrooms providing storage for the tenants of the other flats.

It was a beautiful building and had been transformed into a dream block of flats. Too bad about the people in it.

'The neighbourhood is really going down,' Macho said. 'I hadn't thought it could sink any lower after Gemma Duquette moved in – but now this!'

'Plantagenet Sutton,' Lorinda mourned. 'Are you absolutely sure?'

'Ground-floor left-hand flat.' Macho was certain of his facts. 'I saw the furniture being moved in this morning. No one could mistake that wing chair and lamp table. No one in the business, that is. It's practically his logo.'

'That's pretty conclusive.' She hadn't really doubted him; Macho was an expert gossip. Probably they all were. Keeping tabs on friends and neighbours could be looked on as an extension of their work. What was a book, after all, but the retailing of the alarms, excursions and minutiae of everyday life until it reached a conclusion tidier than any life usually provided? Did they become writers because they were so very interested in gossip? Or did being writers make them preternaturally interested in gossip?

Had-I and But-Known sauntered in and leaped up to sprawl out, one on each arm of Lorinda's chair. She stroked them absently. Roscoe followed and leaped up on Macho's lap. A faint concerted purr began to thrum as background music to their conversation. Outside, dusk began to settle over the village. It was all so comfortable and companionable . . . but for how much longer?

Plantagenet Sutton had come to live in their midst. Life could never be the same again.

'Perhaps he'll hate it here and won't stay long,' she said hopefully.

'We can do our best,' Macho said, 'but the monster has the hide of a rhinoceros. Otherwise, he could never have survived this long.'

'I suppose we'll have to be civil to him,' Lorinda said.

'After all, he hasn't retired yet, has he? Not like Gemma Duquette.'

'No, her fangs have been drawn, but his are still in place and ever ready to go for the jugular.' Macho's eyes narrowed. 'I suspect we have her to thank for his being here. She must have told him about our burgeoning colony. After all, Brimful Coffers is not the first place that would spring to the mind of someone wishing to move to the country.'

'How very true.' Lorinda was beginning to wish she'd never heard of the place herself. The more colleagues and cohorts moved into the village, the less des. the res. seemed.

'If she did it,' Macho brooded, 'that's one more thing we have against her.'

Lorinda nodded, although the main thing Macho had against Gemma Duquette was that she had, not surprisingly, never bought one of his books to serialize in her magazine, *Woman's Place*. Those who had been serialized carried far deeper grudges. Only an author who had seen her work butchered to fit into four to six weekly instalments could really comprehend the depths of hatred Gemma had inspired, especially as the pages sacrificed to expediency had inevitably contained the most inspired passages, the best writing and the most vital plot points – thus making hash of the solution to the mystery.

On the other hand, every suggestion of witless romance, or feeble intimation of sexual attraction and banal dialogue had been retained. Paragraphs disappeared between sentences, consecutive pages went missing between paragraphs – and the screams of anguished authors could be heard in the land. However, despite bitter vows of revenge and dire threats never to allow *Woman's Place* to desecrate another manuscript, those who could continued to sell it first serial rights. Money talked – take it and run and lick your wounds in privacy or in the company of other wounded victims.

And Gemma Duquette was responsible for it all. *Other* magazines were able to publish more sensitive serializations, managing to retain most of the major characters, plot lines and all the other features that were the first things Gemma's deadly hatchet automatically attacked.

'We were so relieved when she retired,' Lorinda remembered. 'We thought we'd never have to deal with her again. And now she's moved into our midst.'

'And brought Plantagenet Sutton along with her,' Macho snarled.

Roscoe stirred restively in his lap and looked up at his master in concern; he was not accustomed to hearing that snarl when Macho was away from his machine and no longer acting out his stories as he wrote them.

'Well, sometimes he gives a good review,' Lorinda said delicately. It was common knowledge that Macho had never received a good – or even a passable – review from Plantagenet Sutton. Quite the contrary, Sutton seemed to reserve his wittiest barbs and most poisonous venom for Macho Magee's books. Macho had good reason for bitterness.

'Sutton the sod!' Macho crossed and recrossed his legs violently. Roscoe bounced to the floor and stalked off to the kitchen, stiff-legged and affronted. Macho didn't notice, too absorbed in his own furious thoughts.

'Sutton the sot!' he hissed.

Lorinda nodded. She wasn't sure about the first accusation, but there was a certain amount of justice in the second. In fact, that might be the root cause of the problem. Plantagenet Sutton had always been a tough critic, but he had not turned into a hanging judge until he conceived the idea of combining book reviews with a wine column and moving to the Lifestyle pages of his Sunday newspaper.

His 'Through a Glass, Darkly' pages had been a great success – with the public. The large photograph of Sutton relaxing in his wing chair, with the lamp table beside him, the lamp casting a benevolent glow over his features and the wide circular table holding a small stack of books, a decanter and half-filled glass, obviously touched a chord deep in the public heart – this was what they thought the Literary Life was like. The wine shippers had had no complaints (except for the occasional suggestion that a bottle might be used instead of a decanter), but the change had been greatly to the detriment of the mystery-writing community.

'Isn't it just our luck?' Fredericka Carlson had lamented. 'Why couldn't the bastard have turned out to be a jovial drunk instead of a nasty one?'

Others voiced the opinion – off the record, of course – that the steaming rancour had set in when Plantagenet Sutton realized that a good review of a wine was likely to bring him a case of the favoured beverage, while a good review for a book brought him no return at all. His opinion of every book had grown more and more venomous, every witticism at the author's expense, every verdict thumbs-down.

'I suppose there's no hope of *him* retiring?' Lorinda was momentarily wistful.

'Not while he can still lift a glass to his lips,' Macho sneered.

'Anyway,' Lorinda tried to look on the bright side, 'in Coffers Court, they're only renting; they haven't bought the leaseholds yet. Maybe they won't stay.'

'We can but do our best to ensure that.' Macho's lips twisted unpleasantly.

'We couldn't do that . . .' Lorinda said uncertainly.

'Maybe *you* couldn't.' She hadn't thought it possible, but Macho's smile became even more unpleasant. 'But would you like to bet how forbearing Rhylla Montague is going to be? She took to her bed for three days after she saw what Gemma had done to her last opus. Then Sutton, in his infinite laziness, reviewed the book from the potted version in the magazine – and slaughtered it. *And* they're all under the same roof now.'

The urgent summons of the telephone saved Lorinda from having to reply. With relief, she rose and crossed to answer it, narrowly avoiding tripping over Roscoe, who had wandered back into the room to make sure he wasn't missing anything.

'Lorinda, have you heard?' Fredericka Carlson's voice was unnaturally shrill. 'I can't believe it! What have we done to deserve this?'

'Steady, Freddie,' Lorinda said. 'Macho is here now. He's just told me. Come over and join us for drinks.'

'We'll need them! Horrors to the right of me, horrors to the left of me – I don't know why I came to this place! I'll be right

24

over!' Freddie slammed down the phone and it seemed only seconds before she was at the door.

'They're going to kill each other, you know,' she announced. 'It's only a question of time – and I'd rather not be around here when they do it.'

'You're just trying to cheer us up,' Macho said. 'They're thick as thieves. Lorinda and I were just saying that it must have been Gemma who told that – that *churl* – that there was a flat going spare at Coffers Court.'

'Not *them!*' Freddie threw Macho a withering look as she hurled herself into Lorinda's vacated chair and automatically began stroking the cats stretched along its arms. 'That would be too much to hope for! I mean, my lot – the next-door neighbours, the other half of the house. I never should have let Dorian talk me into that semidetached. "They're Americans, so they'll only be here three or four months of the year, six at most," he said. "It will be like having a house all to yourself, except that it will be cheaper than a detached," he said. Hah! Bloody hah!'

Had-I and But-Known turned to her with comforting purrs. Roscoe came over to rub against her ankles. As a stray human, owned by no proprietary feline, but always ready to welcome a visiting cat with warmth, snacks and cuddles, she was extremely popular with them.

'Aaah . . . thanks.' She accepted the glass of deep amber liquid and slipped off her shoes, absently scratching Roscoe's neck with a stockinged toe. Relaxation was setting in.

'Are the neighbours being difficult again?' Lorinda looked at Freddie with some concern. Freddie's hairdo was in a disintegrating preshampoo condition, not helped by the way she was running her hands through it, and there were dark circles under her eyes.

'All night,' Freddie sighed. 'Shouting, screaming and throwing things. I didn't get a wink of sleep. Every time it got quiet and I started to doze, they began again.'

'Poor Freddie,' Macho sympathized. 'You should have banged on the wall.'

'I couldn't!' Freddie said. 'They'd die if they thought I could hear them so clearly. Especially with some of the home truths they were hurling at each other. We'd never be able to look each other in the face again.'

'You're going to have to do something,' Lorinda said. 'You can't go on like this. Especially if it's true that they're going to stay here year round this year.'

'Oh, it's true, all right.' Freddie shuddered. 'They're collaborating on a nonfiction book. One of those *A Year In...* efforts with lots of photographs. Guess who's going to do all the work while *he* swans around pointing his camera at everything so that he'll get his name on the title page as coauthor. The last shot to save an ailing marriage. How many times have we seen it?' She shuddered again.

'I'm thinking of moving my bedroom,' she went on. 'If I clear the boxroom and move the bed in there, leaving the bedroom as a dressing room ...'

'You can't squeeze yourself into the boxroom!' Lorinda was horrified. 'There's no window – you'll have no air.'

'Especially if I keep the door closed, which I shall have to do to keep it soundproof.' Freddie nodded gloomily. 'Damn Dorian and all his machinations!'

'Dorian can't be blamed if the Jackley marriage is breaking up.' Lorinda was assailed by sudden doubt. 'Can he?'

'I wouldn't like to swear to anything.' Freddie was suddenly very interested in her drink. 'It's possible that they've just discovered they can't stand each other.'

'And who can blame them?' Macho murmured. Diplomatic relations had been strained ever since Jack Jackley had pointed out the antiquity of much of his hard-boiled American slang. He had been particularly annoyed to be told that 'roscoe' was even worse than 'gat' for a gun. Nor was Jackley's humour appreciated when he suggested alternative names for Roscoe. Nothing on earth could induce Macho to change Roscoe's name to Capone.

'I was so exhausted by the time they decided to call it a night,' Freddie went on, 'that I overslept disgracefully this morning. I didn't wake up until Karla threw the toaster at the wall.'

'How do you know it was the toaster?' Macho always liked to get these little points clear.

'I heard Jack shout, "You'll electrocute yourself!" and then, "Those were the last two slices of bread." It wasn't hard to deduce – that *is* our business, you know.'

'True.' Lorinda and Macho nodded.

'Then there was a long silence. I hoped one of them was

strangling the other with the electric cord, but no such luck. I looked out of the window a while later and saw them setting off for the shops. They had their shopping basket with them –' She forestalled Macho's next question.

'Anyway, I took advantage of the quiet to get some work done. When I heard doors slamming over there again, I decided to get out and do some shopping myself. I had nearly finished and was walking down the High Street when I saw that – that *toad!*' She spat the word out and the cats turned their heads to look at her with a wary interest bordering on alarm. They were not accustomed to that tone of voice from her.

'He was hopping out of the wine merchant's – wouldn't you know it? – and looking too pleased with himself to be true. I'd hoped I was hallucinating, but he spoke to me and said he'd just moved in to Coffers Court and was looking forward to living here amongst all his old friends and colleagues.'

'You should have spat in his face!' Macho was overidentifying with his character again, although the fictional Macho wouldn't have stopped at mere spittle, a few broken teeth were more his style.

'I have a book coming out next month,' Freddie apologized.

'Maybe he'll be nicer when he realizes that he has to live among us and meet us every day.' Lorinda tried to look on the bright – or, at least, hopeful – side.

'Hah!' Macho spat.

Had-I and But-Known jumped down from the arms of the chair and Roscoe joined them on their tactical retreat into the kitchen; the atmosphere was getting too violent around here for a respectable cat to countenance. They didn't even look back when the telephone rang again.

Lorinda recognized the voice the instant it greeted her in the unctuous tones it used when being introduced on television or radio (the waspishness came later, when he launched into the actual reviews). She leaned weakly against the wall, faintly echoing the more pertinent of his remarks, aware that her breathless audience was hanging on every word.

'Yes . . . yes, I'd heard.' She could not bring herself to say, *Welcome to Brimful Coffers.* Apart from anything else, that audience might lynch her if she tried.

'Ye— oh . . . No, no, they're here with me now, as a matter

of fact.' She nodded to the semaphoring arms wildly instructing, *Don't ask him round.*

'Oh, how – how nice . . . Yes, I'll ask them. Just a moment.' She took the precaution of covering the mouthpiece before announcing, 'Plantagenet is inviting us to a party on Saturday night. He's having a house-warming.'

'Warm it?' Macho was still posturing. 'I'd rather burn it down!'

'Oh, hell,' Freddie moaned. 'I suppose we'll have to go.'

'They'd be delighted,' Lorinda said firmly into the phone. 'Eight o'clock? Yes, we'll all be there. Thank you so much.' She managed to replace the receiver before the chorus of groans and complaints broke out.

A sudden gust of wind tore a shower of leaves from the trees and hurled them against the windows like hail. Lorinda watched gloomily as a splattering of raindrops joined them.

It was going to be a long winter.

2

Saturday came all too soon, however. They foregathered at Macho's for a preliminary drink to brace themselves for the house-warming party.

'House-warming!' Freddie snorted. 'Danegeld is what it amounts to.'

'I'd like to geld *him*,' Macho muttered.

'Anyway,' Freddie went on cheerfully, 'I found the perfect present for him at the antique shop. On the principle of sweets for the sweet . . .'

'An antique pendant?' Macho murmured hopefully.

'Better than that. An old gargoyle beer mug! Not only is it hideous, but we all know he wouldn't be caught dead drinking beer. And, since it's an antique and cost quite a bit, he'll never be sure whether I was getting at him or not.'

'Oh, well played!' Lorinda applauded. 'I wasn't nearly so adventurous. I got him an eighteenth-century ship's decanter.' Unimaginative but safe, she hoped.

'The antique shop has been doing a rushing business.' Macho's eyes gleamed wickedly. 'I got him a framed print of the Spanish Inquisition – Torquemada doing his stuff. He can make what he likes of that.'

Roscoe, mindful of his duties as co-host, was padding from guest to guest offering help in disposing of any unwanted items – like the last bite on the cocktail stick. He was not importunate about it – Macho would not have stinted him in the kitchen – he simply wished to remind everyone that further handouts were always welcomed and appreciated.

Lorinda sighed and surrendered to the hopeful eyes, handing over a bacon-wrapped chicken liver she had barely nibbled. Roscoe made quick work of it and looked around for more. No wonder he wouldn't fit through a catflap.

'I wish we didn't have to go,' Freddie said. 'I wish we could stay right here and have a pleasant evening.'

'Think of it as part of the job,' Lorinda advised. 'Like signing sessions and speaking at libraries, schools and clubs.'

'All right for *some*,' Macho said darkly, and Lorinda realized she had been tactless. It was well known that no school or club in its right mind would invite what it imagined Macho Magee's creator to be like to come and address their tender charges.

'She means libraries,' Freddie said helpfully, earning another dark look. The only time Macho had spoken at a library he had nearly been hooted off the stage by some louts who had strayed in to see what he looked like and commented loudly and freely on their disappointment and his deficiencies. The creator of the mountainous bully was not expected to be a weedy individual who could have passed for a university lecturer or tax inspector. In a way, Macho had brought it on himself. When his publishers had insisted on a photograph for the book jacket, Macho, conscious that he might not be exactly what his fans expected, had taken a leaf from the late Craig Rice's book when she was faced with a similar problem and wished to conceal the fact that she was a woman. Thus, coat collar turned up, bundled up in a scarf, hat pulled low and pipe jutting out to mark the approximate location of mouth in a deeply shadowed atmospheric photograph, Macho had presented himself to the world. People could imagine any features or height they liked. And, judging from the behaviour of the louts, apparently they had.

After that dire appearance, Macho had refused all further speaking engagements and confined his bookshop cooperation to signing bookplates. The reclusive reputation he was gaining had done nothing to limit the popularity of his books, and certain of the newer and more studiedly intellectual of the critics were beginning to refer to him as the J. D. Salinger of the mystery world.

'Not now, Roscoe.' Macho deftly caught Roscoe in mid-leap to his lap. 'We have to go out.' He glanced at his colleagues for confirmation. 'We *do* have to go?'

'Much as I hate to admit it, we do,' Freddie said. 'Come on, bite the bullet. At least the wine ought to be good. And maybe even the food.'

'Better a meal of bitter herbs with my friends,' Macho said darkly, 'than a feast with my enemies. Or however it goes.'

'Oh, come now,' Lorinda protested. 'It isn't that bad. Most of the guests *are* our friends.'

Macho deposited Roscoe on the carpet, brushed a few red hairs from his trousers, carefully removed the cocktail sticks from the last two chicken livers and carried the sticks into the kitchen. They heard the clatter of the swing-lid rubbish bin.

'We'll be back soon.' Returning, Macho bent to stroke Roscoe and set the saucer of leftovers in front of him. 'Perhaps very soon.'

Plantagenet Sutton was greeting his guests expansively at the front door of Coffers Court itself, giving the impression that he was master of all he surveyed and not just one of the flats. He was holding his party in the marble-clad entrance hall, which was bedecked with flowers.

The arrivals from London were suitably impressed, while the inhabitants of Brimful Coffers exchanged wry glances.

'Welcome, welcome, so glad you could come!' He greeted them enthusiastically, shaking hands with Macho, planting kisses on Lorinda and Freddie's cheeks. 'Oh, for me? You shouldn't have! It wasn't necessary.'

Lorinda noticed that there was a pile of gift-wrapped parcels on the little table beside him. It might not have been necessary, but it was advisable.

'How well you look,' Freddie cooed insincerely, handing over her Danegeld.

'Ah, Freddie.' He took the gift, weighing it thoughtfully in his hand. 'You have a new one out any moment, haven't you?'

'Next month,' she said.

'Ah, yes. I thought I'd seen it. Well, have a good time.' He turned to the next in line. 'And Lorinda, ah, thank you. And how is the criminous little world of St Waldemar Boniface?'

'Oh . . .' She tried for a becoming show of modesty. 'Still chugging along.'   '

'Now, now, don't sell them short. Why, some of your scenes are almost believable.' He released her hand just as it clenched and greeted Macho.

'Ah, Magee. Same as ever, I see.'

'Why shouldn't I be?'

They faced each other warily, like two mongrel curs, fur bristling, but neither ready to make the first move to attack.

They were too much alike, Lorinda thought, that was part of the problem. Both the same physical type: weedy, undersized, bald and overcompensating by too much facial hair and those ridiculous ponytails. On a dark night, it might be hard for the casual observer to tell them apart unless one of them spoke.

On closer observation, it could be noticed that Plantagenet had gone one step beyond Macho, growing the hair on one side of his head much longer and combing it across his dome, giving the impression from the front that he still had some hair there. The longer hair at the back was gathered into a ponytail, tied with a black velvet ribbon to match his black velvet smoking jacket.

A sudden explosion of light blinded Lorinda and left her blinking into a whirlpool of swirling black dots.

'*Tchaaah!*' With an exclamation of fury, Macho moved away rapidly, his face suffused with rage.

'Don't move!' Jack Jackley called out. 'Get back where you were. I want one more of the two of you together.'

Macho stalked to the other side of the room, seething.

'He's a bit camera-shy, you know,' Plantagenet said, not trying to hide his amusement. Everyone except the Jackleys knew that Macho would go to any lengths to avoid being photographed. 'You'll have to watch your camera now, or he'll have the film out of it and exposed before you know it.'

'The hell he will!' Jackley clutched his camera protectively. 'Nobody touches this camera but me. This little baby is going to provide the complete record of a literary year in England. And this is our first literary soirée.' He whirled suddenly, aimed at a group just entering and unleashed the flash, leaving the new guests blinded, disoriented and blinking on the doorstep.

'Another London train has just come in, I see.' Freddie surveyed the newcomers.

'Representing books or booze?' Lorinda wondered. Both women slid cautiously out of the range of Plantagenet's bonhomie and Jackley's camera.

'Bit of both, I should say.' Freddie frowned judiciously. 'Hard to tell. So many new people are coming along now and a lot of the others are falling by the wayside or retiring. It's one of those Changing of the Guards times. End of an era and all that.'

Lorinda nodded, only half paying attention. They were standing by the door of Gemma Duquette's flat and whining, snuffling

32

sounds, punctuated by the occasional yap, could be heard. It was only a matter of time before the yapping became more imperious.

'I hope they're not going to let those dogs out,' Lorinda said.

'They're bound to,' Freddie said resignedly. 'Some sentimental ass will insist on it. Probably Gemma herself.' The yaps grew more excited.

'They know we're here. Move away.' Lorinda suited the action to the suggestion. 'Maybe they'll calm down.'

'Over here!' Professor Borley, standing by the drinks table, hailed them. 'You haven't got your drinks yet. Let me give you a little tip.' He leaned closer and lowered his voice. 'There's a choice of champagne or red or white wine. I understand this is a classic ploy in wine circles. Those who don't know any better choose the champagne, leaving the truly fine wines for the connoisseur.' He nodded at them wisely.

'Oh, yes?' Freddie looked at the murky red wine swirling in his own glass. 'And who told you that?'

'Why, Plantagenet himself, I'm proud to say. I took it as a word to the wise.' He nodded again for emphasis and took a sip from his glass. 'This is very . . . full-blooded . . . memorable.' He paused. 'But perhaps you ladies might find the white more to your taste.'

Lorinda and Freddie exchanged glances, immediately suspicious. It would be just like Plantagenet Sutton to spread such a story to get rid of his unpalatable rejects.

'Actually,' Freddie said, 'I'm afraid my palate isn't very educated and it's too late to send it to school now. I think I'll just settle for the champagne.'

'So will I.' Looking around, Lorinda observed several knowledgable-looking strangers holding champagne flutes. A good nonvintage was preferable to an unknown red or white.

'Well, I *did* tip you off.' Professor Borley took another sip of his red and nodded appreciatively, but one corner of his mouth twitched in a wince.

'We appreciate it,' Lorinda assured him, registering the waiter's nod of approval as he handed her the glass of champagne.

'Isn't this exciting?' Gemma Duquette came up behind them. 'At last, a proper writers' colony in England! And more and more of our colleagues will join us as they realize that. Mark my words, Brimful Coffers will become a magnet to everyone in the field.'

'Did she say maggot?' Freddie muttered in Lorinda's ear.

'Shhh!' Lorinda nudged her. 'Behave!'

'And what is this I hear?' Gemma cooed. 'There's an exciting rumour afoot that you're thinking of killing off your series character and starting afresh.'

'What?' Freddie stiffened. 'Where did you hear that ridiculous idea? You must be thinking of a couple of other people.'

Lorinda froze. It was a long moment before she was able to lift the glass to her lips and take what she hoped looked like an unconcerned sip of champagne.

'You mean it isn't true? Oh, I'm *so* glad.' Gemma gave her a soul-stripping look. 'Because it doesn't work, you know, my dear. Conan Doyle had to bring back Sherlock Holmes. That should have been the definitive lesson to all of you. You mustn't muck around with a good thing. Your public won't allow it. I realize that the temptation is strong sometimes, but you must *not* think you know better than your public.'

'I'm going to kill *her*,' Freddie muttered under her breath. 'No jury on earth would convict me.'

'Steady on.' Lorinda was barely in control of her own voice. It was true, she brooded. All those joking remarks she had heard at American conventions weren't jokes at all, but the literal truth. 'You can be alone in your own room at midnight in an empty house,' they ran, 'and sneeze. And first thing in the morning, one of the colleagues will be on the telephone asking how your cold is.'

The mystery world was such a small community to begin with, had it been wise to narrow the boundaries still more by moving here to Brimful Coffers?

Too late to ask oneself that now. The move had been made, the mortgage was in place, the die was cast. She had to learn to live with it. With them.

Spasmodic flashes of brilliance lit up the reception area like heat lightning on a summer's day. Lorinda noticed that she was not the only one keeping a wary eye on Jackley as he circled the marble hall looking for fresh victims. Macho had manoeuvred himself behind him while edging closer to the door.

'Not thinking of leaving?' She slid away from the others and moved to cut him off.

'I've been thinking of nothing else all day.' He gave her a hangdog look. 'Too soon, you think?'

'We've only just arrived.'

'Really? It seems like hours.' He sighed and allowed her to lead him over to her group.

Karla, clutching a glass and with an expression of desperate gaiety on her face, also joined the group, obviously positioning herself for the next photograph. Macho quivered and Lorinda caught his arm before he could bolt.

'We were just saying' – Gemma greeted Karla with a bright smile, conscious of the approaching camera herself – 'that it's so easy to become fed up with your series characters that the temptation to kill them off becomes intense. Don't you find that?'

'Not yet,' Karla said. 'But I might if I were stuck with the same one for any length of time. As it is . . .' She shrugged. 'I've got to clear up a three-book contract completing the unfinished manuscript Aimee Dorrow left behind her when she died and writing the next two from her notes, all featuring the endless dreary detections of Miss Mudd. And then there's this nonfiction account of our year in England.' Her voice rose as her husband approached. 'Heaven knows when I'll be able to get back to my own Terri and Toni series again.'

'Smile, everybody!' Jack ordered. 'Show 'em what a great time we're having.' He levelled the camera at them.

Macho ducked behind Freddie just as she raised her eyebrows and gave Lorinda a meaningful look. Precisely what it was supposed to mean, Lorinda wasn't sure.

'Reverting to what we were just saying' – Freddie smiled dangerously – 'I agree that it isn't done to kill off one's series character. Not fair on the readers, they take it so seriously, poor darlings – look at Holmes, look at Van der Valk. But have you noticed the increasing trend to kill off the character's spouse or partner?'

Really, it was unspeakably wicked of Freddie. She even widened her eyes innocently at the Jackleys as she said it. Jack lowered his camera and there was an awkward pause before he laughed loudly. Too loudly.

'Well, we've got the expert on that right here!' He indicated Macho. 'None of his heroines ever make it through the final chapter to get as far as the altar.'

Or, if they did, they were killed off in the first chapter of the next book to provide Macho Magee with a mission of revenge in tracking down the killer and administering his own brand of rough justice.

A ripple of amusement eased the tension. Even Macho joined in, although his face darkened.

'Oh, how delicious they look! I really shouldn't!' Gemma's practised cries of delight welcomed the appearance of one of the catering staff bearing a tray of rather ambitious canapés. Leave it to Plantagenet Sutton to have his party professionally catered. Although, Lorinda noticed, he was using the local caterers, thereby ensuring local goodwill while saving on London prices.

'Hey, that looks good enough to eat!' Jack Jackley laughed immoderately at his own wit. Karla gave a strained smile.

They all gazed in admiration on the neat rows of assorted delicacies before swooping to demolish them. The pinwheel sandwiches of smoked salmon and cream cheese melted like snow in the sun, the flaky oblong boats of creamed chicken and the prawn vol-au-vents also vanished rapidly.

'Don't go 'way.' Jackley caught the waitress's arm as she turned. 'Stay right here. We can finish these all by ourselves.'

'Jack!' Karla's whisper was anguished. 'Please!'

'What's the matter? That's what they're here for: to eat. We're not depriving anybody. There's plenty to go round.' He indicated more waitresses moving into the throng, offering their trays to other guests. 'Eat up – and we'll send her back for a refill.'

Macho didn't need urging. He was steadily devouring one canapé after another with the grim expression of a man determined to salvage what he could from this ghastly evening.

Lorinda helped herself to a round greyish mass, almost the only item left on the tray, and nibbled it cautiously: a marinated mushroom stuffed with crabmeat and tasting, thank heavens, a great deal better than it looked.

'Freddie, darling!' One of the London crowd materialized beside them. 'What a fantastic place. You could have written it yourself!'

'She did.' Suddenly, Dorian was there. 'We all did. And now, like Brigadoon, it has appeared and we've moved in. Beware it doesn't disappear again tonight, taking all of you with it – into the fourth dimension!'

'Oh, Dorian!' The woman laughed skittishly. 'You *are* a horror!' Her gaze shifted nervously to the world beyond the long windows and brightly blossoming window boxes, as though checking that it was still there. Dorian could have that effect on people.

'Only to those I love.' He bussed her cheek smoothly. 'I'm frighteningly polite to strangers and small children.'

'*Must* you keep rubbing it in, Dorian?' Stately as the proverbial galleon, Rhylla Montague glided into their midst and dropped anchor. 'I'm trying to forget – and savour my last few days of freedom.'

'Nonsense, Rhylla,' Dorian said heartily. 'You know you're looking forward to it enormously. Any doting granny would.'

'Don't!' Rhylla shuddered. 'A deadline and a granddaughter, both looming. How am I going to cope?'

'Here we are!' Betty Alvin appeared in their midst, bearing a laden tray. 'I could see that some of you hadn't bothered with lunch, so I liberated this for you.' The invaluable communal secretary thrust the tray at them.

'Hot dog!' Jackley said.

'Hot cocktail sausages, actually,' Macho corrected. They both regarded the bounty for an appreciative moment before diving in. Hot cocktail sausages, satay chicken sticks, giant prawns, sweet-and-sour pork, steak medallions and bowls of tempting spicy dips. Heartier fare than that on the earlier tray.

'Betty, you're a lifesaver!' Rhylla breathed.

'She's spoken for, remember,' Dorian warned. 'She's completely tied up preparing my final draft. There'll be no time for her to play nanny to your bratling.'

'You can't work her twenty-four hours a day!' Rhylla shot him a poisonous glance.

'Neither can you!'

Betty swung the tray around the circle, a faintly anxious frown rippling across her forehead. Lorinda sympathized. It must have seemed like an ideal arrangement when Dorian persuaded Betty to move her freelance secretarial service into the attic flat at Coffers Court, asking only a peppercorn rent and promising an assured group of clients. Now it looked as though Betty was another one questioning the wisdom of having moved into a situation from which there might be no easy escape.

'How thoughtful of you.' Lorinda gave her a sympathetic look as she managed to spear four giant prawns on one toothpick and stood holding them with an innocent expression while she tried to plot the logistics of transferring the toothpick into a napkin and then into her handbag unobserved. The lengths to which being a cat owner reduced one! But she could not pass up those tempting prawns when she imagined the delight of Had-I and But-Known upon being presented with them when she returned. She noticed that Macho had also filled a cocktail stick with the luscious prawns and was gazing at it absently, obviously lost in the same calculations as she. Roscoe, too, loved prawns. It was not that they could not afford to buy them themselves for their pets, it was just that the sudden unexpected treat was greeted with such delight.

With a quick look around and a sudden decisive move, Macho rammed the prawn-laden cocktail stick into his jacket pocket. Lorinda winced. How lucky that Macho was currently between girlfriends. Otherwise some poor woman would have had a fit before delivering the jacket to the dry cleaners.

'Is there another emergency pending?' Betty asked uneasily.

'Nothing to do with you,' Dorian assured her. 'Rhylla has carelessly allowed her son and daughter-in-law to dump the grandchild on her for the holidays. Again.' He smirked heartlessly. 'She's going to find it a little more difficult to entertain the child in a village than in the heart of Knightsbridge, where she could send her off with a pocketful of money and all the theatres, shops, museums and exhibitions of London at her command. You may have to take some time out of your busy routine and actually hold a conversation or two with the child yourself, Rhylla.'

'You know all about it yourself, of course,' Rhylla snapped. 'A bachelor's children are always the best brought up.'

Lorinda noticed that Gemma had taken advantage of the fact that the others were absorbed in the altercation to quietly empty the plate of sirloin medallions into a plastic sandwich bag she had ready and waiting. Lionheart and Conqueror, the pug dogs, would also snack well this evening.

'I wish I'd thought of that,' Lorinda murmured as Gemma caught her watching.

'Come prepared! That's the secret.' With the conspiratorial wink of the veteran of a thousand PR launches, Gemma slipped an extra sandwich bag to her.

'One scavenger to a tray, that's the unwritten rule.' Gemma gave her a gentle push towards a group across the room, who seemed to be London visitors unnaturally concerned about calories – in food, that is. They appeared to have no qualms about the caloric content of champagne.

Taking the hint, Lorinda began circling the room in a delicate stalking operation she recognized she had learned from observing Had-I, the peerless hunter of the two cats. But-Known's qualms about her sister's intrepid activities especially extended to the hunting procedure; although she knew in a vague way that hunting was a Good Thing, But-Known could not bring herself to hunt prey that had to be killed. She was exceptionally generous, however, in her gifts of pebbles, leaves, flowers and the occasional trifle pilfered from a guest's handbag or pocket. That was prowess enough for her.

Behind Lorinda, the heat lightning flashed again and she heard a low growl which, in the absence of any four-legged animals, she had to suspect had come from Macho Magee. But there was also a suppressed hiss among the reactions. Jack Jackley was getting on everyone's nerves. He could not be allowed to go on like this all winter, proposed book or not. Someone was going to have to speak to him about his neighbours' right to privacy. But would that really stop him? Sensitivity to the opinion of others did not appear to loom large in his make-up.

'Lorinda Lucas!' Carelessly, she had passed too close to Professor Borley. He caught her arm and drew her into a corner. 'I've been meaning to talk to you. Now that I'm all settled in, we must fix a time for me to interview you for my new book.'

'Oh. Yes. We must.' Anguished Lorinda watched the tray she had been stalking carried out of reach.

'Over here!' The professor noticed and gestured imperiously to the waitress, who swerved and bore the tray over to them. 'I can recommend the chicken,' he beamed. 'I think it's especially good.'

'Oh. Thank you.' Trapped, Lorinda took a satay stick and then stood holding it helplessly. She realized she could not slip it into the plastic bag with Professor Borley watching – and probably making mental notes for posterity.

'Try the peanut sauce,' Professor Borley instructed. 'Or the sweet-and-sour.' He indicated the bowls of dip. 'They're both very good.'

Recognizing defeat, Lorinda dipped the chicken into the peanut sauce and nibbled delicately. At the back of her mind, Had-I's accusing eyes watched every selfish bite. Had-I was particularly fond of chicken. But-Known favoured prawns. They both loved little surprises.

Don't worry, she promised silently. *I'll bring you your share of the party.*

'Shall we say Monday morning?' Professor Borley was caught up in his own concerns.

'Monday? Morning?'

'Afternoon, if you prefer. This will just be in the nature of a preliminary interview, of course.'

'Preliminary?' Lorinda wished she could stop sounding like an echo.

'I thought we'd start with an overall view of your career. Then, in subsequent interviews, we can get down to the nitty-gritty.'

'Subsequent? Nitty-gritty?' If only she could attribute that sinking feeling in her stomach to impending food poisoning, but she knew that the canapés were blameless. It was due to the prospect of not just one, but a series of interviews with an earnest American academic.

Damn Dorian! This was all his fault. During one of his American tours, he had met Professor Borley and learned of the projected scholarly tome on the wellsprings and influences of popular culture as evinced in the mystery field. With his penchant for collecting people who might be useful, Dorian had kept track of the professor's progress and written to suggest that a sojourn in Brimful Coffers, where he would be surrounded by actively creating mystery writers, might facilitate his research. Naturally, Dorian hoped to figure prominently in the book, if not dominate it. Meanwhile, he had unleashed this . . . this *pest* on the rest of them.

'I'm terribly busy right now.' She mustered her defences. 'Deadline coming up and all that, you know.'

'I understand.' He nodded for emphasis. 'Fortunately, we have plenty of time in hand. I was lucky enough to be able to rent this superb accommodation for my full sabbatical year. I'm anxious to get on with my research, but I can start with one of the others and come back to you when you're less pressured.'

'Yes, that would be fine.' Lorinda felt faintly dizzy. All she wanted to come back to her was the tray of canapés now being carried to the far side of the room.

'Smile,' Professor Borley warned suddenly, baring his teeth.

Too late. As she turned back to look at him, the flash bulb exploded in her face. Again, the after-brilliance and swirling black spots cut off all normal vision.

'That man is a menace,' she muttered.

'He doesn't seem the kind who'll improve on closer acquaintance,' the professor agreed. 'It's a pity his wife is so talented. No one would put up with him for a minute, otherwise.'

'Please excuse me . . .' The spots cleared enough for Lorinda to see a waitress emerging from the improvised caterers' pantry, bearing a fresh tray of the coveted treats. If she moved quickly enough, she could intercept the waitress before the other guests began pillaging the tray.

'Yes, and I've got to . . .' Professor Borley nodded tacit agreement and slid away in the opposite direction, leaving Jack Jackley aiming his camera at thin air.

With a vague smile towards several London colleagues who were waving at her, Lorinda sidled along the marble wall until she reached an alcove suitable for lurking in to ambush the waitress. Around her, fragments of conversation rebounded off the marble walls from a group of critics standing nearby.

'Timetables, my dear, were what killed off the Golden Age. I couldn't believe it when I turned the page and found one in his latest book . . .'

'And genealogy – is there anything more deadly? I always feel as though I'm going to have to face an exam on the family relationships in the morning . . .'

'Series! How much longer is this mad craze for series going to continue? I could upchuck every time I pick up a new book and see it's about the same old dreary . . .'

'It's all due to the fragmentation of modern life in America. All those people, always on the move. They wake up in the morning and can never be sure who's still living in the house next door. Or maybe they're on the way to a new home themselves. A nation on the move – and we feel the reverberations in fiction on the other side of the Atlantic. It gives them the only permanence they have. Series characters are always there, always the same, the community they used to be part of, but which no longer exists in reality – only in their dreams . . .'

'And the books they want to read. Fine for them, but the rest of us have a lower threshold of boredom . . .'

'Or a more stable home life . . .'

'Of course, that's why all those wretched radio and television soap operas are so popular, too. They help provide the stability so lacking in everyday life . . .'

'How much longer can it go on, one asks oneself. Sooner or later, the public is bound to become satiated and the trend will collapse, the way the Gothic boom did when so many writers jumped on the bandwagon it buckled . . .'

'And horror. Don't forget horror . . .'

'And private eyes. There can't be many of them left with a friend, relative or lover to call his own . . .'

Shrieks of laughter hit the marble walls and splintered into brittle shards of knifepoint-lethal cacophony.

The waitress appeared and Lorinda prepared to pounce. It was pounce or scream. At least three of the Judases in that coven of critics had hailed the advent of each of Miss Petunia's adventures with cries of seeming rapture. And this was what they really thought!

No wonder Victorian bank managers had had such a reputation for omniscience. Their customers could never have suspected the acoustical betrayal of those impressive marble walls. One careless word to an accompanying spouse or friend and their doom was sealed, with foreclosure and bankruptcy proceedings in their future.

'I have two cats at home.' With a charming smile to the waitress, Lorinda shamelessly plotted to denude the tray. 'And they'd never forgive me if I didn't bring home some treats for them.'

'Oh, I know.' The waitress smiled back and Lorinda vaguely recognized her as one of the assistants in the local hairdressing salon. 'You've got those two lovely splashy-coloured cats.'

'That's right. The tortoiseshell is Had-I and the calico is But-Known. They're sisters.' Lorinda piled chicken, beef and even cocktail sausages into the thoughtfully provided napkin, prior to transfer into the plastic kitty-bag. For good measure, she took a couple of cheese-and-onion miniature quiches and bit into one recklessly. The cats were indifferent to pastry.

'You want to take some more of these goodies home to your little kitties,' Elsie – yes, that was her name, Elsie – said understandingly. 'There's heaps of food out back – they'll never eat it all. Look' – she thrust the tray at Lorinda – 'you take this round and I'll go back and pack up a takeaway for you to bring home to your cats.'

'Oh, well . . . thank you.' Lorinda caught the tray as Elsie rushed away. What a nice child. She hoped she had tipped her enough last time she'd had her hair done.

'Lorinda! They've pressed you into service, have they?'

'Aren't you kind? How good everything looks.'

The group she had so lately been eavesdropping on greeted her with enthusiasm and took their pick of her wares.

'I hope this doesn't presage a career change for you,' the scrawny female from the *Sunday Special* miaowed. 'I'm *so* looking forward to the next delightful instalment from St Waldemar Boniface.'

Lorinda bared her teeth at her, just managing to bite back a sharp retort that would betray that she knew what they had just been saying.

'Hold it! Don't move!' It was as well she had been warned or she might have dropped the tray. She clung to it grimly as the wild explosion of black dots blinded her again. *Damn!* If Karla really wanted to murder Jack, there would be no shortage of witnesses to swear that she had been sitting innocently at the bridge table with them at the crucial moment.

'Great! The murder writer as hostess! Would you take a canapé from someone who's killed as many people as Lorinda Lucas has? It will make a great caption.'

'Perhaps one of us should collapse at her feet,' the *Sunday Special* suggested acidly. 'That would make a great picture, too.'

'Hey! Terrific!' Jack raised the camera, then lowered it again as no one moved. 'Oh, that was a joke, huh? But it's still a great idea. Why don't we do it?'

This time Lorinda moved, sliding quietly away from the group while Jack was still looking hopefully from face to face. Really, the man was impossible! What had Karla ever seen in him in the first place?

And what was taking Elsie so long? She had to get rid of this tray before Jack came after her again. Lorinda veered over to a marble table that was so much a part of the wall that it seemed to be growing out of it and rested her tray on it, shoving aside two bowls of olives, an ashtray, a saucer of peanuts and a flower arrangement.

'Good work!' She was not alone. Macho materialized at her side, eyes gleaming as he reached for a napkin and began loading it up with chicken kebabs.

'Clever you!' Gemma appeared on her other side and reached for the medallions of beef. 'Just what we needed – a tray of our own.'

'For heaven's sake!' They were shameless. Lorinda cast an anxious glance around to make sure they were unobserved – at least by their host. 'Be careful!'

'I don't care who sees me,' Macho said defiantly, but he took an uneasy look over his shoulder.

'What about who photographs you?' Lorinda pointed out, as a series of flashes went off in the distance. 'Talk about grounds for blackmail!'

'He'd better not try it,' Macho growled. 'Anyway, there's nothing blackmailable about it. It's not a criminal offence.'

'Quite right.' Freddie appeared behind them. 'It may be impolite, in bad taste and a trifle shoddy, but it's not an indictable offence.'

'It's always nice to know what your friends really think of you,' Macho said sourly.

The others regarded Freddie unmoved. It was all right for her, she was petless at the moment. There would be no hopeful little eyes to greet her when she returned home.

'Sorry you disapprove,' Gemma said. 'We can't put any canapés back now though, it would look even worse – and so would they.'

'Never mind.' Freddie shrugged and turned to Lorinda. 'The great Plantagenet sent me over to fetch you. Your editor wants to talk to you.'

'Where is she?' Lorinda looked around. 'I didn't see her here.' A strange man was talking to Plantagenet Sutton, but the familiar face she expected to see was nowhere in sight.

'It's a New York editor, I think,' Freddie said vaguely. 'A new one.'

'Oh, not another new one!' She might have guessed; the permanent tan on the stranger's face marked him out as transatlantic. 'Every time I get a letter from New York, there's a different signature. Can't these people ever stay put?'

'It's happening here, too, these days,' Freddie said. 'Just remember the old adage: Be nice to the people you meet on the way up, you'll meet them again on the way down – and they'll be even more in need of kindness then.'

Plantagenet Sutton and the new editor were both looking in her direction now. Lorinda waved to them and nodded to signal that the message had been received and would be acted upon as soon as possible. Out of the corner of her eye, she saw Elsie approaching with a freshly laden tray and winced inwardly. She moved slightly to one side, so that Macho was shielding her, and hoped the transfer of booty could be made inconspicuously.

'There you are,' Elsie greeted her, and leaned closer to whisper in her ear. 'Too many people around. I'll fill one of those little plastic tubs and leave it outside the back door. You can pick it up on your way home.'

'Wonderful!' Lorinda beamed at her gratefully and went to meet her new editor unburdened and with a moderately clear conscience.

By the time she was able to get away, the party was breaking up. Freddie and Macho were nowhere in sight. The local catering staff had also disappeared and only Betty Alvin and Gordie Crane were still on duty, looking tired and tight-lipped, collecting up the used glasses as soon as they were set down and carrying them away to the improvised pantry behind the screens. A clear signal the party was over.

Plantagenet Sutton's wavering gaze did not quite focus on Lorinda as she thanked him for a delightful party and made her escape.

Outside, she hesitated. The night seemed extraordinarily dark and a chill wind was rising. The moon was hidden behind thick clouds, presaging rain, and trees and bushes rustled ominously. She shivered involuntarily.

The streetlamp marking the turning into the narrow aperture that was Coffers Passage seemed to have burned out. No wonder the night seemed so much darker.

It took her a long moment to argue herself into taking the short cut. Yes, it was dark. Yes, it looked sinister. Yes, it was the sort of thing she groaned about when one of the colleagues sent the heroine into such a foolhardy venture. But this was real life; this was Brimful Coffers, not some urban jungle with danger lurking around every corner. Of course, it was a perfectly safe thing to do and it would enable her to pick up the cats' treats and get home so much more quickly.

She was halfway down Coffers Passage when she heard the faint echoing footsteps.

They were so faint . . . even furtive . . . that she could not tell whether they were behind her or in front of her.

She looked over her shoulder. Nothing moved in the long dark alley behind her. Nor did anything seem to be looming menacingly in the shadows ahead.

There was a perfectly simple explanation. The last guests were still leaving the party, she was hearing their footsteps as they walked along the pavement outside Coffers Court. Sounds carried strangely in the still night air, often distorted and seeming to come from a different direction.

Nevertheless, she quickened her own steps, instinctively tilting forward on to her toes to minimize any sounds she might make. The end of the passage seemed an endless length away; she moved towards it steadily, forcing herself not to run.

As she reached the end of the passage and turned into the back street, she realized that the footsteps were no longer audible. The relief that swept over her left her feeling silly. There had never been any threat in them – why had she allowed them to disturb her so? The dark night and restless wind preying upon her imagination probably, not to mention the lavishness with which the catering staff had dispensed the champagne.

She walked purposefully along the vine-covered wall that enclosed the back garden of Coffers Court and opened the narrow wooden door set discreetly into the wall. It was usually kept locked, but not tonight; the caterers and delivery people would have needed access all evening.

The little round white plastic carton was waiting in a corner of the top step, right where Elsie had promised it would be, just visible in the dim glow of the light from the windows looking on to the garden.

It was heavier than she expected, Elsie must have crammed it full. Just as she began to pick it up, there was a sudden high-pitched burst of unamused laughter from somewhere eerily close at hand.

Lorinda nearly dropped the carton. As it slipped, she heard a faint clink – what else had she dropped? Her groping hand encountered something small and flat and cold. Automatically, she gathered up the object and squinted at it in disbelief.

Pince-nez. . . gold-rimmed pince-nez . . . their broken cord dangling from one side. 'There was only one person she had ever known – or, rather, imagined – who wore pince-nez . . .

The high-pitched mocking laughter sounded again, fading into the distance.

Lorinda thrust the pince-nez into her coat pocket and stumbled down the flagstone path to the door in the wall.

It was some sort of joke. Not funny and in poor taste – as though the autocratic Miss Petunia intended to reprimand her for . . . for . . . ?

Impossible! She really had drunk too deeply of Plantagenet Sutton's champagne to let it affect her like this.

She did not even try to muffle her footsteps as she gained the street and turned towards home. This time she ran.

3

CHAPTER TWENTY

'Oooh!' Marigold squealed, clapping her hands girlishly. 'It all looks so beautiful! Like Fairyland!'

'Not bad, if I do say so myself.' Lily descended the stepladder, hammer swinging carelessly in her hand.

'A beautiful job, my dear.' The vicar's wife always seemed to speak through clenched teeth. 'Although you shouldn't have gone to all that trouble. My husband had planned to –'

'No trouble at all.' Lily beamed. 'Looks good.' Streamers stretched across the ceiling, clusters of balloons bloomed in every corner and fairy lights sparkled everywhere.

'Oh, very good,' the vicar's wife agreed quickly, smartly stepping back out of range of the swinging hammer.

'Yes,' Miss Petunia approved. 'This is going to be one of our most successful bazaars. I can *feel* it.'

The church hall had never looked so attractive, if one did say so oneself. The tables were laden with needlework, knitting, homemade cakes, jams and preserves, books, bric-à-brac, and all the hundreds of offerings designed to charm the pennies and pounds out of pockets and purses.

In one corner an artfully draped sheet represented a gypsy tent, within which lurked a heavily made-up volunteer who (on the strength of having read the two books on graphology and card tricks that comprised the library's entire stock of unorthodoxy) was going to tell fortunes. In the opposite corner, the tombola spun merrily behind a table filled with numbered prizes to be won. A door in the far corner led to the little side room where teas were to be served and the last corner held the steps leading up to the stage where the judging was to be held. The long trestle table was set out on the stage, laden with the pies, cakes, preserves and jams, ready for the solemn procession of judges to taste and pronounce their verdict upon.

'Best part of the whole day,' Lily said, looking around with satisfaction. 'Too bad we have to let the public in to mess it all up.'

Everybody laughed heartily. They always laughed heartily at Lily's jokes. Which was just as well. Lily could become . . . difficult . . . if she thought she wasn't appreciated.

'Let me relieve you of that heavy old thing.' Deftly, Mrs Reverend Christian abstracted the hammer from Lily's hand. 'Now that you've finished with it.' Still laughing gaily, she carried it into the tearoom.

'I *do* feel the Reverend Christian is most fortunate in his choice of a life's mate,' Miss Petunia said, watching her go. 'We must keep watch carefully. Nothing like last year's unfortunate happening must be allowed to mar today's festival.'

'Rotten hard luck on the vicar's wife,' Lily agreed. 'A duff mushroom in the *mushrooms à la Grecque* could happen to anyone.'

'Rather harder luck on poor Mr Mallory,' Marigold twinkled. 'Still, it was a lovely funeral.'

'Although a most premature one,' Miss Petunia said severely.

'Oh, but, Pet, he *was* dead.' Marigold's eyes widened earnestly. 'Everyone said so.'

'I am not questioning the *fact* of his death.' Petunia lowered her voice and her sisters moved closer in order to hear. 'But the *manner* of it!'

'A duff mushroom in the *mushrooms à la Grecque* could happen to anyone.' Lily persisted stubbornly in her defence of the vicar's wife.

'*That* is why it was such a brilliant method of murder!' Miss Petunia pointed out triumphantly.

'Murder!' Lily's eyes gleamed. 'I say, Pet, are we on the trail again?'

'But who – ?' Marigold breathed.

'The least likely suspect, of course.' Lily looked around the hall thoughtfully. 'How about the gypsy fortune teller? Bad lot, those gypsies, anyway.'

'She wasn't here last year, dear,' Miss Petunia reminded her sister. 'Besides, she's not a real gypsy, she's Miss Plotz, the librarian.'

'Then who?' Lily's eyes narrowed, the tip of her nose twitched. Everyone was under suspicion now.

'You will remember that I was one of the judges last year,' Miss Petunia said. 'After Lady Mallerwynn opened the bazaar and did her usual round of the stands, thoughtfully buying something at each, she then went directly to the judging platform on the stage. You might not have noticed it, but she had brought her own silver spoon and silver pickle fork to use in the tastings. The *mushrooms à la Grecque* were the first of the picklings to be judged. They were opened in her presence. When she removed the pickle fork from her capacious handbag, I noticed that there was something soft and small stuck on the tines – so that she shouldn't inadvertently stab herself if she groped quickly for a handkerchief, she *said*.'

'You mean that *Lady Mallerwynn?*' Marigold gasped.

'Precisely! She was, of course, the first to taste – and it would be quite easy for her to *add* a mushroom as well as take one out! Then it was my turn to taste but – as everyone knows – ever since that terrible holiday we had in Athens, I have *never* been able to stomach Greek food. So I simply *pretended* to taste the mushrooms although, naturally, I gave Mrs Christian the highest mark on my scoring pad, for everyone knows she's a wonderful cook. Then poor Mr Mallory actually *did* bite into his mushroom – and we all know the consequences!'

'Lady Mallerwynn!' Lily's fists clenched. 'And she let the vicar's wife take the blame!'

'Oh, it's so unfair!' Marigold cried. 'Especially as poor Mrs Christian is such a martyr to neuralgia!'

'Is she?' Miss Petunia was intrigued. 'How do you know that, Marigold?'

'Haven't you noticed? I have. Every time we're talking together like this and I glance over at Mrs Christian, she's grimacing – bravely trying to hide her pain.'

With one accord, all three turned their heads to stare at Mrs Christian. Sure enough, she was grimacing, wincing – in fact, she flinched.

'Poor woman!' Lily said. 'We must do all we can to help her.'

'Indeed,' Miss Petunia agreed. 'That is why we are here. We must keep careful watch today and miss nothing.'

'But, Pet,' Marigold demurred. 'Lady Mallerwynn isn't here this year, so how could anything go wrong? Besides' – her eyes clouded – 'why on earth should she have wanted to kill poor old Mr Mallory?'

'Ah!' Miss Petunia adjusted her pince-nez and looked at her sister meaningly. 'Just consider the similarity of their two names. It is my suspicion that Mr Mallory, recently retired from a life in the merchant navy, was really the rightful Lord Mallerwynn and heir to all the fortune and estates. Since returning to his native village of St Waldemar Boniface and taking up a hobby of genealogy, he would have begun to realize this and be making plans to lay his claims. If that happened, Lady Mallerwynn would be a Lady no longer, she would be forced to leave the Manor and move to a smaller house, the money would no longer belong to her, her sons would no longer be the heirs apparent . . .' Miss Petunia lowered her voice. 'She might even have to remove them from Eton. That, surely is a motive worth murdering for!'

'Oh, Pet,' Marigold sighed. 'You're so clever!'

'Brilliant!' Lily agreed.

'To your stations, girls. They're about to open the doors and let the public in. We'll have a proper Council of War over tea this evening.'

As Miss Petunia walked past Mrs Christian on her way to stand beneath the stage, she noticed that the vicar's wife was wincing again.

'Jolly good, this.' Lily spread more rosehip jelly on her toasted muffin. 'Different, but good.'

'Delicious.' Marigold helped herself to more. 'Such a subtle flavour. I believe there's a hint of almonds in it. Where did you get it, Lily? I didn't see anything like this on the preserves stand.'

'Vicar's wife gave it to me herself. A new recipe she's trying out for next year. Wanted us to try it. Said she'd value our opinions.'

'How kind of her. *Do* try some, Pet.'

'No, thank you.' Miss Petunia yawned. It had been an exhausting day, with only a few more suspicions to show for it. 'It sounds more like something for spreading on your face than eating. I'll stick with this lovely bramble jam. Is this from the vicar's wife, too?'

'Right you are.' Lily's mouth twitched suddenly. 'Another experimental recipe – in case we didn't fancy the rosehips.'

'Yes ... there *is* something different in it.' Miss Petunia yawned again. 'I can't quite place it ...'

'And there's such a dear little drawing of bramble leaves on the label –' Marigold grimaced suddenly. 'But they don't *quite* look like bramble leaves, do they?'

'Not ... quite ...' Miss Petunia blinked and tried to focus on the label. The drawing reminded her of something ... but she was so tired. She felt that she could fall asleep ... right here in this chair ...

Strangely, both Marigold and Lily appeared to have suddenly become hyperactive. Miss Petunia peered at them muzzily, thinking that they seemed quite revived after their exertions of the afternoon. Even as she watched, Lily leaped to her feet, knocking her chair over, and proceeded to bend over backwards. So athletic, dear Lily!

At the same time, Marigold shrieked and hurled her jelly-laden muffin from her, seeming to go into some form of St Vitus dance. 'The jam!' she shrieked. 'The almonds! It wasn't almonds, it was – aaargh!' She pitched to the floor and, after a bit more twitching, lay still.

Lily now appeared to be doing a Conga on all fours, but was gamely attempting to get to the telephone. She was making strange noises, apparently under the impression that she was communicating something to her sisters.

Miss Petunia watched her progress with interest, gradually realizing that Marigold and Lily had been poisoned by the rosehip jelly. How very fortunate that she had chosen the bramble jam herself.

Just as soon as she could overcome this strange lethargy, she must rise and go to the telephone and summon the doctor. But she could not seem to force herself to move. How odd!

Her vision cleared momentarily and she found that she was staring at the label on the bramble jam. Marigold was right – it was not a drawing of bramble leaves and berries. Miss Petunia frowned at it. It looked familiar ... it was surely ...

Yes ... it was. Deadly nightshade!

But why? And the vicar's wife! Who could have imagined it? Then ... possibly ... that mushroom last year had been meant for *her*, Miss Petunia, and not for Mr Mallory at all. But why?

Why should the vicar's wife . . . want to kill *her?* And Lily? And Marigold?

In her dying moments, Miss Petunia Pettifogg had discovered a new mystery. It was one she carried with her to . . .

> ### THE END

Lorinda straightened and flexed her tightened muscles. Had-I, stretched across her shoulders, mewled a protest and scrambled to a sitting position. But-Known, sprawled across her feet, slid to the floor and stretched.

Lorinda gathered up the pages without her usual feeling of satisfaction. The uneasiness of last night had not quite left her. The gold-rimmed pince-nez, wrapped in a tissue, were filed in the FINAL CHAPTERS folder; she could not wait to bury them under more chapters and forget them.

The phone tweetled abruptly, startling them all. Had-I leaped to the desk and watched the phone intently; she had long suspected that there was a bird in there somewhere. Only the obvious fact that it was completely inedible had kept her from killing and dismembering it. But-Known regarded her sister's posturings with a jaundiced eye; even if there had been a bird in there, it was safe from But-Known.

'Hello?' Lorinda fended Had-I away from the cradle before she disconnected the call.

'Sanctuary,' Freddie croaked piteously. 'I crave sanctuary.'

'Poor Freddie,' Lorinda said automatically. 'Come round and have a drink.'

'I was hoping you'd say that. I'll be right over.'

The cats raced each other into the kitchen where they took up positions in front of the fridge. Two tiny pink tongues flicked out and moved from left to right in unison. They watched Lorinda with greedy anticipation. There was still plenty of booty left from last night's party and they knew it.

'Oh, all right.' She had to open the fridge to get the ice cubes, anyway. The carton of goodies was still embarrassingly heavy. She hoped Plantagenet Sutton never learned how thoroughly his canapés had been plundered. It would not endear his new neighbours to him.

Had-I and But-Known threw themselves enthusiastically into disposing of the evidence, crooning with delight. Lorinda put the carton back into the fridge just as Freddie tapped at the back door.

'Stop me if I'm becoming a bore on the subject,' Freddie said, 'but I think it's getting to be an obsession. I've always heard that there are people who can get along on only three or four hours' sleep a night – isn't it just my luck that a pair of them have moved into the other half of my semi?'

Lorinda thrust a large gin and tonic into Freddie's hand. It was the most sympathetic rejoinder she could think of at the moment.

'Thanks.' Freddie took a deep pull at it and barely paused to swallow before going on with her complaints. 'I've stopped worrying about them killing each other – now I'm afraid they won't. It may be my only hope for a peaceful life again.'

'Perhaps they'll split up and both go away.' Lorinda led the way into the living room. The cats were down to polishing their dishes now and casting hopeful glances; they needed a clear signal that they'd had their lot for the time being.

'That will never happen.' Freddie settled into an armchair. 'They're together until death do them part. Believe me, I've heard enough to know.'

'Oh, well.' Lorinda curled up in one corner of the sofa. 'If that's so, it will certainly provide all of us with a lot of fresh material.'

'All useless,' Freddie said dismissively. 'Most murders are domestic, one spouse killing the other in real life. We all know that. Nothing more boring. No suspense, no questions about whodunit. Open-and-shut case. Straight police procedural and they're yawning all the way to the jail. Nothing in it for us at all.'

'Oh, I don't know,' Lorinda said. 'The way Jack was carrying on last night, I think suspicion might be spread around half a dozen or more people. By the time I left, everyone was going out of their way to avoid him and/or spoil his picture, which was just as good. I thought Macho might brain him with a blunt instrument after he caught him unawares and actually got a

54

full-face shot. He'll give poor Macho a nervous breakdown, if he keeps on like that.'

'That's what the fight was all about when they got home,' Freddie said. 'Karla was furious about the way he'd been behaving and threatened to expose the films he'd taken. Told him it was an invasion of privacy and betrayal of hospitality – which it was – as though he knew about such niceties. Or cared.

'He flew off the handle and accused her of trying to blight his promising career. His promising career – hah!' Freddie snorted. 'He buys a camera and he thinks he's Henri Cartier-Bresson and Richard Avedon rolled into one. Does he imagine anyone would care about his amateur shots if Karla weren't supplying the words?'

'Someone is going to have to have a word with him,' Lorinda said. 'Apart from his wife, that is. She appears to have no effect at all.'

'She maddens him – that's her effect.' Freddie grimaced. 'And vice versa, I'd say.'

'Who'll bell the cat?' Lorinda absently watched Had-I and But-Known stroll into the room, sit down and begin to wash their faces. 'I'd say Dorian – he's their friend, he's the one who brought them into our midst. It's up to him to sort them out. We can't go on like this all winter.'

'Dorian, yes. He got us into this,' Freddie brooded. 'I could strangle him for it.'

'He does seem to have a lot to answer for,' Lorinda agreed.

'More every day. I hope he doesn't have anything else up his sleeve. Anyway' – Freddie brightened – 'I don't think there are any more properties to be sold or let in the village. No more strangers in our midst – '

The sharp peal of the doorbell cut her off. The cats looked up and raced to leap on to the windowsill, jostling the curtain aside as they looked out to see who was at the door.

Someone stepped closer to the window and peered in at the cats, then looked beyond them into the room and waved.

'Only me,' she called.

'Speak of the devil!' Freddie said. 'And she's seen us. There's no escape.'

Lorinda got up and went to open the door to Karla Jackley, who followed her back into the living room, happily unaware that she was not the most welcome of guests.

'I knew you were over here,' she greeted Freddie. 'I saw you cutting across the back gardens. I wanted to talk to you, both of you, so – '

'Gin and tonic all right?' Lorinda asked. 'That's what we're drinking.'

'Just fine, thanks.' She gave Lorinda a grateful smile before continuing. 'I rang Macho, but he had his answering machine on and I don't know whether he was there or not. Or if he was busy working. Oh, thanks.' She accepted her drink and took the other armchair.

'I hope you don't mind my dropping in like this, but I wanted to apologize. For Jack. He was pretty impossible last night. I know he got everybody mad at him.'

There was an awkward silence while they tried to think of something polite and vaguely comforting to say to her, but not so polite or comforting that she would think it was permissible for her husband to continue in that way.

'It's all right,' Karla said. 'I know. I told him so. I – ' She stopped and took an unsteady breath, perhaps dangerously close to tears.

Thank heavens for the cats. With more tact than the humans, they advanced on Karla. Had-I jumped into her lap, But-Known rubbed against her ankles.

'Aren't they darlings?' As Karla bent to stroke the cats, her hair slid forward, masking her expression, but revealing a long horizontal bruise on her neck.

Lorinda and Freddie just had time to exchange a significant look before Karla straightened and faced them again. 'Anyway, just because Jack took the pictures doesn't mean we're going to use them. He'll probably be taking hundreds this winter.'

'Oh, God!' Freddie moaned.

'I know. He's taking them of me, too. I daren't even go down to breakfast without full make-up and not a hair out of place. I'm getting sick of it already. I wish I'd never given him the idea, but he's got the bit in his teeth now and I can't stop him. Believe me, I've been trying to.'

'I believe you,' Freddie said grimly.

'Oh!' Karla wasn't dumb. 'Have we been disturbing you? I've wondered how thick the walls really are.'

'Not thick enough.' Caught, Freddie admitted it. 'Not that I hear much,' she lied hastily. 'Just the occasional thud or crash.'

'I try to keep the noise level down, honestly, I do,' Karla said earnestly. 'But when he gets into one of his aggressive moods . . .' She let the thought trail off, unconsciously raising her hand to rub at the bruise on her neck, now hidden again by her hair.

How did a nice woman like you ever link up with a boor and a brute like that? But it was not a question that could be asked, even though Karla might be willing to try to answer it in one of those exhaustive and comprehensive soul-searchings some Americans indulged in. A more neutral question was safer.

'Where did you meet Dorian?' Lorinda asked instead.

'Oh!' From the way Karla jumped, she might just as well have asked the original question. 'In New York last year, when he came over to do that signing tour. We have the same publisher and we were at a few book stores together. We sort of got to know each other.' She appeared flustered and – was that a blush? She dipped her head again, swinging her hair forward to shield her face.

But-Known allowed one more stroke then obviously decided that her hostess duty was done and strolled over to leap up on the sofa beside Lorinda. Had-I settled down comfortably in Karla's lap, pinning her to the chair.

'He made England sound so . . . so attractive. I'd always wanted to come over and spend some time here and really get to know it. Then, when he wrote and told us about this place, a whole group of mystery writers living together –' She blushed again. 'I mean, in the same community, like the Pre-Raphaelites or the Bloomsbury Set, all like-minded people, friends and colleagues, being creative . . . Oh, I'm not explaining it well.'

'Well enough,' Freddie said dryly. 'Don't forget, we were taken in, too.'

'Anyway, Jack had just lost his job . . . again.' She half swallowed the word. 'So he was free to travel and looking for something to do. I'd just been offered the assignment to complete the book Aimee Dorrow had been working on when she died so suddenly and do another one to see if we couldn't keep the Miss Mudd series going without her, as it was so successful. Jack put the idea of a Literary Winter/Year in England to them and they were interested – provided that I was spending that winter working on *My Name Is Mudd*. To tell the truth, I'm not sure they would have taken Jack's idea on its own, but lumping the three books together in a package, he had a deal.'

'How are you getting on with it?' Freddie asked curiously. 'I mean, someone else's idea, someone else's characters. Doesn't it bother you at all?'

'No . . .' Karla paused and considered the question. 'It's rather refreshing, in a way . . . perhaps liberating is what I mean. It's a challenge to keep a popular series alive, despite the death of the originating author. And it's giving me a chance to try things that would not have been possible within the structure of my own series. Tell me' – she looked at them artlessly – 'don't you ever get tired of your own characters?'

'Do I ever!' Freddie rolled her eyes heavenwards. 'There are days when I could strangle the dear girl with my own hands if she were to appear before me in the flesh. That remark is off the record, of course.' Belatedly, she appeared to remember that Karla might be taking notes for her projected nonfiction book.

'I think everyone must feel that way at some time,' Lorinda said carefully. She shot Freddie a look of complicity. Jack's activities would be relatively easy to monitor, Karla's were going to be a lot trickier. 'There's the classic story of Agatha Christie and Dorothy L. Sayers comparing notes on a railway journey and agreeing that they were heartily sick of Hercule Poirot and Lord Peter Wimsey.'

'It goes with the territory, I suppose.' Karla shrugged. 'I'm lucky to have a chance to escape the mould for a bit, even though I don't break out of it.'

'Have you ever thought of creating a new series?' Freddie's caution was no match for her curiosity. 'A completely new and different character, as opposite as possible to the old one?'

'Perhaps even living in a different country,' Karla agreed eagerly. 'Or even a different century, historicals are big now. Of course I have. Hasn't everyone? The trouble is, one gets so dreadfully locked in. Agents and publishers are convinced the public is too infantile to cope with anything new or different.'

'Unless you use a different name, too,' Lorinda said.

'Then you're faced with building up a new audience all over again,' Freddie pointed out. 'Unless they use one of those weasel lines saying, "Lorinda Lucas writing as . . ." Which rather negates the object of the exercise, I would think.'

'You always hope they know what they're doing,' Karla sighed. 'But I sometimes wonder . . . Oh!'

The telephone rang suddenly and Karla jumped, nearly dislodging Had-I from her lap. Had-I gave her an offended look, jumped to the floor and started for Lorinda, who was rising to answer the telephone. Very unsatisfactory. Had-I settled for leaping to the arm of Freddie's chair, as though that had been her intended destination all along.

'I'm sorry,' Karla apologized, as much to Had-I as to anyone else. 'My nerves are shot to hell these days. I mean' – she gave a wan smile – 'I'm so exhausted from all the packing and travelling and settling in to new surroundings. I'm just not the person I used to be at all. I'm hoping a quiet winter here will soothe me down and recharge my batteries.'

'Hello, Dorian.' Lorinda turned her back to the others, mostly to block off the meaning glances from Freddie. Karla was going to notice, if Freddie wasn't more discreet.

'Dorian?' Karla wasn't noticing anything else at the moment. 'I've been trying to get through to him. I want to talk to him.'

'Yes, it was a lovely party,' Lorinda agreed. 'Just a minute, Dorian, Karla's here and she wants to talk to you.' Karla was already snatching at the phone.

'Oh, God!' Dorian groaned. 'I haven't time right now to –'

'Dore?' Karla had possession of the phone. Lorinda stepped back. 'Do you keep that damned answering machine on twenty-four hours a day? I've been trying to get through to you . . .'

'Freshen your drink?' Lorinda bowed to the inevitable and left the phone to Karla, going over to take the glass Freddie extended. Had-I moved into Freddie's lap and demanded attention, which Freddie duly supplied. Behind them, the conversation – or argument – continued.

'London? I told you I wanted to go up to London the next time you –' Karla stopped, obviously choked off by the retort from the other end of the line. 'But you promised . . .' she wailed.

Freddie winked at Lorinda and bent over Had-I, shaking her hair in a wicked parody of Karla's mannerism. Had-I stretched up a paw and swiped at a lock of hair as though sharing in the joke. Lorinda caught back a laugh and moved hastily towards the kitchen.

When she returned, Karla was still in possession of the phone, but seemed calmer. Dorian was always at his best when spreading oil on troubled waters. Possibly that was all he had been doing in New York and Karla had misinterpreted it as some sort of personal invitation to join him in England and . . . who knew what? Jack's presence would put a damper on most plans.

'Yes, it does sound like fun,' Karla was admitting grudgingly now. 'You won't mind if Jack brings the camera along and records it? I'll try to see that he doesn't overdo the shooting – he just got sort of carried away last night.'

There was a short silence while Karla nodded agreement to whatever was being said on the other end of the line, then she turned to Lorinda. 'He wants to talk to you,' she said, holding out the phone.

Not surprisingly, since he had telephoned her in the first place. 'Thank you,' Lorinda said dryly, taking the phone.

'Lorinda?' Dorian asked cautiously. 'Have I got you now?'

'Yes, Dorian.' Lorinda watched Karla resume her seat. 'What is it?'

'Forgive the informality, but it's an invitation. I've decided to have a little Guy Fawkes party on November fifth. Small and old-fashioned. Just our crowd, potatoes roasting in the bonfire, loads of sausages, perhaps a few sparklers but no fireworks. I thought those of you with beasties could bring them along to share the sausages – so much less messy than trying to wrap up titbits to take home to them, don't you think?'

'How kind.' So he'd noticed that and was going to rub it in. He wouldn't say anything to Plantagenet Sutton, of course, but he was not above insinuating that he might. Dorian liked to keep people off-balance. She wondered if he had been responsible for those pince-nez. It was just the sort of thing he might do.

'It sounds like a lovely party. I'll be delighted, but I think the cats had better stay at home. You might not have fireworks, but others in the village undoubtedly will. I don't want them frightened or worried.' Or startled into running away in territory that was still unfamiliar to them. Dorian didn't have to worry about such problems with his tropical fish, but pet owners with lively four-legged companions were in a different category.

'I suppose you know best.' Dorian obviously didn't believe it for a moment. 'Pity. I thought they'd enjoy it.'

'Another time, perhaps, when the proceedings aren't likely to get so noisy.'

Had-I and But-Known came over to sit at her feet, blinking at her as though realizing they were being discussed. Lorinda blinked back and it seemed to satisfy them. They slumped down into a sleeping position and closed their eyes.

'Yes, Freddie's here, too.' Lorinda answered Dorian's next question. 'Do you want to speak to her or shall I just pass your invitation along?'

'I've already heard it,' Freddie said. 'And, yes, thanks, I'll go to his party. There obviously isn't going to be anyplace else to go that night.'

Karla drew in her breath in a shocked hiss. Lorinda nodded and conveyed Freddie's acceptance, suitably bowdlerized.

'Ooops!' Freddie gave Karla a severe look. 'That was off the record, you understand.'

'Look,' Karla said, 'I'm beginning to get a pretty good idea of what you think of me and I'm not happy about it. Jack and I are two different people, you know. I don't approve of everything he does and he –' She broke off and lurched to her feet.

'I'm sorry. I told you my nerves –' She raised a hand to her head. 'And I'm getting a ghastly headache, it keeps coming and going . . . I can't get rid of it.'

'I'm sorry,' Freddie apologized in turn. 'It's the idea that you're doing a book about your winter with us that's unnerving me. Plus the fact that we have Professor Borley prowling around with the same intention. I'm not very tactful and I know it. I don't like the feeling that I've got to watch everything I say.'

'You might trust *me* more,' Karla said reproachfully. 'I wouldn't do that to you – any of you. I'm not some kind of investigative reporter. It's just going to be a light-hearted informal history of a year in England. And I'll make sure Jack clears the photos with you before we use any of them.'

'That's something.' Lorinda and Freddie exchanged glances, repressing the information that Macho would never authorize any picture of himself for publication.

'Perhaps it would be a good idea if we passed the word along,' Freddie said helpfully. 'It might make life easier.'

'Oh, would you?' Karla asked gratefully. 'I'd try to tell people myself, but I don't often get a chance to get out without Jack. He'd *kill* me if he knew I was apologizing for him and making promises about his photographs.'

'We'll take care of it,' Freddie assured her. 'Everyone will be glad to know that they're not going to spend the winter under *two* microscopes. Professor Borley and his interviews will be bad enough.'

Lorinda felt an uneasy qualm. Something about this situation was . . .

'Thank you. Oh, thank you,' Karla said. 'I'd be so grateful. After all, I – I don't have any friends here yet. And I do want people to like me.'

'Of course.' There was something quizzical about Freddie's smile, but only someone familiar with her expressions would know that.

'Well . . .' Karla looked around restlessly. 'I'm sorry, but my headache is getting so much worse. There's nothing for it but to go home and lie down in a darkened room. But I'm so glad to have had this talk with you both.'

'Yes.' Lorinda and the cats escorted her to the door and saw her out.

'Poor dear,' Lorinda said, returning to the living room. 'She hasn't a clue about Dorian's "arrangements", has she? Or do you think he's ready to turn over a new leaf and settle down?'

Freddie snorted. 'I think our Dorian prizes the quiet life too much to change it now. And he's too much of a snob to swap a titled lady in London for a not-yet-divorced American termagant.'

'You don't think you might be too hard on her? She's trying so desperately to fit in. And she *is* rather sweet, isn't she?'

'Oh, absolutely charming,' Freddie agreed. 'You'd never dream that she'd even *heard* some of the words that have come through my walls when she's in full screech.'

'We can all have a surprising vocabulary when we lose our tempers – and that husband doesn't seem to bring out the best in her.'

'*That's* the understatement of the year. Only . . .' Freddie looked thoughtful.

'Yes?' Lorinda prompted.

'Do you ever get the feeling that you've just been very cleverly manipulated?'

4

By the fifth of November, Lorinda was in no mood for a party. Not after the week she had just endured.

First, Had-I had suddenly begun moping about the house, resisting But-Known's invitations to play, picking at her food and sleeping most of the time. Just as Lorinda was about to take her to the vet, she had begun retching and heaving and had slowly disgorged an enormous hairball. No wonder she had been so uncomfortable.

Then Freddie had dropped in frequently with further complaints about the Jackleys. So had Macho, who couldn't stop worrying about the pictures that Jack had taken.

'I've got to get those photographs,' he brooded. 'And the negatives. My Macho Magee would break in, burgle the house, take what he wanted and perhaps smash up some of the furniture as well – but I haven't had any experience in that sort of thing. Do you think I should send Jackley a solicitor's letter?'

Now, at her feet, But-Known looked up anxiously and gave an experimental little throat-clearing cough. After all, *she* might be incubating a hairball, too.

'Oh, But-But, baby.' Lorinda stooped and gathered the little calico into her arms. 'Haven't you been getting your fair share of attention this week? I'll try to do better, I promise.'

In the distance, a string of firecrackers rat-tat-tatted into the dusk and But-Known flinched.

'All right,' Lorinda soothed, holding her close. 'It's all right.'

Nearer to the house, a rocket hissed up into the darkening sky. Had-I leaped up on the windowsill and hissed back. The rocket burst with a thunderclap into a shower of scintillating multicoloured sparks. Had-I jumped down, skittered across the room, leaped to the top of the desk and gazed up at Lorinda indignantly.

'Sorry, my darlings.' Still cuddling But-Known, she reached out a hand to ruffle Had-I's fur gently. 'I'd stop it if I could, but it's out of my control. This is Guy Fawkes Night.'

And she had promised to go to Dorian's party. Now that the night had arrived, she would have preferred to spend a quiet evening with the cats, providing a reassuring presence against their fears. However, it was not to be. Dorian had rung from London last night to assure everyone that he would be back today and remind them that he was expecting them at the party. The best she could do was to shut the cats in the bedroom with plenty of food, close the curtains and leave the party early to get back to them. Not the most satisfactory solution, but it would have to do.

She carried But-Known into the bedroom, Had-I followed close at her heels. They both settled at the foot of the bed while she changed. A hasty phone consultation with Rhylla and Freddie that morning had resulted in general agreement that trousers and heavy pullovers under jackets would be the most suitable clothes against the chilly night. If the festivities moved indoors, the jackets could be removed.

The cats sniffed suspiciously at the gourmet cat food she set out for them and turned their backs on it. She was going out against their wishes and bribes were not going to pacify them – at least not while she was watching.

'Suit yourselves,' she said, as they leaped back on the bed and settled down. 'It's there when you want it. I'll get back as soon as I can.'

Lorinda had just added a gold chain around her neck and freshened her lipstick when the doorbell rang. She went downstairs to greet Freddie and Macho, who had come to collect her.

'I must admit,' Freddie said, as they crossed the High Street, 'it *is* rather nice to be able to walk to places.'

'No need to worry about your drink when you're not driving,' Macho agreed. 'I'll wager Sutton takes full advantage of it tonight.'

'No takers,' Freddie said. 'That's a sucker bet, if I ever heard one.'

'Yoo-hoo, wait a minute!' a voice called out behind them. Gemma Duquette bustled up. 'Oh, good, now we can all arrive together. I hate making an entrance on my own.'

'Join the club.' Freddie moved over.

'Trust Dorian,' Macho said bitterly, as they climbed the hill on the other side of the High Street, 'to ensconce himself in the Manor House before any of the rest of us got a look-in at the property market in the town.'

'It's only a *small* manor house,' Gemma said defensively. 'And he's worked very hard.'

'So have we,' Freddie said with a trace of belligerency.

'Of course, of course,' Gemma said hastily. 'I'm just so delighted and grateful that Dorian thought of me when he found that Coffers Court still had some flats available. I can't tell you how good it is to be able to settle down among the friends and colleagues I've always worked with.'

'Better than King's Langley, I suppose,' Freddie muttered.

'What? Oh, Dorian – ' He had opened the door to them. 'What a splendid idea for a party. Guy Fawkes Night – how I've been looking forward to it!'

'About as original as most of his ideas,' Macho grumbled sotto voce, before advancing to offer a limp handshake and even limper smile.

'Come in . . . come in . . .' Dorian looked beyond them with a slightly nervous air, then seemed to relax as he realized no one else was with them. 'Drinks are being served out on the terrace . . . just make your way through.'

The drawing room doors opened out on to the long paved terrace with its stone balustrade and steps leading down to the lawn where an enormous stack of wood larded with rolled newspapers, kindling and magazines waited. On top, the traditional dummy sprawled uncomfortably awaiting its fate.

The drawing room doors were wide open – so much for any idea of taking off their jackets; it was nearly as cold inside as out. A fire was laid in the fireplace, but not yet lit.

Lorinda was relieved to see that a barbecue had been set up in a corner of the terrace; they were not going to have to stand at the edge of a roaring conflagration waving their sausages on toasting forks and trying to dodge stray spurts of flame. Foil-wrapped potatoes nestled among the burning coals; obviously they had been cooked in a proper oven and the baking process was being finished in the barbecue, no waiting until the bonfire died down and then scrabbling in the ashes for potatoes which might be only half baked.

'How civilized.' The relief in Freddie's voice betrayed that she also had had her reservations about an old-fashioned Guy Fawkes party. 'Leave it to Dorian. We can eat properly and enjoy the bonfire without having to play around its edges.'

'Over here!' Plantagenet Sutton, presiding over the bar, called imperiously. 'What are you having?' Three drinks trolleys had been pushed together to form a bar on which was displayed practically every liquor known to man. 'Name – dare I say? – your poison.'

'Oh, no,' Freddie groaned. 'How I hate coyness. Especially in postmenopausal males.'

'Not so loud,' Lorinda cautioned. 'You're up for review next.' A fugitive gleam in Gemma's eye reminded her that any incautious remark might be repeated later, probably with embellishments, to the person concerned. There was also the possibility that Gemma would take inspiration from the activity around her and decide to write her memoirs.

'We know what yours is,' Plantagenet smirked, waving a bottle of tequila at Macho. The worm curled up at the bottom rolled about wildly.

'Not tonight,' Macho growled, hunching his shoulders defensively. 'I'm in a bourbon mood tonight.'

'Still a good Macho choice, eh?' Plantagenet winked, reaching for the Wild Turkey. He left the tequila ostentatiously in the front row of bottles, where everyone could see that it had never been opened. In sharp contrast, the Wild Turkey was well depleted.

Macho snatched his drink with a growl of acknowledgement which was not quite thanks.

'Now I'll serve the ladies – sorry, women.' Plantagenet turned to them with a beaming smile. 'No sexist nonsense here, I hope you notice. Macho made a decision, so he was served first. Have you browsed around all these fascinating bottles enough yet to have made your choices?'

'I'll stick to gin and tonic, thanks,' Lorinda said quickly, before an enraged Freddie could say something she'd be sorry for later.

'Oh, perhaps just a teeny splash from that rather exotic purple curlicue bottle.' Gemma evidently felt that she had to live up – or down – to the Little Woman typecasting. She knew her *Woman's Place*, as she often used to jest. Lorinda wouldn't have risked it herself, that bottle looked *too* exotic; she wouldn't put it past either Dorian or Plantagenet, or both, to have slipped a few perfume bottles in amongst the collection.

'I'll have a whisky mac,' Freddie said, 'on a night like this.' A cold wind gusted across the terrace, in the distance more fireworks exploded and stray rockets soared into the sky.

'Ah, yes.' Plantagenet distributed the requested drinks. 'Nice night for a murder, eh? With all the background noise, no one would notice the proverbial shots ringing out.'

'Red herrings,' Macho growled. 'Check out that dummy on top of the bonfire first.'

'What a good idea.' Plantagenet beamed at him, carefully refilling his own glass from a bottle secreted on the lower shelf of a trolley. 'Why don't you climb up and make sure? Be careful, that structure looks quite rickety to me. And, of course, you mustn't let yourself be trapped on top when the torch is set to the kindling at the base.'

'I know who I'd like to see on top of that bonfire,' Freddie muttered.

They all turned to survey the bonfire, instinctively looking at the sprawled dummy. A sudden flash brought on the familiar light-splattered blindness.

'Great shot!' Jack Jackley shouted. He and Karla had obviously been circling the bonfire, taking shots from different angles, and had come round it in time to catch the group on the terrace looking at it.

'Alternatively,' Plantagenet said thoughtfully, 'you could strangle the victim with his own camera strap. You wouldn't need background explosions to cover that. It would be nice and quiet – and a public service.'

Hmmm, interesting to know that Jack was also getting on Plantagenet's nerves. One would never suspect him of objecting to being photographed anywhere, any time. Perhaps he felt he wasn't looking his best tonight.

Trailing in the wake of the Jackleys, more guests appeared; Rhylla Montague, talking with Professor Borley and Jennifer Lane, who owned the village bookshop. There were several other villagers as well, who had already learned that it was safer to be behind Jack and his camera than in front of him.

Karla made a helpless apologetic gesture as she and Jack stepped up on to the terrace. Lorinda noticed that, although Karla seemed to wish to dissociate herself from her husband, they were wearing matching outfits. Both were dressed in cream-coloured jeans, cream turtleneck pullovers and fawn jackets, making them faintly ghostlike in the darkness. They obviously had no idea of the effect on their costumes of the smuts and ashes that would be flying through the air as soon as the bonfire was lit.

The others were sensibly dressed in dark clothing and wore amused expressions every time they glanced at the Jackleys.

'I got some great shots of that Guy Fawkes dummy,' Jack said complacently. 'It sure looks lifelike.'

'Come and get your drink now,' Plantagenet invited, becoming more proprietorial by the moment. Perhaps he had refilled his own glass often enough to forget where he was and actually did think he was the host.

'O K,' Jack said. 'I guess I've got both hands free for a little while now.'

'No more pictures until they light the bonfire,' Karla said. 'Remember, you promised.'

'Not unless something happens that's too good to miss,' Jack said. 'I've got to keep alert, you don't get second chances on a really good shot.'

'What do you think might happen?' Karla exhaled a long breath of exasperation. 'Freddie's going to dance naked on a tabletop?'

'Not tonight,' Freddie said, 'it's too cold.'

'Here we are!' Dorian appeared in the far doorway and marched through the drawing room, holding aloft a flaming torch.

'Oh, gawd!' Freddie said. 'He thinks he's lighting the Olympic flame.'

Nevertheless, it was quite an entrance. He had taken all the attention away from Plantagenet Sutton and reclaimed his rightful position as host and Master of the Revels.

Dorian was followed by Betty Alvin and Gordie Crane, who were almost staggering under the weight of enormous trays laden with dishes piled with sausages, each pile thoughtfully labelled with a brief description of the sausages on offer. It was clear that Dorian had spent part of his time in London at a gourmet sausage establishment. Trust Dorian – no common-or-garden-variety bangers at *his* Bonfire Night.

'On the table,' Dorian directed, indicating the long trestle table set up beside the barbecue. 'Everyone can choose their own and have them cooked to order.' He stepped back and leaned against the stone railing, obviously gratified as his guests crowded round with cries of appreciation.

'Burgundy pistachio sausage . . .' Freddie began reading the tags. 'Pork, prune and cognac . . . steak and Guinness stout . . . duck with apricot and orange . . . smoked salmon . . . venison and wild mushroom . . . wild boar with Calvados and apple . . . There's something for everyone here.'

'There's even a *green* sausage!' Jack Jackley peered at it mistrustfully. 'I'm not eating that. How long have you had these things? Is your refrigeration working?'

'That's John Nott's sausage.' Dorian was amused and superior; it was obviously a reaction he had hoped for. 'From his *Cook's Diary* of 1720. The green is fresh spinach and it also contains eggs, marjoram and savory. You'll be missing a treat if you don't try one.'

'Jackley walked right into that one,' Macho said with satisfaction. 'Dorian was hoping someone would fall for it. Did you notice how he had the recipe right on the tip of his tongue?'

'Yeah?' Jackley had noticed, too. 'Well, whatever it is, you can find another sucker. I'm not eating anything that gives me cold chills to look at it.'

'*I'll* try one.' Karla gave her spouse a dismissive glance.

'It's hard to know what to choose,' Professor Borley said. 'They all look fantastically exotic. But, tell me, what do vegetarians do on Bonfire Night?'

'Here comes the vegetarian selection now,' Dorian said, as Betty Alvin reappeared with another tray. 'You'll find mushroom and tarragon sausage, chestnut and orange . . . a Welsh sausage of Caerphilly cheese and leek . . . then there's one made with courgette, coconut and spices . . .'

'Sorry I asked.' Professor Borley held up his hand as though quelling an unruly classroom. 'I think I'll settle for the venison and wild mushroom.'

'I intend to have a bite of everything,' Rhylla Montague announced. 'This spread must have cost dear Dorian a fortune and the least we can do is take advantage of it so that he can charge it up to research.'

'Dear Rhylla, how kind of you to be so concerned about

my finances,' Dorian murmured. For a moment, their glances crossed like swords.

'Well,' Rhylla said, 'are you going to stand there like a human torchère all evening, or are you going to light the bonfire?'

'Oh, I'm going to light it.' Dorian swept a glance around the terrace. 'In fact, I think it's time. Jack,' he called, 'are you ready to record the great moment?'

'Yeah. Sure. Coming.' Jack brought up his camera in a reflex action as Dorian flourished his torch, sending a shower of sparks into the air.

'I'd better go with them,' Karla said. 'It's supposed to be the record of my year. I mean, our year. One of us ought to be in the picture.' She hurried away to join the group following Dorian down the steps and on to the lawn.

'I wouldn't want to get too close to that bonfire myself.' Rhylla set her drink down on the stone balustrade and surveyed the scene below. 'It looks as though it might collapse if someone sneezed on it.'

'Dorian should stick to his level of competence,' Macho said. 'He's just about adequate as a writer; he has no flair at all for carpentry or building.'

'Actually, that bonfire is quite well constructed.' Gordie Crane joined them. 'I built most of it myself. It only looks so ramshackle because he allowed the local children to come along and throw their contributions on to it. That's why it has all those bits sticking out in odd places.'

'Children?' Rhylla looked around nervously. 'Where?'

'Oh, his hospitality didn't extend to inviting them to the party.' There was a trace of bitterness in Gordie's voice, perhaps because he wasn't a guest himself. 'He fobbed them off by saying that their parents would have their own plans for private parties, but they must be sure to look out of their windows when the bonfire was going well and they'd be able to see the guy burn.'

'All heart, our Dorian,' Rhylla said.

'I hope he has that dummy firmly anchored in place. It would ruin his evening if it slid to the ground without catching fire.' Macho sounded as though he hoped the opposite; it would not ruin *his* evening if Dorian's plans went awry.

'It will remain in place, I assure you.' Gordie seemed to resent the implied slur on his handiwork. As well he might. His expertise in all practical fields was the reason he was here. One of the truly useful people Dorian had collected, he was able to build bookcases, solve electrical problems, fix the plumbing and deal with all the other mechanical faults that baffled the rest of them. ('Invaluable,' Dorian had said. 'He can even mend broken-down typewriters. If the part isn't available any more, he'll hand-craft it himself.' To writers nursing along obsolete machines to avoid the day they had to grapple with new technology, it was the major point in Gordie's favour.) Dorian had used his influence to have Gordie installed in the basement flat at Coffers Court as resident caretaker, on call for any emergencies among the rest of the literary inhabitants of Brimful Coffers. Gordie's only flaw was that he cherished ambitions to be a writer himself and imagined that living in their midst would help him achieve his goal. It was a delusion Dorian encouraged for fear of losing the services of such a peerless handyman.

'The dummy will stay in place,' Gordie insisted firmly. 'I made sure none of the children got near it.'

'Children!' Rhylla sighed.

'Your granddaughter must be due any moment now, isn't she?' Lorinda obligingly picked up the cue.

'Three suitcases arrived this morning. Can Clarice be far behind?'

They watched as Dorian circled the bonfire, his torch dipping rhythmically to ignite the firelighters strategically concealed at intervals around the perimeter. Camera flashes recorded each flare of tinder and kindling. Crackling noises began to drown out the laughter and comments below.

'Gordie! The sausages are burning!' Betty Alvin's sharp cry made Gordie whirl about and dash for the barbecue grill where the first sausages were blackening and splitting.

'Oh, don't let Dorian see them!' Betty wailed in dismay. 'They cost a fortune – he'll be furious. Here, hide them in the warming cabinet. We'll eat them ourselves later.'

'I'll take one,' Macho said. 'I like them well done and crispy, anyway.'

'I'll help dispose of the evidence,' Freddie agreed.

'We all will.' Lorinda could say no less.

'Oh, bless you!' Betty Alvin looked at them hopefully. 'You needn't actually eat them. Perhaps you could take them home for your cats.'

'Oh, I don't think so.' Lorinda looked at the blackened lumps and shuddered. She was in enough trouble with the cats for leaving them tonight. Their probable reaction if she brought home such burnt offerings made her cringe. They wouldn't speak to her for a week.

'No, no, won't be necessary,' Macho agreed quickly. His Roscoe was also accustomed to much better fare. 'We'll eat them ourselves.'

'And *that* won't be necessary, either.' Gordie forked the ruined sausages into a pile and concealed them in a paper napkin. 'I'll slip down and throw them on the bonfire later.'

'Oh, that's a good idea!' Betty Alvin's relief betrayed that she hadn't been looking forward to choking down the burnt food herself. 'Don't get caught. Wait till Dorian is out of the way. He's sure to take some of the guests into his study to show off his tropical fish. That will be the best time to make a move. Then he won't get furious over the waste –'

'He can afford it.' Grimly, Gordie whisked the greasy bundle out of sight and set out a fresh row of assorted sausages on the grill just as the others returned to the terrace.

'It's well alight.' Dorian surveyed the scene below with the satisfaction of one who had done an excellent job. As a finishing touch, he had rammed the point of his torch into the ground beside the bonfire to burn itself out. 'Now, how are things proceeding here?' He cast an expert eye over the grill. 'Ah, splendid!'

Gordie nodded acknowledgement, his mouth a tight line. Much too soon, he turned the sausages over, frowning with a concentration that proclaimed he was too busy to talk.

'More drinks!' Dorian ordered. 'Bartender!' It was not quite a joke. 'You're falling down on the job. Fresh drinks for everyone!'

'Coming right up!' Plantagenet bared his teeth at the guests crowding round the bar. 'Step up and name your poison!' There was no doubt who he would like to poison.

Dorian smiled blandly and stepped back, not relinquishing his own glass to be refilled.

'Keep the home fires burning, dear boy,' he murmured to Gordie. 'I think I'll slip into my study for a few quiet moments and feed the fish.' He moved away.

'Feed himself, he means,' Betty Alvin translated when he was safely out of earshot. 'His ulcer has been acting up again. He has a plate of sandwiches waiting in there for him. These sausages are too rich and spicy for him to risk.'

'He'll be out of the way for a while, then.' Gordie handed the barbecue fork to Betty. 'Hold the fort while I dispose of the corpus delicti.' He retrieved the guilty bundle from its hiding place and started down the terrace steps with it.

Lorinda was not the only person to have noticed the byplay. As Gordie stooped to bury his parcel in the bonfire, a flash illumined the scene. Gordie straightened up in a whiplash motion and whirled to glare up at the terrace.

'Good one.' Jack lowered the camera and gave him a cheery wave. 'You're doing a great job,' he called. 'Keep that fire stoked.'

Gordie's lips moved; it was probably just as well that his voice didn't reach the terrace. He pushed the bundle farther into the bonfire with a stick and kicked a few embers over it before returning to the terrace and resuming his place at the grill.

Jack had wandered away and was taking more pictures, his earlier promise to Karla evidently forgotten – if he had intended to keep it at all. Karla, deep in conversation with Rhylla, did not appear to notice.

'If he comes near me, I'll break his camera,' Macho said, moving defensively behind Lorinda. 'How much longer do we have to stay? I'm ready to leave now.'

'Have something to eat first,' Freddie soothed. 'They've begun serving. Look! Jack's first in line. He won't be able to eat and take pictures at the same time. You're safe for another half hour. Come on, it's better than going home to the microwave.'

She had used a telling argument. Macho followed her meekly. Lorinda, swerving to avoid Karla, ran straight into Professor Borley.

'Allow me.' He took possession of her glass and passed it to Plantagenet. 'How is the book coming along?'

That was a question she did not wish to answer. She smiled vaguely and was rewarded with another question she did not want to answer.

'Is it possible to set a time for our interview?'

How about when hell freezes over? 'Oh, not just yet,' she said quickly. 'I'm at rather a tricky bit just now.'

'And you don't want your concentration broken.' He nodded

sagely. 'Well, just let me know when you're ready. I hope it will be soon.'

Lorinda smiled falsely again and accepted her now-refilled glass. The urge to kill was rising in her. She wondered whether she could strangle Miss Petunia with her own pince-nez cord.

Then she wished she hadn't thought of that. The spectre of those pince-nez, the broken cord dangling, rose at the back of her mind. Perhaps someone had already tried ... NO! No, it wasn't possible. She took a deep breath as the world seemed to tilt suddenly and reality began to slide away.

'Are you all right?' Professor Borley asked anxiously. 'You've gone so pale.'

Freddie and Macho walked past, laden with booty from the barbecue, and signalled to her. *They* were reality. She watched them take over the stone bench set against the wall of the house at the other end of the terrace, where they would have the best view of the proceedings while remaining apart from them.

'Can I get you anything?' Professor Borley put a steadying hand on her arm. 'You're not going to faint?'

'No, no, I'm all right.' She was suddenly aware that Plantagenet Sutton was watching her with a sardonic smile. Was it possible that he had put something in her drink?

'I just felt a little faint.' If he had, she was not going to give him the satisfaction of letting him see that it had affected her. 'The ... the smell ...'

The bonfire was burning merrily and crackling festively, but the smell of scorched meat wafting from it was slightly repugnant. She was not the only one fanning the air with a protesting hand. She watched as the flames licked upwards towards the sprawled dummy.

'Lorinda,' Freddie called. 'Your sausages are getting cold.'

'Perhaps I ought to sit down,' Lorinda excused herself, sliding away from his grasp.

'A. B.' Gemma was ready to pounce; she pronounced it Abbey.

'Come and get your bonfire food. It's delicious.' Hand on Professor Borley's elbow, she firmly guided him over to the grill.

Plantagenet had abandoned his post and was helping himself to a selection of sausages. Betty Alvin was looking around to make sure the others had all been served. They had.

Dorian had rejoined the party, wandering about amiably,

holding a plate with a safe bland baked potato and a small sausage he had no intention of eating. He appeared faintly on edge, with a curiously expectant air.

'He's up to something.' Freddie had noticed it, too. She looked around suspiciously. 'What's the betting?'

'No takers.' Macho narrowed his eyes thoughtfully. 'He was being very insistent that we should bring the cats along – as though I'd let Roscoe out on a night like this. Do you think that might have something to do with it?'

'It might. He seemed quite annoyed,' Lorinda remembered, 'when I told him Had-I and But-Known were staying in their own home with tranquillizing saucers of cream tonight.'

'Gemma didn't fall for it, either,' Freddie said. 'And thank heavens for that. A couple of overexcited pugs chasing around would be all we needed.'

'He probably hoped they'd start chasing the cats and add a bit of excitement to the party.' Macho was darkly suspicious. 'Not that this party couldn't use something to liven it up.'

'Oh, it's not that bad,' Freddie defended. 'The food is good. It isn't actually raining and, so long as we stick together, the company is agreeable.'

'That's about to change,' Macho said darkly, as Plantagenet Sutton headed towards them.

'Anyone want a fresh drink?' he offered. 'We're switching to wine now. Dorian wasn't sure what to serve but, for an outdoor occasion like this, I advised a good rough chianti or rioja – about the only wines tough enough to hold their own with spicy sausages.'

'What a good idea,' Lorinda responded automatically, realizing that the others, their eyes glazing over with boredom, were not going to bother to answer.

'Yes. Yes, he was a trifle disappointed, I fear. It's his first big party here, isn't it? He wanted to make a splash, but it would be an insult to good wine to waste it on –'

A high piercing scream cut him off. All eyes turned to mid-terrace where Jennifer Lane was pointing to the top of the bonfire, still screaming.

'Oh, my God!' Freddie gasped.

The dummy on top of the bonfire was moving.

Slowly at first, it writhed on the blazing pyre, then began jerking as though in agony as the flames engulfed it. A strange hissing sound came from it, like the whistling exhalation of a thousand last breaths. The stench of burning meat became overpowering.

'Do something!' Jackley bellowed, leading the rush from the terrace.

The women screaming, the men shouting, they dashed to the base of the bonfire, then wavered, unable to approach closer because of the heat and the flames.

'Hang on a minute.' Freddie caught Lorinda's arm as she started to run. Macho and Plantagenet had already bolted along the terrace and down the steps.

'But we've got to *do* something,' Lorinda protested. 'We've got to *try* –'

'Steady on,' Freddie said. 'I'll panic when Mine Host does.' She nodded towards Dorian, who was standing at the top of the steps, sipping his drink and looking down with amusement at the scene below.

Some of the men had begun kicking at the wood at the base of the fire, trying to collapse it. Jack and Karla glimmered like twin ghosts as they ran around to the other side of the bonfire, obviously hoping that it wasn't burning so furiously there.

'Where's the garden hose?' someone shouted. Gordie broke away and ran towards the garden shed.

'Call the Fire Brigade!' someone else shouted.

Dorian gave a wave of acknowledgement and stayed where he was.

'Nice night for a murder,' Freddie said between clenched teeth. 'But not even Dorian would have the nerve to –'

With a gigantic roar, the dummy burst apart, sending rockets thundering in every direction. Most of them erupted into the sky, but some fell back and slithered down the bonfire or snaked along the lawn. The explosions were deafening.

The world was a sudden terrifying nightmare, a war zone thrust into their midst. Abruptly, everyone deserted the bonfire and, covering their ears or trying to shield their faces, ran for the shelter of the house as out-of-control rockets showered their coloured starbursts all around them. The sky was alight with a display that must have been visible miles away. An ear-splittingly noisy display. If it had this effect on humans . . .

'And Dorian wanted us to bring our pets along,' Lorinda said bitterly. The mental pictures running through her mind didn't bear watching: Had-I and But-Known, Roscoe, Lionheart and Conqueror, terrified out of their wits, bolting away into the darkness, running for safety and winding up lost, alone, frightened, hungry . . .

'Relax.' Freddie patted her arm. 'It didn't happen. You're all nice responsible pet owners, so Dorian didn't get his cheap laugh. What does he know about pets and responsibility? That tank of stupid fish is just about right for him – he's a cold fish himself.'

The excitement was almost over now. Only a sporadic rocket issued from the heap of rags to explode against the sky. Shrieks and gasps were giving way to nervous ripples of laughter.

'That was quite a show, Dorian. You really had them going for a minute.' Plantagenet spoke as though he hadn't joined the panic-stricken rush to rescue the dummy himself. He was busy behind the bar again. Not surprisingly, there was a rush for more drinks.

'I can see that having you around is going to liven up the village no end.' Jennifer Lane spoke with a certain amount of reserve. Lorinda remembered that the bookshop had a resident cat; had Jennifer been urged to bring it along? 'You're going to keep us on our toes.'

Dorian was smiling blandly, nodding approval as Gordie spread the last of the sausages on the grill. Betty Alvin appeared from the kitchen regions carrying a tray of fruit-and-whipped-cream tarts, to be greeted with appreciative cries. The bonfire was dying down, the flickering glow not quite lighting the terrace any more. Most of the light was streaming out from the drawing room, most of the guests were gravitating to the warmth and comfort inside, where someone had ignited the logs in the fireplace. One of them cast a lingering glance back to the guttering bonfire.

Once again, shrill screams rang through the night. This time the finger was pointing to the pale ghostlike figure lying face down in the smouldering embers of the dying bonfire.

In that silent horrified moment before people began dashing forward, the edges of the fawn jacket smouldered, blackened and lit with a pale flickering flame.

5

'I wish I didn't feel so damned guilty,' Freddie said. 'Here I've been moaning for weeks about all the noise and fighting and wishing for some peace and quiet – and now that I've got it, do I feel pleased? No, I just feel guilty.'

'It wasn't your fault,' Macho said. 'And it isn't as if he were dead. It's a good thing he threw up his arm to protect his face as he fell. The arm is badly burned, but he'll be able to use it again ... eventually. And,' he added with satisfaction, 'the camera is a complete write-off.'

'But,' Freddie said, 'there's such a thing as ill-wishing.'

'In that case, it's my fault,' Macho said. 'I'll guarantee I wished him iller than you did.'

'Oh, stop it, both of you!' Absently, Lorinda held out a potato crisp for Roscoe to nibble. 'You're beginning to sound like Dame Isolde Llewellyn!'

'You needn't be insulting,' Freddie said.

Dame Isolde Llewellyn was Rhylla Montague's series character, a concert harpsichordist and possibly a spy, and, even more possibly, a white witch with a sideline of dabbling in spells and mixing strange potions to ensure love or other useful reactions. (How else had she been created a Dame before her fortieth birthday?)

'Poor Rhylla.' Macho was diverted. 'Imagine having a grand-child descending and a deadline in the same month.'

'I saw her driving past this morning, looking rather martyred,' Lorinda said.

'She's gone full-tilt at the martyr's crown,' Freddie said. 'She even stopped to pick up Karla to drop her off at the hospital on her way to the station to collect Clarice. Karla will take a taxi back when she's had enough of cheering the patient. That shouldn't take long. Since the accident didn't actually kill him, she's pretty annoyed with him for his clumsiness.'

Had-I and But-Known strolled in from the kitchen, where they had been sampling Roscoe's rations, licking their chops. Had-I halted abruptly as she saw Lorinda cosseting Roscoe; her eyes narrowed. Ostentatiously, she marched over to Macho and jumped into his lap. Automatically, he began stroking her.

But-Known reacted more with sorrow than anger. She gave Lorinda an accusing look, then slowly walked over to leap up on to the arm of Freddie's chair. Equally automatically, Freddie reached out to rub her ears.

'God, how I miss my darling little Horatio,' she sighed. Her eyes misted over. 'It's all very well having your darlings come visiting, but I want a cat of my own.' She brightened. 'Now that we're getting settled in, perhaps I could manage one. If you'd be willing to look after it occasionally when I have to go up to London or over to New York?'

'No trouble at all,' Macho agreed quickly.

There was a moment's silence, while Freddie blinked several times, as though restraining tears. Macho visibly grew more nervous; he hated tears.

The throb of a diesel engine outside broke into the uneasy atmosphere, promising relief.

'A taxi!' Macho leaped out of his chair, sending a protesting Had-I tumbling to the floor. 'That must be Karla. Why don't we invite her to join us for tea?' He dashed for his front door and they heard him hailing her.

'A cup of tea and the company of friends.' Karla smiled at them as Macho shepherded her into the room. 'Just what I need right now.'

'How is Jack?' Lorinda asked.

'Jack?' Karla looked at her blankly. 'Oh, Jack! That stumblebum! As well as can be expected, what else? If he'd been paying attention to what he was doing for one moment, it would never have happened.' She flung herself into an armchair and closed her eyes.

The others took the opportunity to raise eyebrows at each other. The verdict seemed a bit unfair on poor Jack, who had been trying to rescue what he thought was a live victim on top of the bonfire. He hadn't even paused to take any pictures.

Roscoe was more forgiving. He abandoned Lorinda abruptly to scramble on to the arm of Karla's chair and rub against her bowed head. Like Macho, he hated tears and emotional upsets. His anxious chirrup penetrated her gloom.

'Hello, sweetheart.' She reached for him. Roscoe braced himself against her grappling embrace and gave her a friendly head-butt on the chin.

'It *was* careless of Dorian to plant that torch where someone could trip over it,' Lorinda said.

'No one else fell over it,' Karla said broodingly. 'Only idiot-boy.'

'You're sure tea will be enough?' Macho returned from the kitchen with another cup and saucer. 'If you'd like something stronger . . . ?'

'Tea will be fine,' Karla said. 'I'm not that devastated. I'm just damned annoyed.'

'At least Jack's being taken care of on the National Health.' Freddie offered comfort. 'Just imagine if this had happened in New York.'

'Don't!' Karla shuddered so violently that Roscoe meowed in protest. 'He let our health insurance lapse! That's another little gem he sprang on me just before we left the States. He forgot to pay the premiums – he says!'

Freddie whistled softly and looked quizzically into her own cup, as though hoping the tea leaves might reveal what some of the other gems had been.

'Well, you won't need it this year,' Macho said cheerfully. 'You can pick it up again when you go back –' He broke off; Karla's look of fury had struck him like a blow across the face.

'Tell me –' Lorinda tried to lower the temperature by changing the subject. 'How are you getting along with Miss Mudd?'

'Don't ask me!' Karla swung violently to face her. Roscoe protested faintly. 'I hate the damned creature! I always did!'

'Then why did you take on the series?' It was a tactless question, but it slipped out before Lorinda could stop it.

'Money, of course.' Karla's face shuttered. 'And . . . there were other considerations.'

'The Mudd books are money-spinners,' Macho conceded. 'I'm not surprised the publishers want to keep them going. There's a lot of that about these days. They've even been reviving long-defunct series characters and farming them out to new writers.'

'New writers, I can understand.' Freddie surveyed Karla thoughtfully. 'Anything to get a foot in the door. But you have a successful series of your own. You can't need to take on someone else's.'

'Oh, yes. Toni and Terri – the all-American backpackers, hiking their way around the world and into adventure and murder.' Karla gave a short mirthless bark of laughter. Roscoe twitched uneasily. 'How I've grown to hate the little bastards!'

'We all feel like that at times, I'm sure.' Lorinda tried not to think of the guilty chapters lurking in her filing cabinet.

'You have no children of your own?' Freddie asked. 'No teenagers? No adolescents you've left behind in boarding school?'

'You mean, am I sublimating? Are my backpackers really the kids I never had?' Karla laughed bitterly. 'No, we had a son. He was killed in a car crash when he was ten. Jack was driving. Everything began going downhill after that.'

'I'm sorry,' Freddie said inadequately, obviously regretting ever having raised the subject.

'What about you?' Karla challenged her. 'All of you? I know your work, but I don't know anything about any of you personally. Just the little bits I've been able to piece together since we moved here. If you're going to question me, fair's fair. Freddie, you've obviously spent some time in the States – there's a trace of a familiar accent, plus an Americanism every now and then. What about *you?*'

'You got me!' Freddie grimaced. 'I did a stint in advertising in New York. Had quite a pleasant life there for nearly a decade: plenty of money, nice apartment, darling cat, not to mention the obligatory affair. Then' – she shrugged – 'everything seemed to go wrong at once. The cat died, the lover went off with a new and improved younger model, the landlord raised the rent to an even more extortionate level – and the advertising agency was taken over, with the usual claims that nothing was going to change, even as the new upper echelon began eyeing the existing talent to see who they could do without. I can read the handwriting on the wall as well as anyone else. I had enough put by to support me for a couple of years while I found out whether I could really write a book. I took the money and ran. Back here, where I still had some family and friends.'

And where she could lick her wounds in privacy and rebuild her life, Lorinda thought. It was more than she had ever heard Freddie tell about herself, although she had pieced most of it together from hints Freddie had let drop. That was really the proper way to find out about other people, she felt, not this pouring out of facts Americans seemed to require.

'And you?' Lorinda flinched as Karla faced her relentlessly.

'There isn't much to tell,' Lorinda said slowly. 'I was a late child, an only child. My parents were nearly fifty so I came as quite a surprise to them. By the time I'd graduated from university, my mother was quite ill and my father couldn't cope. Fortunately, I was able to write while I looked after them. I did a few other books before I dreamed up Miss Petunia and her sisters. They did well enough here and were a great hit in the States. So that's what I've been doing ever since. Between that and caring for my parents, it rather cut me off from my own generation and ... well ...' She emulated Freddie's shrug. 'Eventually my parents died ... and here I am.'

'How sad.' Karla's perfunctory tone really meant, 'How boring.' She turned avidly to Macho and waited expectantly.

'This is rather painful ... I don't usually talk about it.' He was not going to disappoint her. He took a deep breath and sent the ghost of a wink to Freddie and Lorinda.

'My wife and I were teachers at a mission school in Africa. This was some years ago and we had no idea of the underlying tensions that were about to tear the Continent apart. Even when the revolutions and uprisings began, they were in distant parts of the country. Oh, we heard the usual rumours of atrocities and, as the unrest crept closer to our territory, we even began to discuss the advisability of returning to England. But it still didn't seem quite possible that it could happen to us ... and so ... we left it too late.' He shuddered and covered his eyes with one hand, head bowed.

'We were armed by then, of course. We weren't complete fools. We knew trouble was coming closer every day. We sent out a call for help just as the Mission compound was besieged – and then we prayed. As the days dragged past and our supplies grew low, we began to fear that no one had heard our pleas for help. Our ammunition was even lower than the food – and we'd maddened the rebels by our resistance. There would be no mercy for us when they broke through our defences.'

'How terrible!' Karla's eyes were round, her breath ragged. 'But you made it all right. You're here.'

'*I'm* here,' Macho said brokenly. 'But my wife ... and not

just mine. You see . . . we knew . . . the drill. You loved her, so you saved the last bullet . . . for *her*.'

'No!' Karla's eyes opened even wider.

'We all knew what had to be done. When the terrorists breached the barricades and swarmed into the compound, we retreated into an inner room . . . and then . . .' He had not uncovered his eyes, his voice quavered.

'Then I put the gun to her temple . . . she smiled at me . . . I pulled the trigger. All around me, I could hear the other shots and the crash of the front door being broken down. Then . . . I . . . we . . . heard the sound of helicopters swooping down on us. Help had arrived . . . too late.'

'Oh, my God!' Karla gasped in horror.

Why didn't we think of something like that? Lorinda and Freddie met each other's eyes in gleeful collusion. *Good for Macho!* It was a lot more exciting than admitting that he had been a schoolmaster teaching history in a minor public school when his wife ran away with his best friend.

'Oh, you poor –' Karla began.

'Please –' Macho lurched to his feet and waved a hand, stopping her. 'I . . . I'm afraid I . . . It's brought it all back. Forgive me –' He rushed from the room.

'Oh, I'm so sorry.' Karla began apologizing to those remaining. 'I didn't mean to upset him. I had no idea –'

Roscoe gave her an accusing look and jumped from her lap, pursuing Macho into the kitchen.

'Now even the cat is mad at me,' Karla mourned.

'I think it will be better if we never speak of this again,' Freddie said gravely.

'Yes, of course. I agree.' Karla was still shaken, her own troubles forgotten. 'I'm so sorry. I wouldn't for the world have –'

There was a muffled clatter from the kitchen, followed by the sharp crack of an ice-cube tray being broached. Had-I and But-Known were instantly alert. That meant the fridge door had been opened and Roscoe was already on the scene and might be getting treats. They abandoned their posts and headed purposefully for the kitchen.

'I think maybe –' Karla stood, then hovered indecisively. 'Maybe I ought to leave now? Maybe we all ought to?'

'No need for that.' Freddie was settled comfortably and had identified the activity around the fridge as surely as the cats had. 'Macho will be all right. And we can't leave him now . . . to his memories.'

'Oh! Maybe that wouldn't be kind . . . ?' Karla looked to Lorinda for confirmation.

'Here we are.' Macho returned, carrying a tray with ice bucket, glasses, cheeseboard and crackers. Roscoe sauntered along beside him, waving his tail complacently, as though he had organized the refreshments all by himself. Had-I and But-Known followed behind, their gaze firmly fixed on the large chunk of cheddar that they especially favoured.

'Oh, well . . .' Karla sat down again.

'Time for something stronger than tea,' Macho announced, setting his tray down on the coffee table. The cats moved forward and began circling the table in an elaborately casual manner while Macho mixed the drinks.

'Have some cheese,' he urged. 'Not you!' He pushed Roscoe's questing muzzle away. 'Guests first. Where are your manners?'

'Oh . . . thank you.' Karla cut a triangle of cheddar nervously, obviously not accustomed to three pairs of little eyes watching her every movement. They were waiting for her to drop it. Had-I spoke sharply and she obliged.

'Oh, I'm sorry.'

'Quite all right,' Macho said cheerfully. 'Won't be wasted.' Three blurs of fur pounced, proving him right. 'Nothing to clean up, either. Quick, cut yourself another piece while they're busy.'

'Uh –' She wasn't fast enough. Three little heads were craning over the rim of the coffee table, watching her avidly. Happy the cats with a clumsy and easily unnerved guest. 'I'm not really hungry, thanks.'

'Come here, you little bully,' Freddie said, unfairly sweeping But-Known, the least aggressive of the lot, into her lap.

'That goes for you, too.' Lorinda captured Had-I, immediately negating the reprimand by slicing off a sliver of cheese and holding it for her to nibble at.

Roscoe crouched and soared into Macho's lap the instant he sat down. There was a generous chunk of cheddar waiting for him.

Contented purrs provided background music as the well-trained humans finally got to their own cheese and drinks.

'This is nice,' Karla admitted. 'I've never seen so many cats all together at the same time. Don't they get on well together?'

'Had-I and But-Known are females,' Lorinda pointed out. 'So

Roscoe thinks they're his harem – and they think he's there to do their bidding. It works out very well.'

'Yes, but aren't they all –?' Karla looked uncomfortable. 'Well, *fixed?*'

'What has that got to do with it?' Freddie asked. 'All their instincts are firmly in place. The fact that the apparatus has been removed and they can't do anything about it is largely immaterial. They're all quite happy. They enjoy each other's company and they don't know anything different.'

'Yes, I've heard people say that before. But what if something upsets the balance? I mean,' Karla persisted, 'Rhylla was saying that her granddaughter was bringing her own pet along. The kid has only had it a short time and it probably hasn't had anything done to it yet. Won't that upset the applecart?'

There was a thoughtful silence. Rhylla hadn't told any of them about that. Perhaps an entire cat – whether male or female – might indeed upset the delicate balance.

'Anyway, it's only temporary.' Freddie tried for the silver lining. 'Child, plus pet, will only be here two or three weeks until she's sent off to her parents and new school in the States. Not much can go wrong in that length of time.'

There was another thoughtful silence. A cat could be mortally offended in ten seconds flat – and carry a grudge for years. It would be too bad if the harmony were to be disturbed for the sake of a transient child.

'I'll ring Rhylla in the morning,' Lorinda said. 'Clarice will probably want to keep her little darling indoors for the first few days anyway, while it gets used to new surroundings. It's only sensible.'

'Of course –' Macho began, then stopped abruptly.

'Yes?' Freddie encouraged.

'No, nothing. Just a stray thought.' Macho shook his head and leaned forward to cut off another chunk of cheddar, which he shared with Roscoe. 'I'll save it for the next book,' he said, using the formula they had evolved for evading awkward moments.

'Yes, and what about the next book?' Karla's glass was empty; she raised it to her lips in a draining motion and Macho leaped to refill it. 'Are you still doing that stupid Macho Magee – and how much longer do you think you can get away with it?'

It was the first indication they had had that she had been drinking before she joined them.

'Long enough.' Macho regarded her impassively. 'I have

85

enough put by now to see me through comfortably, even if political correctness finishes off Macho Magee.'

'Are you sure that's good enough?' Karla asked earnestly. 'Would that satisfy you? Would that make you happy? Could you bear not writing any more? Or . . .' She paused and regarded him challengingly. 'Or are you secretly planning another series . . . like so many of us?'

She had hit a nerve. Freddie stirred restively. Lorinda looked off into the distance. It was not only the cats, she thought, who might find a disruptive influence in their midst. And they had thought the danger might come from Gemma and Plantagenet.

'I feel I might be able . . .' Macho spoke slowly '. . . to spread myself further. Perhaps one always wonders whether there might be . . . another string to one's bow.'

'You can say that again!' Freddie leaned forward. 'Sometimes I get so fed up with Wraith O'Reilly, I could kill her!' She paused, as though listening to what she had just said, then shrugged. 'Not that it would make much difference – the damned creature's half a ghost already.'

It was so true, they were glad Freddie had said it herself. Wraith O'Reilly, an orphaned flame-haired Irish girl, living in New York City, but with her heart back in Ireland, drifted through the dark canyons of the city only half aware of the perilous shadows around her. Her hobby was exploring old graveyards, collecting epitaphs. Protected only by her innocence and a thoroughly unwarranted belief in the goodness of human nature (the girl never learned!), she encountered the dregs of society and the Four Hundred, treated them equally and solved their murders largely through a fey intuition before drifting on to the next case, still wondering whether the rose bushes she had planted in the garden of the little cottage in Galway Bay were still flourishing.

'Sometimes I think I should go the whole hog,' Freddie said, 'and have a *real* ghost to take on the cases. How would that be for retribution from beyond the grave? Nothing too gory or recent, of course.' Her eyes grew thoughtful. 'A revenant from an earlier century – and aristocratic, of course. An English title, that always goes down well. Duke the Spook. He's been lounging around the ancestral pile a few centuries, getting more and more bored. Then an American heiress rents the castle for the summer and moves in with her not-so-loving family and hang-ers-on. One of whom is trying to murder her. She doesn't realize this, but the Duke does.'

Lorinda realized with surprise that Freddie had actually given a great deal of thought to the subject; she was seriously considering a new series.

'Although the heiress doesn't know it, she's a bit psychic – and this draws the Duke to her side. What he finds going on around her, keeps him there.' Freddie leaned forward, eyes sparkling, her residual American accent became more pronounced, her hands waved in great swooping gestures. She must have looked like that when she was pitching ideas at the advertising agency.

'You see, the Duke was done in by a relative he'd thought he could trust, so this gives him motivation. He wasn't able to save himself, but he ought to be able to save her.'

'Especially with the supernatural powers he'll have at his disposal.' Macho nodded, catching her enthusiasm. 'It would work.'

'Naturally, as he grows fonder of her, he has to fight the temptation to say, "The hell with it," and let her cross over to his side where they can be together in a way they can't be if she lives. But she's young and she's got a long life ahead of her – and he's got nothing to do but hang around anyway. He can wait and, now that he's found her, life – or what passes for it with him – isn't so dull any more.

'So he saves her life, traps the villain and waves her goodbye as she flies back to New York. But the bond between them is too strong ever to be broken. The next time she needs him, he's there. And the next, and the next. Neither time nor distance can part them. And the beauty of it is, the Duke provides a continuing love interest while allowing her to have a fresh romance with each book – which comes more or less to grief because the Duke is so jealous that he ruins it for her, which allows her to have a new heart interest in the next book without doing anything so crude as killing off the last one. (Sorry, Macho.)

'So there you are –' Freddie spread her hands in a finale. 'How does that sound for a new series?'

'It sounds like *The Canterville Ghost* meets *Blithe Spirit*,' Karla said briskly. 'With perhaps a touch of *Mrs Muir* thrown in.'

'Oh!' Freddie blinked and reared back, like a cat who had just had a bucket of cold water thrown over it.

'Nothing wrong with that,' Macho said quickly. 'Everyone knows there's nothing new under the sun – and it didn't sound all that familiar to me. By the time Freddie has fleshed out the characters and background, it will be completely original. And a lot better than taking over someone else's character or – '

'So that's what you think of me!' Karla flushed a dull red.

'No, no!' Macho was aghast. 'I wasn't getting at you. I was just speaking generally. I mean, look at all the Sherlock Holmes books there have been since he went out of copyright. He's become a minor cottage industry – even more so than in his heyday when only Conan Doyle was writing him.'

'And hating him,' Lorinda could not stop herself from pointing out, even as she decided it would be more tactful to move on to a safer subject. 'Then there are all the actual historical figures some authors are turning into detectives; they're resurrecting anyone they can think of. The poor old Prince of Wales, before he became Edward VII, has been waltzed around so many mysteries, I've lost track. And he featured in a stage play about the Baccarat Scandal, too.'

'I've considered the Prince of Wales myself,' Karla said thoughtfully. 'Not that one, the one who became Duke of Windsor. It's a great period and he had an American wife. But they've been used in several books already – usually wartime thrillers.'

'Yes . . .' Macho frowned. 'But those are hit-and-run affairs, as it were. If you were to try to settle down to using them as continuing characters, you might run into difficulties.'

'It's safer to take a peripheral character and push them to the front,' Karla agreed. 'And just use the serious historical figures for walk-on parts. That's why I thought it might be a great idea to – ' She stopped and actually looked over her shoulder before continuing. 'To use Aunt Bessie as the detective!'

'Who?' Macho looked blank.

'Wallis Simpson's Aunt Bessie. Just think of it, there she sat in Baltimore while her dear niece pours out her soul to her in all those letters she wrote constantly because Aunt Bessie was the only person she could truly confide in. All that intrigue and plotting going on around her, too much for her to make sense of because she was right in the middle of it and most of the plotting was against her. But Aunt Bessie could read between the lines and recognize the assassination plot forming – '

'What assassination plot?' Macho looked dazed.

'Surely somebody would have had the bright idea that, if they killed Wallis, the King would come back in line and their troubles would be over. But astute Aunt Bessie, the careful reader, foils the plot and the Duke and Duchess sail off happily into the sunset – and Aunt Bessie visits them frequently in their exile. Do you realize they were actually living in Nassau at the time of Sir Harry Oakes's murder? Why couldn't Aunt Bessie solve that? – everybody else has. And then they lived in postwar New York and Paris!' Karla sighed happily. 'The possibilities are endless.'

'Maybe.' Freddie threw her own bucket of cold water. 'But can you get control of the Aunt Bessie character?'

'I'll have to look into that. But I can't do anything about it right now.' Karla looked over her shoulder again and then, mistrustfully, back at them.

'This is all highly confidential, you know,' she said earnestly. 'You're not to mention it to a living soul. Especially, Jack. So far as he's concerned, I'm deep in the Miss Mudd books and haven't another idea in my head. I don't want him to know I'm even *thinking* about a new series.'

'Fine with me.' Freddie shrugged. 'So long as you keep your mouth shut about Duke the Spook.'

'Deal!' Karla held out her hand and they shook hands briefly. 'And you two?'

'I wouldn't dream of mentioning anything under discussion this afternoon.' Macho ran his finger down Roscoe's spine and Roscoe's answering rumble seemed to agree. But-Known, stretched along the back of Macho's chair, reached out a paw to toy with the black velvet ribbon tying his ponytail.

'I'm not going to say anything.' Lorinda hugged Had-I a bit tighter. Certainly, she had nothing to say to Jack; they all spent most of their time avoiding him – and his camera.

'When is Jack coming home?' Freddie voiced the question lurking at the back of their minds.

'Soon. Too soon.' Karla's face shuttered. 'Whenever it is, it will be too soon. It's so nice and peaceful without him.'

Freddie nodded agreement before catching herself. Fortunately, Karla hadn't noticed. It was obviously more peaceful living next door to Karla on her own, but what would happen when Jack came back again? Jack, in a weakened state, no longer so well able to defend himself against Karla's violent attacks?

And, thinking of attacks ... had Jack really tripped over Dorian's abandoned torch? Or had he been pushed?

6

CHAPTER TWENTY

Miss Petunia adjusted her pince-nez and glanced at the fob watch pinned to her lapel. She knew this was a very busy day for them, but surely Lily and Marigold were unusually late in returning home from Saints Etheldreda & Dowsabel Abbey, the foremost Academy for Young Ladies in all the British Isles, where they had the great honour to reign as gym mistress and art mistress, respectively.

If they didn't hurry, they wouldn't have time for tea before they had to go down to Peppercorn Meadow, where the start of the Hot Air Balloon Race would mark the opening of the annual and greatly anticipated St Waldemar's Fayre. And this year they were all invited to ride in the Saints Etheldreda & Dowsabel Abbey balloon. So exciting!

Then the front door slammed and Miss Petunia smiled fondly as her sisters bounded down the hallway and into the room like overgrown puppies.

'The afternoon post has come! And we've each got a letter!' Marigold squealed in girlish excitement, waving the letters. 'They must be invitations! Just look at that lovely formal handwriting, sort of a cross between backhand and copperplate. How I wish my pupils could write as artistically as that.'

She tore her envelope open, the others opened theirs more sedately . . . then a curious silence filled the room.

'Oh! Oh! Oh!' Marigold crumpled her missive in both hands and hurled it from her, bursting into tears.

'AAAARRGH!' Lily gave one bellow of rage and went pale.

She looked around the room as though seeking something – or someone – to kick.

Miss Petunia closed her eyes, her lips tightened, but she remained completely silent. The enormity of the situation was too great for words.

Only the sound of Marigold's sobs rent the air.

'I take it –' Miss Petunia brought herself to speak at last. 'I take it that we have all received the same sort of insult?'

'It says –' Marigold choked. 'It says that everybody in town knows that I'm bone-stupid and that I dye my hair!' She burst into a fresh torrent of tears.

'What nonsense!' Miss Petunia comforted. 'Everyone knows that you are extremely bright and talented.'

'Your hair colour is natural,' Lily growled. 'No one could possibly have any doubt about that. It hasn't changed a bit since we were children.'

'I don't dye my hair!' Marigold shook her head vehemently, sending the red-gold curls bouncing. 'I don't need to! My hair-dresser gives it only the teeniest brightening rinse – to enhance its natural colour.' Her lower lip quivered piteously. 'It isn't dye. I would never stoop to dyeing my hair!'

'There, there,' Miss Petunia soothed. 'It's just silly spiteful malice. No one could possibly believe a word of it.' She took a deep breath and turned to Lily. 'What does *your* letter say?'

'Spite . . . malice . . . just like you said.' Lily shuffled her feet uneasily and looked away. 'Calls me a psychopath . . . brings up that slur about Old Gumboots.' Her hands clenched convulsively.

'How beastly! How horrid!' Marigold forgot her own troubles. 'Miss Gumbrell slipped on that treacherous cliffside path. Everyone knows that. It was the merest coincidence that it happened so soon after your quarrel and that you were standing nearby with your vaulting pole.'

'Indeed!' Miss Petunia said severely. 'Only a sick mind could put any other interpretation on the accident. Why, you and the headmistress are on the best of terms. She even gave you the promotion you wanted and so richly deserved as soon as she got out of hospital.'

'No hard feelings. Proves it, doesn't it?' Lily relaxed somewhat and looked Miss Petunia squarely in the eyes for the first time. 'And what does your letter say?' she inquired innocently.

Miss Petunia closed her eyes and shuddered. Although she had taken only one quick look at that scurrilous letter, it seemed that every outrageous word was printed in letters of flame across her mind. She shrank from communicating it, but Lily and Marigold had confided in her – they had a right to know.

'It said that I was an evil, obnoxious, wicked, nosy, interfering old bitch, forever shoving her nose into things that were none of my business.'

'You're not old!' Marigold cried loyally.

'The idea!' Lily growled. 'Look at all the crimes in St Waldemar Boniface that would have gone unnoticed – and unpunished – if it hadn't been for you.'

'And,' Miss Petunia continued grimly, 'that the world would be a better place without me.'

'That's right!' Marigold's eyes widened with recognition. 'I forgot. Mine ended that way, too.'

'So did mine.' Lily was still growling. 'Do you think it's a threat? Think we ought to call the police?'

'Oh, no!' Marigold protested, horrified. 'We might have to show them the letters. I couldn't bear it!'

'You're right, dear,' Miss Petunia said. 'We don't want to bring the police into this.'

'Handle it ourselves, then?' Lily's eyes gleamed. 'Put our heads together and –'

Oh, the hell with it! It was too beautiful a day to kill anyone – even Miss Petunia.

Lorinda pushed back her chair and filed the uncompleted chapter. The cats had disappeared ages ago, obviously out and about their own business. She didn't blame them. The day was bright and clear, the air crisp and invigorating. They were heading into winter and there might not be many more days like this. It would be a shame to waste it. She collected her wheeled wicker shopping basket and set out for the High Street.

Everyone seemed of the same opinion. The High Street was bustling. Before she had reached the greengrocer's, she had exchanged greetings with several villagers, waved to Freddie, who was across the street, standing in front of the bookshop watching Jennifer Lane assemble a new window display, and observed Plantagenet Sutton going into the wine merchant's.

Wheeling her basket out of the dark fragrant cavern of the greengrocer's, she nearly ran down Macho, who was too busy trying to control a struggling, protesting Roscoe to watch where he was going.

'*There* you are!' He greeted her as though she had just returned from the missing. 'We've got to have a Council of War. I can't believe Rhylla wouldn't have warned us. It was the least she could do. She must be out of her mind.'

'*Mrreow-aaaoeh-rraarr* . . .' Roscoe also decided she was the right person to register a complaint with. He struggled briefly again to escape Macho's tight clasp.

'Irresponsible!' Macho brooded.

'*Mrrrr-rrrrm-mmrrr* . . .' Neither of them were happy.

'What is it?' Lorinda looked from one angry face to the other. 'What's happened?'

'I didn't think you knew,' Macho said. 'And you ought to. It's your problem, too. You're going to have to lock up Had-I and But-Known. I'm taking Roscoe home now to shut him in – and he isn't going to like it.'

'What's wrong?'

'Rhylla's monstrous grandchild. Have you seen her pet?'

'No.' It was a rhetorical question, but Lorinda answered it anyway, ghastly visions forming in her imagination. 'What is it – a pit bull?'

'The police could deal with that.' Macho dismissed such a puerile worry. 'It's worse, much worse.'

'For heaven's sake, tell me!' Sometimes she could shake him.

'*Rrrreeeooowww* . . .' Obviously, Roscoe felt the same way.

'That revolting child has for a pet . . .' Macho paused for dramatic effect. 'A white rat! *And* she walks around with it perched on her shoulder.'

'Oh, no!'

'Oh, yes! Fortunately, I was doing some shopping when I saw Roscoe . . . acting suspiciously . . . trailing the child down the High Street. Then I saw why.'

Roscoe hunkered down in his master's arms and closed his eyes, absenting himself from the situation. He continued to emit a low rumbling sound that was not quite a growl, but definitely was not a purr.

'I caught him in mid-air as he sprang.' Macho shuddered. 'If he had landed with all claws extended on that rat . . . on that child's shoulder . . .'

'Oh, dear!' The picture was clear and irresistible.

'I'm glad you think it's so funny,' Macho said coldly. 'Have a real laugh: your two are staking out Coffers Court right now, waiting for the child to return. If they catch her, it could be the start of our first village feud.'

That wiped the smile off Lorinda's face. 'I'd better get over there,' she said.

'Yes, you really had.' Macho, having spread alarm and despondency, now seemed in a better mood. The same could not be said for Roscoe, who was still bemoaning lost opportunity. 'Ring me when you've got them safely locked up. Someone is going to have to have a serious talk with Rhylla.'

Had-I and But-Known were perched in the window box outside Gemma Duquette's living room, whiling away the time by tormenting the maddened pug dogs inside.

'And just what do you think you're doing?' she asked sternly.

Had-I gave her an innocent look and flicked an insouciant tail, sending the pugs into fresh paroxysms of yapping. But-Known tugged a petal off one of the chrysanthemums and offered it to her placatingly.

'Well, you can stop that right now and come home.' But it was easier said than done. She could not carry two cats and pull the wheeled basket at the same time. It was no use putting them into the basket, they knew how to flip the lid back and escape. Jumping in and out of the basket was one of their favourite games on a wet afternoon and, if they were home when she returned from shopping trips, they always rushed to claw open the lid and inspect her purchases.

They eyed the basket now, with some interest, but not enough to deflect them from their original plans. They remained firmly rooted in the window box, Had-I squashing a few small asters beneath her rump.

'Home,' Lorinda repeated with more firmness than she felt. They knew she was in no position to enforce her command.

Inside, the yapping grew to a crescendo and the window was opened suddenly. Gemma leaned out to see what was disturbing her pets. She did not look well.

'Shoo! Scat!' She waved her hands at the cats before noticing

94

Lorinda, then stopped guiltily. 'Sorry,' she said, 'but they're upsetting the dogs. Come in, why don't you, and have a cup of coffee?'

'Oh, I don't think –' But the cats had already accepted the invitation. They leaped through the open window and there were sounds of canine hysteria at this brazen invasion of their territory.

'Oh, God!' Gemma's head disappeared as she turned to join in the fray. 'Conqueror! Lionheart! Stop it! Stop it this minute!'

Lorinda sighed and moved on to the imposing front door. It was locked. She pushed the doorbell for Gemma's flat, but the noise of skirmish could be heard out here; there was little chance that Gemma would hear the bell or remember that Lorinda was there until things quieted down.

'Allow me.' Plantagenet Sutton came up behind her silently and inserted his key in the lock. There was a clank of bottles from his basket as he swung open the door. 'Visiting someone?'

'Gemma,' she replied. 'I'm afraid my cats are already in there.' It was useless to pretend otherwise – the noises behind the other door were quite explicit.

'Those damned mutts!' He frowned. 'This wouldn't be such a bad place if only it were quiet.' He lingered as Lorinda knocked loudly on Gemma's door.

'You'll never make her hear that way,' he remarked, always a critic. He took out a wine bottle and hammered on Gemma's door with it.

'All right! All right! I'm coming!' The door opened and Gemma stood there, distraught and harassed. 'Oh, it's you. What do you want?' She glared at Plantagenet Sutton.

'A little peace and quiet,' he replied. Lorinda scuttled around him; the battle inside the flat promised to be more manageable.

'I'm sorry,' Gemma said, 'but they're overexcited and –'

'That's all very well, but they're always overexcited. You ought to have some consideration for your neighbours. If you can't control your animals, at least you might cut their vocal cords!'

'Well, really!' Gemma gasped in outrage. 'If you weren't in the throes of a perpetual hangover, a little healthy noise wouldn't bother you!'

It was definitely safer inside; it even sounded quieter now. Lorinda parked her shopping basket in the tiny entrance hall while Gemma and Plantagenet continued to trade insults. The dogs advanced into the hallway to reinforce their mistress. Had-I and But-Known had sprawled in a corner of the sofa, well pleased with their bit of excitement.

'You're disgraceful,' Lorinda told them. 'Absolutely disgraceful.'

The door slammed and Gemma marched back into the living room, quivering with indignation and flanked by Conqueror and Lionheart.

'This was such a nice place before *he* moved in!' She sank into one of the armchairs, leaned back and closed her eyes. Suddenly she looked drained, her brief spurt of energy exhausted. Her hair was dishevelled and she was still wearing her dressing gown.

'Are you all right?' Lorinda felt vaguely alarmed.

'It was something I ate yesterday, I think.' Gemma spoke without opening her eyes. 'I'm better now, but I had a terrible night. I'd only just got to sleep when the dogs woke me.'

'I'm sorry.' Lorinda apologized for her cats.

The dogs settled themselves, one on each side of Gemma's chair and looked up at her. Conqueror whimpered anxiously.

'Are you sure you're all right? Did you call the doctor? Can I get you anything?' Lorinda's unease grew. Gemma did not look better, she seemed to be getting paler.

'No, no. Just let me rest for a minute. Plantagenet is so exhausting. Oh –' Gemma's eyes opened. 'Actually, there *is* something you could do, if you wouldn't mind –?'

'Yes? What?'

'Would you take Conqueror and Lionheart walkies? Poor dears, we've usually been out hours ago. Just down to the end of the High Street and back will do.'

'Of course.' Lorinda would have agreed to far more than that. 'No, don't get up. Just tell me where you keep their leashes.'

'They're hanging on the hook underneath my raincoat. Thanks awfully.' Gemma smiled weakly. 'I'll have that coffee I promised you ready when you get back.'

'Don't bother, it's all right. Why don't you go back to bed? You look as though you could do with some more rest.' Lorinda found the leads and attached them to the dogs' collars while Had-I and But-Known looked on with interest and a certain air of superiority. *They* didn't need to be tethered to a human before being allowed out of the house.

'Coming?' Lorinda asked them.

Had-I yawned and stretched out on the cushions. It was nap time. But-Known wavered, but yawns were catching; she gave one of her own and slumped down atop her sister.

'They're all right.' Gemma also yawned. 'Let them stay.'

'They're just going to sleep now,' Lorinda agreed. 'I'll collect them when I bring the dogs back.' The dogs were already prancing and pawing at the carpet, eager to be off. 'Come on, you lot.'

Three lampposts along the High Street, Lorinda saw Freddie walking slowly towards them with a strange look on her face.

'You're not going by the old graveyard, are you?' she greeted Lorinda.

'I wouldn't dream of it.' It was a popular dog-walk with some villagers, but Lorinda felt it lacked respect. 'Why? Is Clarice in there?'

'Clarice? What's she got to do with anything?' Freddie looked puzzled, then her face cleared. 'Oh, is she one of those ghastly children who like to play tricks?' She seemed quite happy with the thought.

'Not that I know of. She has other alarming traits. Apparently, she has a white rat for a pet and likes to carry it around on her shoulder.' Lorinda reined in the pugs who were sniffing enthusiastically at Freddie's shoes.

'That's going to add some spice to life around here,' Freddie said. 'What are you going to do about the cats?'

'It won't be easy.' Lorinda sighed. 'I just hope Clarice's parents settle down quickly in the States and send for her in very short order.'

'I wouldn't trust those dogs with a rat, either.' Freddie looked at them critically. 'They may not be terriers, but they still have the hunting instinct. What are you doing with them, anyway?'

'Walking them for Gemma. She isn't well. Something she ate, she thinks.'

'People aren't careful enough about refrigeration in this country.' Freddie still seemed preoccupied by problems of her own. 'I'm always seeing packets of frozen food abandoned on supermarket shelves by dimwits who've changed their minds. Then some even dimmer employee comes along and puts them back into the freezer without knowing how long they've been sitting there and whether they've defrosted or not. I'm only surprised there aren't mass outbreaks of food poisoning. They haven't a clue here.'

'I see what you mean.'

'*They* haven't a clue!' Freddie laughed mirthlessly. 'I should talk. Neither have I. I'm stuck in Chapter Six and I don't know what that damned Wraith O'Reilly is going to do next – and neither does she. It's beginning to haunt me.' Freddie glanced over her shoulder in the direction of the old graveyard. 'Sometimes I think *she's* beginning to haunt me.'

Lionheart tugged at his leash, Conqueror whined his impatience. They were ready for the next lamppost, making their wishes clear by pacing about restlessly.

'You'll feel better as soon as you get into the next scene,' Lorinda comforted. 'I always do.'

'*If* I ever get into the next scene.' Freddie's despondency was not to be dismissed so lightly. She seemed to be leading up to something.

Ordinarily, Lorinda would have waited and encouraged the impending confidence, but Conqueror chose that moment to dart behind her, looping his leash around her ankles and pulling it tight. She caught at Freddie's arm to steady herself as Lionheart began to circle in the opposite direction.

'I'd better get along and let you finish with those brutes and take them back where they belong,' Freddie said.

'I *would* like to get rid of them,' Lorinda agreed, trying to untangle herself. 'This dog-walking is trickier than it looks.'

'You're spoiled because cats take care of themselves. And I'd advise you to stick to cats.' Freddie watched critically as she struggled to extricate herself. 'You're better off.'

'I'll be all right so long as we don't run into Clarice and her white rat. I'm not sure I could control them then.'

'I'm not sure you can control them now.' But Freddie did not offer any help. In fact, she began backing away. 'Well . . . good luck.'

At the end of the High Street, the dogs were still restless and unwilling to turn back. She knew that Gemma often set them free to run in the woods, but she didn't dare; they might not return when she called – and how could she go back to Gemma and confess that she had lost the dogs?

'Come on!' She tugged at the leashes, half dragging the pugs as they stiffened their legs and tried to make a dash for the woods. 'Come *on* . . .'

'Having trouble?' She hadn't seen Professor Borley approaching. 'Allow me.' He took a leash in each hand, gave them a sharp jerk and announced, 'Heel!'

The pugs looked up at him in surprise and decided to obey.

'Right,' he said. 'Where are we heading?'

'Back to Coffers Court.' Lorinda fell into step beside him. 'I want to get them home before Gemma starts worrying.'

But Gemma was asleep when they entered the flat. She did not appear to have moved since Lorinda had left.

The cats were also where she had last seen them – fast asleep on the sofa – although, typically, Had-I had struggled out from under and was now on top of But-Known.

'Those cats have the loudest purrs I've ever heard.' Professor Borley had released the pugs and they scampered into the room ahead of him, charging straight for Gemma.

'That's not the cats,' Lorinda said. 'It's Gemma snoring.'

'Snoring?' Professor Borley crossed to the chair where Gemma slumped.

Conqueror pushed a wet nose against the limp hand dangling off the arm of the chair and seemed upset when there was no answering caress. He began to whimper on a sharply rising note of panic.

But-Known sat up abruptly, tumbling Had-I to one side. Both cats became wide-eyed and still, watching.

Lionheart jumped into Gemma's lap and began to lick her face frantically.

Gemma did not stir; the heavy stertorous breathing continued.

'It was something she ate.' The tension began to infect Lorinda. 'She said she'd been sick all night, but that she was better now. Surely, it can't still be affecting her?'

'That depends on what she ate.' Professor Borley's face was grim as he laid the back of his hand lightly against Gemma's grey, clammy face.

'Who's her doctor?' he asked.

'I don't know.'

'Then who's yours?'

'I don't have one here. Yet. Perhaps she hasn't one, either.

We haven't lived here all that long, you know. We're still in the process of getting ourselves organized.'

Professor Borley's look told her she wasn't doing a very good job of it. Lorinda felt herself growing defensive.

'What makes you think Gemma needs a doctor? She told me she'd had a terrible night; she needs all the sleep she can get to catch up.'

'Sleep, yes. A coma, no.' Professor Borley frowned at her. 'What number do you ring for an ambulance?'

'An ambulance?' Lorinda shrank from the thought. 'Surely, that's a bit excessive? Gemma . . . ?' She moved over to look down at the woman. 'Gemma . . . ? Gemma . . . can you hear me? Do you want an ambulance?'

'Do you want the responsibility of denying her medical aid?' Professor Borley asked sternly. '*You* can't do anything to help her. Can you?'

The ambulance arrived quickly, the paramedics were swift and efficient. Gemma looked a little better even as they lifted the stretcher and carried her outside, but her eyes were still closed.

'Any idea what she might have taken?' The steely glance accompanying the question left no doubt of the medic's meaning.

'Taken?' Lorinda looked at him blankly. 'She said it was something she ate. She thought it was food poisoning.'

'Hmmm.' His eyes were openly suspicious. 'We'll see.'

'She might have taken something by mistake,' Lorinda said. 'When she got up in the night. If she didn't put the light on . . . an accident . . .'

'Another accident? Pretty careless people around here.'

He could be right. A cold chill swept over Lorinda as she looked at the situation from his point of view. This was the second time an ambulance had sped to Brimful Coffers to carry away one of its newer residents.

'The rest of you better start being more careful,' he said. 'Things come in threes, you know.'

'That's the sort of superstitious remark I wouldn't expect from a medical man,' Professor Borley said, but the medic had gone. They heard the ambulance door slam, the engine start, then the whine and whoop of the siren as it drove away.

Conqueror gave a mournful howl and Lionheart crouched with a pitiful whimper.

'What is it? What was that?' The door across the magnificent marble entrance hall opened and Plantagenet Sutton stood in the doorway of his flat, blinking. 'What's going on here?'

'They've just taken Gemma away in the ambulance,' Lorinda said. The siren must have roused him, although it was strange that he could have slept through its arrival and the noisy invasion of the paramedics.

'Gemma? Gemma?' He might never have heard of her. He blinked again, reinforcing the appearance of someone who had just woken up.

Conqueror emitted another howl; Lionheart decided to join in.

'For God's sake!' Plantagenet winced and raised one hand to his head. 'Can't you shut those mutts up?'

'Maybe *you'd* like to try,' Professor Borley challenged.

Plantagenet lifted his head and directed a venomous glance at the academic, who smiled blandly back. Plantagenet scowled, obviously realizing that he could not exact vengeance on someone whose work never came to him for review. He shifted his threatening gaze to Lorinda.

It told her she was doomed. Guilt by association. In the unlikely event of her next book winning the Nobel Prize, Plantagenet Sutton would still revile it as the most meretricious, unworthy, inept, misbegotten piece of arrogance that the world had ever had foisted on it. He would be merciless and utterly damning – and all because she had had the misfortune to witness him bested by Professor Borley.

'You do well to raise the subject.' Borley was not through yet. 'What *is* going to happen to the dogs while their mistress is in hospital? Someone is going to have to take care of them.'

'Don't look at me!' Plantagenet retreated into his flat, slamming the door behind him.

Lorinda realized that Professor Borley was now looking at her.

'Oh, no,' she said quickly. 'I can't take them. I have the cats.'

'That's what I thought,' he said gloomily, following her into Gemma's flat. The pugs scampered ahead of them, going straight to Gemma's chair. Despite the fact that they had just seen her carried out and loaded into the ambulance, they still seemed to expect to find her there.

'They're missing her already,' the professor said mournfully. 'Poor things.'

Had-I turned to her sister and made an obviously uncomplimentary remark. But-Known agreed. They eyed the dogs coldly.

'If you took the dogs home with you,' Borley tried again, 'you could keep them outside in the garden. The cats wouldn't mind that, would they?'

Had-I and But-Known turned to stare at him with incredulous icy contempt.

'Sorry,' he apologized to them quickly. 'It was just a thought.'

'Think again,' Lorinda said. 'What about Gordie? He'll have duplicate keys to all the flats – and it's his job to look after everything. Surely, he can feed and walk the dogs for a few days?'

'I'm afraid Gordie isn't the pillar of reliability he used to be, now that he's got that new red-headed girlfriend. You'll notice there's been no sign of him, despite all the commotion here.' Professor Borley frowned uneasily. 'She's much too old for him, of course, but they seem to be quite happy. I suppose one shouldn't be judgemental about such things. It's their business, after all.'

'Quite right,' Lorinda agreed abstractedly. Had-I and But-Known were sliding cushionwards again, ready to go back to sleep.

'No, you don't,' she warned them. 'We're going home.'

'Betty Alvin!' Borley said, on a note of inspiration. 'She'll take care of the dogs.'

'Betty already has her hands full,' Lorinda said. 'Dorian is coming to the end of his new book.' There might be more demanding employers than Dorian, but not many. He monopolized Betty at the best of times; now that he was coming to the end of a book, he undoubtedly turned into the proverbial Fiend in Human Form. Perhaps they all did. It was a wonder poor Betty was able to stand it. It was certainly unfair to expect her to take on any more tasks at such a time.

'In any case, I'm not going to be here next week. I have business to attend to in London and I'm leaving in the morning.' It was a spur of the moment decision but, as soon as she said it, she knew it was the right one. She needed a respite. When

102

she returned, she would be better able to usher those ghastly Sibling Spinster Sleuths to the victorious conclusion of another case and a happy ending for everyone except the trapped villain.

'Tomorrow?' Professor Borley looked aghast, realization seeping in that he was going to be left holding the pugs.

'Home,' Lorinda said sternly to the cats. Had-I twitched an ear and wriggled deeper into the cushions. Lorinda sighed and started for the door.

'You can't leave them here!' Professor Borley sounded close to panic at the thought of yet more animals to look after.

'I don't intend to.' Lorinda reclaimed her shopping trolley from the hall and wheeled it back into the living room. She positioned it beside the sofa and flipped back the lid. But-Known opened one wary eye and closed it again.

'Inside,' Lorinda ordered. Both cats remained motionless. She knew they were aware of her because they had stopped purring.

'All right, we'll do it this way.' She lifted Had-I and lowered her into the basket. But-Known gave a faint mewling protest at receiving the same treatment, then they both moulded themselves to the lumpy bags of vegetables and returned to their semicomatose state. Lorinda lowered the lid and wheeled the basket towards the door.

'Umm . . .' Professor Borley was at the window and appeared to be about to say something, then changed his mind. 'I suppose,' he offered instead, 'I could walk the dogs before bedtime tonight . . . and open a can of dog food.'

'That would be fine,' Lorinda agreed. 'Gemma may be able to come home by tomorrow. It might just be a case of having her stomach pumped and then they'll release her to recuperate at home. I'll ring the hospital later and find out how she is.'

'I hope you're right,' he said gloomily. 'She looked pretty awful to me.'

Since Lorinda was the one moving, both dogs followed her hopefully to the door. Perhaps she could be persuaded to take them for another walk.

'Ummm . . .' Again, Professor Borley seemed about to say something. He trailed after the dogs, looking undecided.

'It might be a good idea to open that dog food now,' Lorinda suggested. 'Fill their bowls and then you can slip out while they're eating.'

'That wasn't what –' He stepped back nimbly, trying to

restrain the pugs as she swung the door open and wheeled the shopping basket into the marble hall.

And halted abruptly. Clarice was crossing the hall to the lift, her white rat perched on her shoulder, its little red eyes gleaming wickedly as it turned its head to look at Lorinda.

'Hello.' Clarice changed course, veering over to the group in the doorway.

'No!' Lorinda gasped. 'No, go back!'

'Don't you like rats?' Clarice asked innocently, delighted with the effect she was creating. 'Boswell won't hurt you. He's really quite tame. He won't bite. Wouldn't you like to pet him?'

'No.' Lorinda backed into Professor Borley as she tried to pull the shopping basket back into Gemma's flat.

Too late. The lid on the basket began bouncing as strong little legs fought to brace themselves on the vegetables and leap upwards. Two indignant yowls told Clarice what they'd like to do to Boswell. The dogs added their yelps.

'Back! Get back!' Lorinda pushed at the little muzzles thrusting out of the basket.

'Steady, boys.' Professor Borley fought to keep the dogs from rushing into the hall. 'Steady there.'

'Oohhh . . .' Clarice began backing away. The rat squeaked, recognizing danger, and tried to burrow down the neck of Clarice's sweater.

Clarice screamed as it clawed frantically at her neckline.

Had-I was head and shoulders out of the basket now, hurling a challenge that reverberated off the marble walls. Unusually, But-Known was right behind her. The dogs slipped around Professor Borley and skittered free into the hall.

'WHAT THE HELL IS GOING ON OUT THERE?' Plantagenet Sutton threw open his door, which was his mistake.

Clarice screamed again and hurled herself towards the sanctuary of the open door, so much closer than the lift. The dogs pursued her, in full cry.

Lorinda wrestled the cats back into the basket and jammed the lid shut with her heavy shoulder bag, then raced for the front door.

Plantagenet staggered backwards as Clarice rushed past him.

The dogs hesitated momentarily as Lorinda opened the front door, distracted by the sudden choice. Professor Borley swooped on them and gathered them up.

'I always knew I wasn't interested in keeping pets,' he said. 'Now I know why.' The wriggling bodies under his arms struggled to escape.

The door across the hall slammed shut. Plantagenet Sutton was behind it – with Clarice and her rat. He wouldn't appreciate that. He was even less of a pet person than Borley, and Lorinda doubted that he cared much for children, either.

'You were at the window,' Lorinda accused Borley coldly. 'You must have seen Clarice coming into the building. Why didn't you warn me?'

'I thought of it, but you had the cats in the basket and I thought it would be all right. They couldn't see the rat.'

'Haven't you ever heard of a sense of smell?' Lorinda bumped the trolley over the threshold and out into the High Street. 'And the fact that animals have a much keener one than we do?'

'Well, yes, but I didn't think –'

'Precisely, Professor Borley!' Lorinda turned and walked away briskly, feeling that, for once, she had had the last word.

7

CHAPTER TWENTY

'I suppose you are wondering why I have brought us all together like this,' Miss Petunia said slowly. Her heart was heavy as she surveyed her siblings. Lily, so strong and self-assured; Marigold, so dainty and delicate, with her bright blue eyes and red-gold hair. It was unbearable, unthinkable, that they should be threatened in any way.

'In your own private study,' Marigold breathed with awe. 'Oh, Petunia, this is such an honour!' Her bright blue eyes danced around the room, taking in every aspect of the rarely visited *sanctum sanctorum*. 'Oh, there's Daddy's precious amethyst-quartz lamp! I always wondered what had happened to it.'

'You'll tell us when you're ready,' Lily said with supreme confidence. 'Mind if I borrow this copy of the Oxford English Dictionary? Had one of my own once; don't know whatever became of it.'

'Now settle down, girls.' Miss Petunia's fond smile turned a trifle wintry. 'This is important. I want your full attention. In fact' – she paused portentously – 'this may be the most important problem we have ever faced in our whole lives.'

'Oh, goody!' Marigold clapped her hands girlishly. 'We've got a new case!'

''Bout time we had another,' Lily said. 'Been getting a bit boring lately. Important, eh? Lots of money involved?'

'Far more important than mere money,' Miss Petunia said solemnly.

'Ooooh!' Marigold's eyes grew round.

'What could that be?' Lily was sceptical.

'It is, literally,' Miss Petunia told them, 'a matter of life and death. Ours.'

'Somebody threatening us again?' Lily clenched her fists. 'We've dealt with that before. Soon see him off.'

'Ah, yes.' Miss Petunia removed her pince-nez and tapped them against her chin thoughtfully. 'I fear it may come to that.'

'Oh, tell us about it,' Marigold said eagerly. 'I'm dying to hear all about it. Only . . .' Her delicate brow furrowed. 'I just must make a telephone call first to . . .' She blushed delicately. 'To my new friend.'

Lily growled deep in her throat. 'He's not good enough for you.'

'I fear it will not be possible to ring anyone.' Miss Petunia called them to order. 'I have turned the telephones off. It is vital that I have your complete and undivided attention.'

'Petunia!' Marigold gasped. 'You've never turned the telephones off before!'

'We have never faced such a crisis before.'

'That's a bit thick!' Lily growled. 'Are you sure?'

Miss Petunia gave her the sort of look she rarely had occasion to turn upon one of her sisters, her cohorts. Like any miscreant, Lily quailed before it, but only momentarily.

'Sorry,' she apologized. 'Lost my head.'

'I trust not,' Miss Petunia said. 'Such a calamity is what we must now unite to prevent.'

'Oh, Petunia!' Marigold gave a dramatic little shiver. 'You sound so solemn.'

'It is a solemn moment.' Miss Petunia bowed her head. 'And one I never expected to see. However, it has arrived and we must deal with it as best we can.'

'But, Petunia, what is it?'

'Come on, woman.' Lily, as ever, was impatient. 'Out with it!'

'I have considered this deeply for some time.' Miss Petunia replaced her pince-nez and looked from one sibling to the other. 'I fear the conclusion I have reached is inescapable. But first, I must ask you some questions. Sit down.'

Lily thumped down instantly into the comfortable armchair. Marigold flitted about for another moment, poising herself to perch on the edge of the desk, but deterred by Miss Petunia's severe look, she settled on the footstool at Lily's feet instead.

'Yes, Petunia?' she breathed.

'Are both of you quite comfortable?' Miss Petunia asked.

'Fine,' Lily said gruffly. 'Springs seem to be loosening up a bit though. Probably need reupholstering in a couple more years.'

'Oh, yes, this is –'

'Never mind the furniture!' Miss Petunia snapped. 'Not now! I mean, are you comfortable within yourselves? Have you been feeling at all strange at times recently? Are you uneasy, perhaps unhappy, without being able to put your finger on any reason for it?'

Lily and Marigold exchanged long glances.

'Have you,' Miss Petunia persisted, 'been having strange dreams lately?'

'Fancy your knowing that!' Marigold gasped.

'Nightmares, more like,' Lily admitted.

'Ah, yes.' Miss Petunia bowed her head. 'Yes. It is, indeed, as I had feared.'

'Yes, nightmares!' Marigold agreed, going pale. 'I keep dreaming that we're coming to the end of a case and – and then – everything starts going wrong. Terribly wrong.'

'Awful things start happening.' Lily stirred uneasily. 'People we thought were our friends show themselves as enemies. People we thought we were helping aren't grateful. Every hand turns against us.'

'And we all die,' Miss Petunia said. 'Horribly.'

'Petunia! You don't mean you're having them, too?' Marigold cried.

'Time to change our diet,' Lily said. 'No more cheese at bedtime. Get more exercise. Good healthy fresh air will blow all those demons away.'

'I think not,' Miss Petunia said. 'I fear the problem is far more deep-rooted than that. It strikes at the core of our very existence. Our continuing existence.'

'Oh, Petunia!' Marigold's blue eyes brimmed with the remembered tears of terrified awakenings. 'What can you mean?'

'Got to put a stop to it,' Lily said gruffly. 'Can't go on like this.'

'*Can* you stop it, Petunia?' Marigold's trusting eyes turned to her eldest sister, fount of all knowledge and support. 'How?'

'Why?' Lily wanted to know. 'Why should this be happening?'

'There, indeed, is the nub of the matter,' Miss Petunia said slowly. 'I fear that our Chronicler – I will not call her our Creator, for, surely, we have always existed in a life of our own – has grown tired of us. At the moment, she is merely playing with the idea . . . toying with us . . . but I fear that we are coming to the parting of the ways.'

'Oh, Petunia!' A small shriek escaped Marigold. 'Whatever shall we do?'

'We shall survive,' Miss Petunia said grimly. 'At whatever cost.'

'Quite right.' Lily flexed her muscles.

'Not yet, dear.' Miss Petunia laid a soothing hand on her sister's arm. 'First we must consider our options and come to a democratic decision.'

'Well said!' Lily straightened her back and glared around challengingly. 'So what do we do?'

'Oh, dear!' Marigold burst into tears. 'It's all so terrible! I can't bear it!'

'There, there, old thing.' Lily patted her heaving shoulders awkwardly. 'Don't take on so. It will come out all right in the end.'

'I don't see how,' Marigold choked. 'If our – our Chronicler – wants to get rid of us –'

'Someone else will take us up,' Miss Petunia said firmly.

'Oh, Petunia!' Marigold raised her tear-drenched face hopefully. 'Do you really think so?'

'Our fans will insist on it,' Miss Petunia said confidently. 'And our publishers,' she added as an afterthought. 'We are far too popular to be allowed to . . . to . . .' She found herself unable to complete the sentence; the enormity of the thought was too much for her. She closed her eyes briefly.

'Steady on,' Lily said. 'It isn't going to happen. We won't let it.'

'You're right, of course.' Dear Lily, always so supportive. Miss Petunia opened her eyes again and almost smiled. 'There is no question but that a new Chronicler will emerge to continue the relating of our adventures. It's done all the time. Look at Miss Anastasia Mudd – she's carrying on stronger than ever.'

'Yes . . .' Marigold looked doubtful. 'But will it be that easy for us? Might not Lorinda Lucas fight the idea? And she *does* hold the copyright. Miss Mudd is a different case. They had to find a new Chronicler for her because her old one died.'

'Precisely,' Miss Petunia said.

'Oh, Petunia, what *can* you mean?' Marigold's voice quavered.

'As I have said, we are in a life-or-death situation. We must face that fact and prepare to act accordingly. If the choice is between our Chronicler and ourselves . . .'

'Petunia!' Marigold buried her face in her hands.

'You mean – ?' Lily gave a long low whistle.

'Precisely,' Miss Petunia said again. 'I fear we are left with no other choice in the matter. Lorinda Lucas *m*

u

s

t

d

i

e . '

She had never written that! Not one word of it!

The pages slid from Lorinda's nerveless fingers and slithered across the carpet with the dry rustling sound of a snake gliding through the undergrowth.

Had she?

Lorinda backed away from the scattered pages even as Had-I and But-Known advanced to inspect them.

No! Her mouth shaped the word soundlessly. *No!* Something struck her in the back and she gave a muffled shriek before realizing that she had backed into the wall.

But-Known gave a final sniff at the papers and seemed to understand that she was needed elsewhere. She strolled over and brushed against Lorinda's ankles, offering comfort.

'Oh, But-But.' She bent and gathered the little calico into her arms, holding her close. But-Known twisted to stroke her head along Lorinda's chin. The little body throbbed and a soft deep purr rose like a benediction. Lorinda hugged her tighter.

110

I can't be going mad. Can I?

The dark terror lurking at the back of every human mind assailed her. She clung to But-Known and looked around her little study, hub of her new home, her peaceful ordered life. Was it all about to implode on her? Had the tenuous link with reality snapped? She earned her living from her imagination; was the mind that had given her that imagination now turning on her like some rogue cell battering at an immune system that was failing to contain it?

Her imagination – was that it? Surely, she could not have read what she thought she had read. She was overtired, stressed – her imagination was playing tricks on her. Her imagination – not her mind. Just a little blip. Perhaps the onset of a nervous breakdown? No, that wasn't a very reassuring thought, either. Nor was the next thought she had.

She was going to have to read those pages again. Make sure that they actually said what she thought they had said.

She forced herself to approach the scattered pages, fighting down the dire realization that she was in a no-win situation. It was bad if the pages remained as she had first read them; it would be worse if they didn't.

'All right, move.' She shifted Had-I, who was sitting on two of the pages, putting But-Known down beside her. The pages shook only slightly in her hands as, carefully looking at nothing but the page numbers, she put them in the right order. Then she retreated to sit at her desk and stare into space for a long moment before she looked at them again.

Yes, they were the same. Unexpectedly, she was aware of a feeling of relief, mingled with a growing anger.

This was some sort of elaborate joke. It had to be. And it wasn't funny. But who would do such a thing? And how had they known – ?

She rose abruptly and crossed to the filing cabinet. It looked the same. One didn't tuck a betraying scrap of paper into the crack of a drawer or paste a hair across it in ordinary life. Only in the sort of books she and her colleagues wrote – and any one of them could imitate each other's style for a few pages.

She pulled out her Final Chapters file and immediately knew that someone had gone through it. The gold-rimmed pince-nez glasses were missing.

Miss Petunia had come back to reclaim her property!

Lorinda pushed the thought away. She must not give in to such an idea. She was not completely mad. Not yet. While she could still function, she must. And when she found the perpetrator of this abysmal joke . . .

She thrust the file back into place and took a large manila envelope instead. She put the counterfeit chapter into it and looked around for a safe place to hide it.

The cats watched with great interest as she pried up a corner of the carpet and slid the envelope to lie flat beneath it. Not very original, perhaps, but what was the point of that when the joker who wrote those pages probably knew as much about crime and concealment as she did?

She should have hidden the pince-nez better. She should never have put them in that file. *She had put them there, hadn't she?* Without them, she could not prove they had ever existed. But they had. She could not have hallucinated such a thing. *Could she?* She could see them now, even down to the tiny '14k' imprinted in the gold rim.

Unfortunately, no one else could see what was in her mind's eye. And she would sound like a fool if she tried to tell anyone about it. That was what the joker would be counting on.

Had-I walked gingerly over the replaced carpet, testing it with tentative paws, as though it might collapse beneath her. But-Known sat on the desk, looking down on her intrepid sister and giving her familiar impression of a Victorian Miss wringing her paws at the recklessness of a daredevil.

Lorinda tested that patch of carpet herself, treading on it firmly. There was no telltale rustle of paper and no obvious difference in the thickness of the carpet. It would do.

The best way to handle the situation now was to ignore it, give no sign that she had ever seen those pages, and disappoint whomever was waiting for some sort of reaction from her.

An unpleasant feeling remained with her. Perhaps because Someone had violated the privacy of her home as surely as any burglar: sat at her desk, written on her machine – hijacked her characters. Although the escapade could be written off as a joke if anyone admitted it, there was an underlying malice that was disquieting. Someone had read through her files, invaded her home in her absence.

Who? Not Freddie. Automatically, she exonerated her friend. But who?

She had been in London for the past week, attending to all the errands she had been postponing since her move to the country. A visit to her dentist, giving a talk at a suburban library, lunch with her agent, doing research at the London Library, dinners with friends and catching up with theatregoing. She had even done some Christmas shopping. The week had sped past and she had enjoyed it thoroughly, knowing that Freddie would be looking after the cats.

It had never occurred to her that someone might be needed to watch the house. Freddie had the only duplicate keys. She would never have allowed a stranger inside, probably not even a friend. Of course, there was always that time-honoured pretext: 'I loaned her a book and I need it back.' Yes, even Freddie might have fallen for that one. She would have to find out if anyone had tried it.

If anyone else *was* involved. The quiet terror stirred at the back of her mind again. If she hadn't written that chapter herself before she went up to London and then forgotten about it, blotted it out of her memory. People could do things like that.

But they were cases of split personalities, perhaps even multiple personalities. Fighting against themselves, hating themselves, doing strange things to punish themselves for transgressions only they knew or cared about. She couldn't be one of those – could she?

She drew a deep, unsteady breath; then another, somewhat steadier. She must not give in to these thoughts. That way lay madness. If madness was not already . . .

Had-I and But-Known, who had been curled up on the corner of the desk, suddenly sat up and turned towards the doorway, eyes bright and alert, seeing, as cats do, something invisible to the human eye. The back of her neck prickled. She watched the empty doorway with apprehension.

Had-I abruptly stood and leaped to the floor, followed by But-Known. They advanced to the door in time to greet Roscoe as he sauntered in and touched noses with them.

'Oh, Pud.' Lorinda went limp with relief. 'I didn't hear the catflap.' Left to himself and without being harried by his female friends, Roscoe could negotiate the catflap, moving slowly and taking his time.

The wild thought swept into her mind and she dismissed it instantly. Of course, it wasn't possible for anyone to squeeze in through the catflap. Poor Roscoe could barely make it himself and he was nowhere near the size of an adult human being – or even an adolescent human. Apart from which, adolescents entered with intent to remove, not add to, the contents of a house.

The cats finished their silent communion and turned to look at her with faintly accusing stares. What had they been saying to each other? And why were we wasting so much time, energy and money in trying to contact whatever might exist in outer space when we couldn't even communicate properly with the warm friendly creatures living beside us?

I can explain everything, she felt like saying defensively. But she knew that she couldn't – and so did they.

The ring of the telephone came as a lifeline. She snatched it up quickly. 'Hello?'

'Oh, good, you *are* back. Freddie wasn't quite sure –'

'Macho, yes.' She had not realized how much she had tensed until she felt herself relax. 'Yes, I got back late last night. And I've been out shopping this morning, replenishing the larder.'

'Good ... good.' Macho sounded somewhat abstracted. 'Er ... have a nice time in London?'

'Oh, yes. Saw a lot of friends, got a lot of things done. I'm glad to be back, though.' Surprisingly, she found that she meant it; the place was beginning to feel like home. At least, it had been. 'I haven't caught up with Freddie yet. What's been happening while I've been gone? Have I missed anything interesting?'

There was a curious silence at the other end of the line. 'Oh ... nothing much,' he said eventually. 'We've all got invitations to an early Christmas Party at Dorian's on the nineteenth, because he's off on a cruise over the holidays. If yours hasn't arrived –'

'I haven't gone through my post yet.' She glanced at the pile of envelopes on her desk. 'I was planning to do that this evening.'

'Oh ... good, you'll find it then. Er ...' he was elaborately casual. 'I don't suppose you've seen Roscoe anywhere around?'

'He's right here with the girls,' she said. 'He came in a few minutes ago.'

There was an explosive exhalation of relief.

'Macho, what is it?'

114

'Oh, nothing, nothing. I'm glad to know he's sa—there. I haven't seen him all afternoon. I was getting – I mean –'

'I was just about to open some of the gourmet cat food I brought back from London for a treat for them,' she said. 'Why don't you come over? You can have a drink, of course.'

'Oh, yes. Yes, I will. Thanks. I'll be right over.' He put the phone down.

She had just reached the kitchen when he appeared at the back door. He looked over his shoulder, then caught the door before she opened it fully and slid through the narrow aperture. Inside, he stood with his back against the wall and slowly turned his head to scan the room.

'Macho, what's wrong?' She was shocked by the change in his appearance. In the week since she had last seen him, he had grown haggard with dark shadows under his eyes. Furthermore, although it was a pleasantly misty mid-December day outside, with the red tinge of the setting sun colouring the mist, Macho was behaving like someone out of a *film noir*.

'Wrong?' For a moment, he was his old fussy self. 'Why should you think there's anything wrong?' Then the invisible atmosphere settled round him again. He stared at the far doorway with haunted eyes, a fugitive wrapped in the deep gloom of a perpetual midnight, with danger lurking in every shadow.

'Ah! There you are!' He dashed across the room as the cats appeared in the doorway and scooped up Roscoe, holding him close. 'I haven't seen you for hours.'

Roscoe looked up in mild surprise at finding himself thus clasped to his master's bosom. He stretched up to touch noses with Macho and began purring.

Had-I and But-Known strolled over to sit at Lorinda's feet and stare meaningly at the small stack of gourmet cat-food trays she had brought them. If it was cocktail time for humans, it was treats time for felines.

'Game with turkey.' Lorinda picked up the top container and read the contents. 'How does that sound to you?'

It sounded good to Roscoe. He twisted free of Macho's arms and hit the floor, bouncing over to take his place beside the others.

'So, what's been going on while I've been away?' Lorinda divided the cat food into three neat portions, then glanced down doubtfully at Roscoe. He was watching her in bright-eyed anticipation, licking his chops. He could polish off one of those small containers all by himself.

'Hasn't Freddie filled you in yet?' Macho sounded surprised.

'I still haven't seen Freddie.' And that was unusual; she had expected to see or hear from Freddie before this. Of course, she had arrived home last night too late for visiting and perhaps Freddie had rung this morning while she was out shopping.

'Freddie isn't looking too well lately,' Macho said. 'She seems a bit . . . stressed.'

'Oh?' That was surely the pot calling the kettle black. Perhaps Macho hadn't looked in a mirror lately. Lorinda set the saucers down on the floor. Had-I inspected the size of her portion and gave her a wounded look. 'You can have seconds, if you want,' she told her, then led Macho into the sitting room while the cats hunched over their treat.

'What would you like?' If she poured fast, they might have time for a few sips before the cats came in to demand more.

'What do you have?' He peered suspiciously at the small collection of bottles. 'There's no tequila there, is there?'

'Sorry, no. Do you want some?'

'God, no!' He shuddered. 'I never want to see or hear of the stuff again!' He spoke with bitter vehemence and looked over his shoulder again as he did so. Lorinda wondered if that was becoming a nervous tic.

'I'll have a dry sherry,' he decided. 'A large one.'

'Trouble with the new book?' she asked sympathetically, handing it to him and pouring one for herself.

'The publishers want to call it *Blondes Die Screaming*.' He took a deep swallow and brooded into his glass. There's no blonde in the book and I told them anyone would die screaming when a serial rapist-murderer went to work on them.'

'What did you want to call it?'

'Does that matter?' He *was* in a mood. 'I'm only the author.' He flung himself into an armchair and stared into space. After a moment, he twitched and looked over his shoulder. 'What was that?'

It was only the sound of cats' dishes moving around the kitchen floor as tongues scraped to get every last morsel off them. If Macho couldn't identify that familiar sound, he must be in a bad way.

'Macho, what is it?' She tried again. 'Is there anything I can do?'

'Do? Do?' He gave a snarling bark of mirthless laughter worthy of his PI hero in a cornered moment. 'There's nothing anyone can do. Except –' He raised his head and looked at her strangely.

'Yes?' she encouraged.

'Lorinda, if anything . . . happened to me, you'd take care of Roscoe, wouldn't you? I mean, adopt him. He gets on so well with your two, it wouldn't be like going to a stranger. I think he'd be happy here.'

'Macho, are you ill?' *Dying?* she meant. Had he been informed that some fatal disease was unexpectedly numbering his days?

'No, no.' He caught her thought. 'Not that. It's just that I may be put – have to go – away.'

'*Put* away?' She pounced on his slip of the tongue. 'Macho, what *is* it? What have you done?' He was an erratic driver, but usually quite careful. Had he killed someone in a moment of inattention in the night fog? A hit-and-run? She could visualize him panicking when he realized his victim was dead and instinctively bolting for home and safety. Then, with time for reflection, realizing the full horror of his position (MACHO MAGEE RUNS AND HIDES, the tabloids would scream) would dawn on him. With his knowledge of police procedures, knowing that they were waiting for the results of their forensic tests to filter through, wondering what evidence he might have left behind – flecks of paint, tyre treadmarks, hairs from his beard – that would lead inexorably to him, there was no wonder he was a nervous wreck, constantly looking over his shoulder.

'Nothing!' he declared vehemently, as though suspecting the trend of her thoughts. 'I've done nothing. Yet. And nothing may ever happen. But, if it should –' He looked at her pleadingly, 'Roscoe –?'

'*Prrryaaa??*' Roscoe padded into the room, drawn by the sound of his name. He leapt into Macho's lap and settled down purring. Had-I and But-Known were right behind him. They looked at Lorinda thoughtfully, then settled on the hearthrug in front of the fire. They had obviously decided against agitating for any more food right now, realizing that they would have to share it with Roscoe if they did.

'Of course I'll take him.' She could reassure Macho on that

point. 'It will be no trouble at all.' Apart from having to get a larger catflap installed.

'Thank you.' He sank back in his chair, running his fingers through Roscoe's fur. 'It may never happen,' he muttered. 'It may all be just my imagina—'

'Macho!' There was something terribly familiar in his attitude. 'What –?'

The back door slammed. 'Had-I! But-But!' Freddie's voice carolled. 'Come and get it!' The cats rose unhurriedly and strolled towards the kitchen.

'We're in here, Freddie,' Lorinda called. 'Come and have a drink.'

'Oh, no!' Freddie appeared in the doorway, looking guilty. 'You're back. I'm sorry, I wouldn't have burst in like that if I'd known. I thought you were coming back tonight.'

'Last night,' Lorinda said. 'Don't worry, it's all right.' What was not all right was Freddie's appearance. She looked grey and drawn. What was going on around here?

The cats, sensing that they were not about to get another feed, turned and went back to their spot before the fire.

'Are the Jackleys still fighting?' Lorinda asked.

'They're trying, but some of the old fire has gone.' Freddie curled up on the sofa. 'Jack still has one arm in bandages – he can't throw things the way he used to.'

'Maybe not, but they're obviously disturbing your sleep again.'

'If you think I look bad,' Freddie said. 'Wait till you see the others. Gemma looks terrible – I think they let her out of hospital too soon.'

'What was wrong?' Lorinda felt guilty; she ought to have rung Gemma this morning.

'Nothing the medics seemed to be definite about. They half-way agreed with her own diagnosis of something she ate, but they didn't rule out an extreme allergic reaction to something, or even one of the new mystery viruses that are breaking out all over.'

'No one else seems to have caught it,' Macho said. 'So it was probably an allergy.'

'And Rhylla is really in trouble.' Freddie dismissed Gemma's problem as inconsequential. 'Her son and daughter-in-law telephoned last week to say they were having such a good time without the sprog that they've booked themselves a second-honeymoon skiing holiday in Colorado over New Year. She's stuck with the brat and the rat until well into January – and I don't know which is upsetting her more.'

'Oh, no!' Lorinda was horrified. 'What will that do to her deadline?'

'Nothing good,' Freddie said gloomily.

'Look on the bright side.' Macho cheered up for the first time all afternoon. 'It may upset Rhylla – but it will drive Plantagenet Sutton absolutely crazy.'

'That's right.' Freddie also brightened. 'He hates rats. Funny that, you'd think he'd have some fellow-feeling for them.'

Had-I's ears twitched and she raised her head.

'Go back to sleep,' Lorinda advised. 'Boswell is out of bounds.'

Had-I lowered her head slowly, with the air of a cat who had her own ideas about that.

'I thought I'd drive over to Marketown for some shopping,' Freddie announced. 'Either of you care to come along?'

'Now?' Macho looked askance. He might have a hero who acted on impulse – a door kicked down here, a jaw broken there – but he preferred to plan his own days well in advance.

'Say . . . ten minutes?' Freddie offered.

'Two will do it.' Lorinda was already on her feet. 'Just let me grab my coat and bag and I'll be right with you.'

'Sorry –' she heard Macho say as she left the room. 'But I want to finish a chapter before dinner. Another time . . .'

It was not until Lorinda was safely tucked into the passenger seat beside Freddie that it occurred to her that it might not be wise to leave the house unattended. Dear as the cats were, they were of no use as watchdogs.

But the car was rolling smoothly down the High Street and it was too late to do anything about the situation except worry. She wished she had not thought of it. She turned to make a remark to Freddie and gave a muffled shriek.

Freddie was driving with her eyes closed.

'What is it?' Freddie's eyes flew open, she looked fearfully in the direction of the graveyard they were passing. The car swerved. 'Did you see it?'

'See what?' Lorinda was startled. There was genuine terror

in Freddie's eyes as she stared deep into the old graveyard where the mist was thickest. 'Freddie, what's wrong?'

'Nothing, nothing!' There was an echo of Macho's anxious evasion in Freddie's immediate defensive denial. 'Why should anything be wrong?'

'Freddie! Watch the road!' The front tyres scraped against the kerb.

'Sorry.' Freddie braked violently, then they lurched backwards. 'Not paying attention. I'll be all right as soon as we get on the open road.'

'I hope so.' Lorinda bit down on a sharper remark. Freddie was still looking fearfully over her shoulder at the old graveyard. It was clearly not a moment for either levity or reproach. Freddie was deeply disturbed.

'Freddie –' A sudden thought disquieted her. 'Don't tell me the old graveyard is haunted!'

'All right.' Freddie returned her attention to the road. They rounded a bend and the graveyard was out of sight. 'I won't tell you.'

'Well . . . is it?' She remembered Freddie's strange attitude towards the graveyard when she had been walking Gemma's dogs, just before she went up to London.

'Who knows?' Freddie shrugged. 'Stranger things may have happened in Brimful Coffers. I wouldn't put anything past this bloody place.'

'But what is it?' She tried to pin Freddie down. 'If there were any sort of legend about the place, surely Dorian would have told us about it?'

'Told us? He'd have seen to it that we were charged extra for the privilege.' Freddie's bravado was growing, the farther away from the graveyard they travelled.

'Have *you* seen whatever it is?' Lorinda would not be diverted. 'Has anyone else seen it?'

'No one is admitting it, not that I'd blame them.' Freddie shrugged again. 'In fact, the subject has never been raised. I don't blame anyone for that either.'

'But *is* there anything to talk about?' A spectral sighting might explain Macho's curious behaviour – although not, perhaps, his intense anxiety over Roscoe. In the annals of haunting, human beings were often menaced, but not animals. It took vampires for that.

'Perhaps someone is playing jokes.' Lorinda put forward the idea cautiously. Misery loves company and she realized that she would be a lot happier if she thought she wasn't the prankster's only target.

'Ha-ha-ha,' Freddie said bitterly. 'I may die laughing.'

'But what exactly have you?' – Freddie swerved the car sharply, throwing her against the seatbelt, cutting off her breath.

'You had the right idea,' Freddie said. 'Get out of this place for a while, sweep the cobwebs out of your brain and come back with a fresh perspective.'

'I'm not sure I could claim –'

'Maybe I ought to go up to London for a week or two myself.' Having changed the subject, Freddie was not going to go back to it. 'Tell me what show I ought to see.'

8

It was days before Lorinda could force herself to take up work on the book again. Had-I and But-Known watched with interest as she approached the desk, taking one step backward for every two steps forward. They had not seen this performance before.

'All right, all right,' she assured them. 'I'll get there. Don't rush me.'

It didn't help that the cats had decided that their favourite spot to curl up was the place on the carpet beneath which the envelope lay hidden. They weren't trying to keep her attention focused on the spot, she knew, and no one who came into the study would think anything untoward about it. They were probably settled there because the envelope and pages provided another layer of insulation, making that spot on the carpet slightly warmer than the rest of it.

She hesitated over the pile of paper beside her typewriter, and lifted the top sheet with a hand that trembled only slightly. It was blank. She quickly riffled through the other pages. Blank, all blank. She exhaled a quiet sigh of relief.

The cats shifted into a more comfortable position and waited for her to sit down in her office chair. They seemed to relax when she did so. It had been several days since she had occupied her familiar place. All was right with their world again. What about hers?

Cautiously, she began to tap at the keys, still half fearful that control might be snatched away from her. After a few paragraphs, the knot in the pit of her stomach began to loosen. Miss Petunia settled her pince-nez firmly on the narrow bridge of her long thin nose, Lily growled, Marigold tossed her red-gold curls and burbled, and none of them showed any signs of taking on a sinister life of their own.

With increasing confidence, Lorinda settled down to making

up for lost time. Her fingers flew over the keyboard, she scarcely noticed when the sky began growing darker.

The cats grew restive. Had-I strolled over, head-butted her ankles and eyed her lap, inaccessible since the chair was pushed well under the desk.

'Later,' she said absently to Had-I's protest.

But-Known knew better than to try to disturb her, but was equally disgruntled. Nose to nose, the cats communed for a moment, then turned and left the room purposefully. Lorinda barely registered the subsequent plop of the catflap as she continued working.

When, at last, she raised her head and came back to the present, the room beyond the desk lamp was dark. In the early-night blackness outside, lighted windows glowed in Macho's cottage and in the larger semidetached occupied by Freddie and the Jackleys.

Lorinda sighed, stretched and pushed back her chair. As though that were a signal, the doorbell and the telephone rang simultaneously.

'Hello?' The phone was nearest. 'Hold on a minute, will you? The doorbell's ringing. I'll answer it and get straight back to you.'

'Oh-oh!' It was unmistakably Freddie's voice. 'I'll get right over there. You may need reinforcements.'

'What?' But Freddie had already rung off. The doorbell rang again, more insistently.

'I'm coming!' she called, hurrying down the stairs to throw open the door.

'I thought you might need some help.' Macho stepped inside and looked around – at floor level. 'Where are they?'

'What on earth –?' She could see Freddie hurrying up the path with an anxious expression on her face.

'Keep calm and don't worry,' Freddie said quickly. 'If the pugs had done it, Gemma might be in trouble but, remember, a cat owner is not responsible for anything her cats do. That's the law.'

'Do? Law?' That sinking feeling was back in the pit of her stomach. 'What have they done now?'

'She doesn't know yet,' Macho said. 'They haven't –'

Flip-flop. . . flip-flop. . . The catflap sent its familiar message, followed by a questing, '*Mrraahhaarrmm?*'

'In here –' Lorinda began, but Freddie and Macho were already rushing for the kitchen door. She followed, more slowly, in their wake.

'*Not* in here, you little wretch!' Freddie said. 'Not on the nice clean carpet.'

There was a muffled indignant feline protest as Freddie executed some fancy footwork, blocking the threshold.

'Oh, no!' Lorinda had a full view of the scene now: two triumphant cats standing over one plump furry white body with glazing red eyes.

'I saw it from across the street,' Macho said. 'I shouted at them, but they paid no attention.'

'They wouldn't,' Freddie said. 'Not even Lorinda could have stopped them at that point.'

'You saw it, too?' Lorinda asked faintly.

'It was hard to miss. Clarice's screams were enough to wake the dead.'

'Oh, no!' Lorinda flinched as the telephone shrilled. 'If that's Rhylla, what can I say?'

'Just grovel,' Freddie advised. 'And remember, it's not your fault.'

'Hello . . . ?' Lorinda breathed a sigh of relief. 'Oh, Elsie . . . Yes . . . yes, I know. They've just come in with it . . . yes. Yes, it looks very dead . . . Well, thanks for trying to warn me.' She had barely replaced the receiver when the phone rang again.

'Hello . . . ? Oh, Jennifer . . . right past the bookshop, did they? Yes, yes, of course I want to know. They're back now and they've brought it with them. Thanks, anyway.' She began to replace the receiver, then thought better of it and set it down beside its base.

'What did you do?' she asked the cats bitterly. 'Take a lap of honour with the damned thing?'

Had-I wriggled her shoulders and preened; she was delighted with herself. But-Known sensed criticism and moved a few inches away from her sister, distancing herself.

'*Prrryaaaah?*' Had-I began to notice that she was not receiving the appreciation that was her due. She reached out and prodded the limp white lump. '*Prrryaaaah?*'

'Yes, yes, good girl.' Macho bent and patted her head consolingly. It was all right for him, he didn't have to face the full brunt of the social horrors in store. Lorinda shuddered.

'Well, she is,' Macho defended. 'If the place were overrun by an infestation of rats, you'd be bloody glad to have her on duty. She isn't to know the difference between a pet rat and a wild one. She might even have thought the rat was attacking Clarice. If it had been, she'd have been a heroine.'

'Good scenario,' Freddie said. 'Would you like to try to explain it that way to little Clarice?'

'Perhaps after she's calmed down a bit,' Macho said.

Lorinda shuddered again. The doorbell rang more insistently. But-Known backed a little farther away from Had-I and her victim.

'I'll get the door,' Freddie said.

'Now what do we do?' Lorinda asked despairingly.

'When we lost one of the hamsters at school,' Macho said, 'we found it distracted the boys' attention wonderfully if we gave it a full military funeral. Matron,' he added hopefully, 'always sewed a nice black velvet shroud for it.'

'You can forget that one,' Freddie said, returning. 'I wouldn't even sew for myself, let alone a dead rat. And neither would Lorinda.'

'Who was it?' Lorinda asked.

'Nemesis!' Freddie rolled her eyes heavenwards. 'We've just paused to blow our little nose and dry our tears. They'll be with us in a minute.'

Had-I, with a thoughtful look, got up and strolled away. But-Known had already disappeared. The abandoned corpse lay in the centre of the kitchen floor.

'B O S W E L L !' The agonized cry tore through the air, propelling Clarice into the room and to her knees by Boswell's side. She burst into noisy anguished sobs.

Rhylla came into the room more slowly, a long-suffering look on her face. She watched her granddaughter's histrionics with a certain wry amusement.

'You wouldn't think, would you,' she remarked sotto voce, 'that she's only had the thing three weeks? She originally wanted a Gila monster, but her mother, I'm happy to say, put her foot down.'

'Boswell . . . Boswell . . .' The broken-hearted wail rose and fell. 'My poor little Boswell.' The scene was rather marred by a

125

sudden sidelong glance from Clarice to gauge the effect she was having on her audience.

'Is she going into the theatre when she grows up?' Freddie asked with interest. 'She'd do a smashing Lady Macbeth.'

'More of a touch of *East Lynne* there,' Macho observed critically. '"Dead, dead, and never called me Mother" – you know. The Drama Society did it at school one year.'

Two small furry faces peeked around a corner and wisely decided to withdraw again. The sobbing continued unabated.

'Would she like a glass of water?' Lorinda offered diffidently.

'Fortunately, she's too young for anything else,' Rhylla said. 'I, however, am not – and I would appreciate a large measure of the strongest liquid you have on hand. Or perhaps Macho would donate one of his slugs of tequila.'

'That isn't funny!' The colour drained from Macho's face, his eyes blazed.

'Well, I'm sorry.' Rhylla was taken aback. 'I meant Macho, your character. I know you wouldn't have the stuff in your house.'

'Who told you that?' His face burned with hostility.

'You did.' Rhylla was affronted. 'Often.'

They glared at each other wordlessly for a moment, while Clarice's sobs dwindled to an occasional hiccough as she became distracted by the sudden inexplicable animosity between the two adults. Lorinda took advantage of her distraction to slide a paper towel over the small corpse.

Clarice did not seem to notice. She rose slowly to her feet, seemingly absorbed in some new thought. She raised her head and faced her grandmother challengingly.

'*Now* can I have a Gila monster?' she demanded.

'Over my dead body!' Rhylla snapped.

For an instant, something nasty flashed in the depths of Clarice's eyes. If looks could kill, that Gila monster would have been riding on her shoulder in the morning.

'Keep looking at me like that, young woman, and you won't get your pocket money, either!' Already in a bad mood from Macho's unwarranted attack, Rhylla was not prepared to tolerate dumb insolence.

Not for the first time, Lorinda envied the cats. How nice, how wonderful, how peaceful to be able to melt away at times of strife and not reappear until the atmosphere cleared and the world was calm again.

While Clarice seethed, trying to settle on a form of mutiny that would not bring reprisals, Macho had recovered his composure. With a conspiratorial nod to Lorinda, he slipped behind Clarice, scooped up the remains of the late Boswell and made an inconspicuous exit through the back door, closing it silently behind him.

He need not have bothered. The battle order had changed and Clarice moved forward without a backward glance at her erstwhile pet. The threat to her pocket money outweighed all lesser considerations.

'I'll tell my mother,' she threatened.

'Go right ahead,' Rhylla said. 'You can also tell her that I now recognize some of the mistakes I made with her husband and I am not about to repeat them with you.'

The one consolation was that they were moving steadily towards the front door. If nothing impeded their progress, they would soon be gone.

'Who was it,' Freddie murmured, 'who said that children keep you young?'

'Someone who never had any!' Rhylla snapped, slamming the door behind them.

'All this,' Freddie said into the silence, 'and Dorian's party tomorrow night, too.'

'I think I'll go back to London,' Lorinda said.

As though in protest, Had-I and But-Known reappeared. After a quick, almost disinterested, glance at the empty spot on the kitchen linoleum, they cut their losses and followed Lorinda and Freddie into the living room where they made it clear that it was time for laps and loving. They barely contained their impatience while Lorinda poured drinks.

'I don't know,' she sighed, as Had-I sprang into her lap and curled up. 'I suppose Dorian meant well, but I don't think this was one of his better ideas.'

'Only you could give Dorian credit for meaning well,' Freddie said, shifting slightly to accommodate But-Known. 'I must admit I'm not looking forward to this party. I keep remembering what happened at his last one.'

'At least there won't be a bonfire for anyone to fall into.'

'There's always the fireplace.' Freddie would not be reassured. 'He's sure to have a blazing fire in it.'

The party went smoothly, however, helped by the fact that Jack Jackley was still unable to operate a camera. Unfortunately, he appeared to have developed a form of paranoia; he stood with his back against the wall, clutching a large drink he had poured from a fresh bottle, insisting on breaking the seal himself, and obviously intended nursing through the evening lest any other drink offered to him might be noxious.

'Honestly, he makes me *sick!*' Karla came up to Lorinda and Freddie, eyes flashing. 'He's so afraid something's going to happen to him. He didn't even want to come tonight.'

'Well, something *did* happen to him at the last party,' Freddie said. 'You can see his point.'

'If he hadn't been so damned clumsy –' Karla gulped savagely at her drink. 'And then he tries to pretend he's not so stupid by claiming someone pushed him! Who'd want to? That's what I asked him – and he couldn't answer me.'

Lorinda and Freddie stared thoughtfully into middle distance, no more anxious to answer the question than Jack had been, even though they were not in such a vulnerable position for reprisals.

'Dorian's parties are always so marvellous!' The uncritical voice at their elbows made them turn, and quick bright smiles spread across their faces. No author was going to dispute an issue with the proprietor of the town's only bookshop. Jennifer Lane beamed back at them. 'He's certainly revitalized this town. He's so full of wonderful ideas!'

They all agreed automatically and with some relief. At least she was changing the subject. Not even Karla would continue her complaints in front of a third party who was so innocently sure that they were all one big happy family.

'Gemma, feeling better?' Lorinda turned her bright social smile on Gemma Duquette, who was wandering past, clutching a glass of white wine.

'Oh, yes, thank you.' Gemma joined the group gratefully. 'I'm still being careful, though.' She raised her glass. 'This can't hurt me, I'm sure. I'd have had orange juice, but I'm afraid it's just that little bit too acid for my stomach right now.'

'Can't be too careful,' Freddie agreed. 'You had a nasty do. What was it, do you know?'

'I wish I did. Probably some new virus going around.' Gemma flinched as Betty Alvin appeared beside them with a tray. 'Oh, no, I couldn't possibly dare!' She regarded the king prawns and spicy dip with horror. 'It's more than my life's worth. I must be very careful, you know. I'm really still convalescent.'

The others had no such inhibitions and rapidly depleted the tray. 'I'll get a refill,' Betty said reassuringly. 'There's plenty more out in the kitchen.'

Perhaps there was, but the party was low on catering staff, Lorinda noticed. Poor Betty and Gordie were doing overtime . . . again. Betty didn't seem to mind, but Gordie appeared vaguely discontented. He hovered near Dorian, as though hoping for an introduction to the prosperous-looking strangers Dorian was being so attentive to that they had to be publishers. Poor Gordie. She wondered just what Dorian had promised him when he lured him into moving to Brimful Coffers and acting as general factotum, as well as his caretaking duties at Coffers Court.

There were fewer Londoners at this party. Presumably, now that the weather was worsening, with freezing conditions and even snow forecast for tonight, they preferred not to risk getting stranded in the country. They would undoubtedly be back in full force for any parties Dorian gave in the summer. There was, of course, a good sprinkling of townspeople.

Plantagenet Sutton, as had become usual, had usurped the bar, leaving Dorian free for socializing. Bursts of ostentatiously coarse laughter were resounding from another corner where three males from London were obviously recounting the latest dirty jokes.

A slight movement at waist level caught Lorinda's eye, and she saw Clarice edging closer to the riotous group, anxious to be in on any jokes going around. Since everyone had been invited to the party, there had been no baby-sitter available and Rhylla had had to bring her along. It was more than possible that Rhylla would regret it – especially if Clarice picked up any of those jokes.

Professor Borley appeared to be in a quandary, looking from group to group, nearly overcome by an embarrassment of riches. So many authors at his fingertips, as it were. It was a hard choice to make; he swerved towards Lorinda's group, then detoured in response to something Plantagenet called to him. He went over to the bar and they conferred earnestly.

Rhylla was trying to be nice to Jack Jackley, who did not appear to be appreciating her effort. He looked around restlessly and almost smiled.

Rhylla followed his gaze, arriving at the source of his amusement just as a further shout of raucous laughter brought a nervous, slightly puzzled smile to Clarice's face. Rhylla gasped and swooped across the room to snatch a protesting Clarice away from the circle of deeply embarrassed men who belatedly became aware of her presence.

'*Wha-at?*' Freddie's outraged squawk wrenched Lorinda's attention back to the group.

'Oh, yes.' Jennifer smiled nervously. 'Hasn't he mentioned it to you yet? I believe he's going to announce it tonight. Just informally, of course. He'll announce it again at a proper launch, with full media presence, once we have all the details finalized.'

'I'll finalize him!' Freddie muttered.

'Oh, I don't know.' Karla had brightened. 'It sounds like a really great idea to me.'

'You're not trying to work,' Freddie said.

'I *beg* your pardon!' Karla drew herself up huffily. 'I am working my butt off. Especially since Jack got home. I practically have to feed him half the time. He can't even cut his meat, the way his hands are.' There was more annoyance than sympathy in her voice. It was clear that any help Jack got from his wife was reluctant and under protest.

Freddie twitched her eyebrows and looked away.

'It won't be so bad,' Jennifer said. 'It shouldn't interfere with your work.'

'I'm afraid I've missed something here,' Lorinda said softly to Freddie. 'What are we talking about?'

'I thought you were too calm.' Freddie did not bother to lower her voice. 'The crux of the matter is that Dorian is planning to turn Brimful Coffers into a sort of Literary Disneyland-Cum-Zoo. With us as unpaid employees and captive exhibits.'

'*Wha-at?*' Lorinda found herself echoing Freddie's earlier incredulous gasp.

'No, no, nothing of the sort. Freddie exaggerates.' Jennifer sent Freddie an impatient glance. 'Honestly, the schedule won't be intrusive and you needn't participate in any of the events unless you want to. There'll be the usual signings at the bookshop as your new books are published – you'd do that anyway. And giving the occasional talk to tours passing through and perhaps joining them for drinks and dinner.'

'What tours?' Freddie asked ominously.

'Oh, just fans.' Jennifer shied back nervously. 'People who really admire you and your works. They'll be small tours and only stay in town a night or two before going on to take in the usual historical sites and have a few days in London ... and meet other authors in other places ...' She trailed off, perhaps sensing that her audience was not as enthusiastic as she was.

'Did she just say what I thought she said?' Unnoticed, Macho had joined the group.

'You heard.' Freddie was grim.

'Did you just arrive?' Lorinda tried for a more social tone.

'I had to ... settle Roscoe first,' Macho said.

'Isn't he well?'

'He's fine – and he's going to stay that way.' Macho's mouth tightened. 'What I want to know is what's going on here?'

'We're just finding out ourselves,' Lorinda said.

'Treachery!' Freddie glowered at Jennifer. 'Sheer outright treachery. We've been set up!'

'Oh, no, you mustn't think that.' Jennifer was sinking under the combined weight of their disapproval. 'I – I've explained it badly, that's all. When Dorian makes his announcement, it will all be much clearer.'

'Dorian ...' Macho shifted his brooding gaze to their debonair host, now raising his glass as though in a toast to his companions. 'The plot thickens.'

'Raising the time-honoured question: since when have you lisped?' Freddie also turned to glare at Dorian.

'Gad! He'll be running school parties round next!'

'No, no, not for quite a long time yet, not until we really ... get ... going.' Jennifer faltered to a stop as she realized she was making things worse.

'I promise you –' She tried again. 'It won't interfere with your work. You can just give them a talk at the library and later their teachers will take them on a walk around town. They'll enjoy seeing where all the real authors live.'

'Maybe they'll enjoy seeing all the FOR SALE signs,' Freddie snarled.

'Oh, no! You can't do that! Please!' Jennifer was stricken. 'Hilda Saint has already taken out a second mortgage to enlarge and refurbish her guest house. And I've doubled my inventory in preparation.' She was close to tears.

'I may kill him,' Macho said thoughtfully.

'You'll have to get in line,' Freddie snapped.

Lorinda found herself too deep in gloom to say anything. It was all very well for Freddie to talk glibly of selling, but who could bear to go through all that upheaval again? Apart from which, who was going to buy? The housing market was currently deader than the victims in their books. That was why they had been able to buy the desirable residences in Brimful Coffers at favourable prices. The market might recover in time, but right now there was unlikely to be anyone interested in buying.

'I don't know what you're all fussing about,' Karla said. 'I think it's a great idea. You English don't understand about publicity and public relations. It's not enough just to write the books any more – you have to get out there and sell them!'

'I'm willing to get out there,' Freddie said. 'I'm just not willing to allow packs of strangers in here.'

Karla looked exasperated as the others nodded agreement. 'You've got to make some concessions,' she said. 'Personally, I'll be delighted to go along with any arrangements Jennifer and Dorian care to make. And so will Jack.'

'Jack?' Jennifer looked somewhat less than enchanted at this assurance. 'Er . . . does he write under his own name?'

'Not yet,' Karla said. 'He's concentrating on his photography right now.'

He was concentrating on his drinking, actually. Jack and Plantagenet were behind the makeshift bar and seemed to have struck up an unholy alliance. Sniggering like schoolboys, they were lifting up the less popular bottles, scrutinizing the labels carefully and pouring dollops into an array of glasses lined up before them. They appeared to be trying to invent a new cocktail. The contents of some of the glasses had already acquired a lethal colour. Lorinda made a mental note to stick to the champagne.

'Attention! Attention!' Dorian suddenly tapped the swizzle stick he affected against a bottle, calling them to order. 'Attention, everyone!'

The hubbub of conversation died down and faces turned towards him expectantly.

'Here it comes,' Freddie muttered.

'Some of you –' He frowned in their direction. 'Some of you may think you already know what I'm going to say. But I think I may yet have a surprise in store for you.'

'Make a change from his books.' Macho was muttering, too.

'Shhh!' Karla hissed and moved away, virtuously distancing herself from her unruly companions. She turned her enraptured gaze on Dorian, ostentatiously giving him her full attention.

'Crawler!' Freddie muttered.

'Shhh!' Gemma moved away to join Karla. Jennifer looked as though she would like to, but the authors were part of her stock-in-trade and she was caught in the proverbial cleft stick.

The bottles continued clinking at the bar, an occasional snicker also sounded. Jack and Plantagenet were having a wonderful time, perhaps a better time than anyone else at the party. Karla flicked a disapproving glance in their direction. Jack would undoubtedly hear more about this when she got him home.

'Yes, well . . . for those of you who are interested –' Dorian dismissed them. 'And this is of great import to the *real* authors amongst us –'

Jack raised his head and glared at Dorian; he considered that working with Karla made him an author, too. Gordie Crane flushed a deep red and set his tray down on the nearest table with a thud. Plantagenet Sutton seemed no less offended; presumably he felt that his two or three Christmas-stocking fillers – scarcely more than booklets copiously illustrated with whimsical drawings by his newspaper's top cartoonist – about wine put him in the 'real' author category.

'We have an exciting year ahead of us . . .' Dorian, happier now that he had managed to offend a few guests, went on to announce what they had already heard.

Most of them. Rhylla, who had been kept fully occupied with Clarice and had not yet plugged into the gossip circuit, straightened abruptly. She looked over to Freddie, as though for confirmation, and her mouth tightened, her jaw jutted forward.

'But what you may not have heard,' Dorian concluded, 'is that our numbers are about to be swelled by yet another recruit to our happy colony. Unfortunately, she can't be here tonight so that I can introduce her personally, but she will be with us in the course of the week, direct from her triumphal tour of Australia and New Zealand. I know you will all be delighted to welcome Ondine van Zeet into our midst.'

A bottle crashed to the floor and shattered. Heads turned towards the bar, but Jack and Plantagenet were both standing motionless and expressionless. It was impossible to tell which of them had dropped the bottle.

The audience began an automatic round of applause as they realized Dorian had finished his speech.

'Who?' Unfortunately, Karla's voice could still be heard.

'Ondine van Zeet.' Dorian strolled over to join them. 'Otherwise known as the Un-woman,' he added roguishly, anticipating her response.

'The Un-woman?' Karla walked right into it. 'You mean – ?'

'No, no, nothing like that,' he assured her. 'You must know of her and her Un-books.' He waited and was not disappointed.

'Un-books? You mean she isn't really an author, either?'

'Don't be unfair,' Freddie said to Dorian. 'Ondine was just starting to be published in the States when I left. There wasn't the great storm of publicity she gets here – she's just another author over there. It's not surprising if Karla hasn't caught up with her yet.'

'Ah, yes,' Dorian said. 'Ondine is very popular in Britain and the Commonwealth, but it sometimes takes the Americans a long time to catch up with writers who aren't home-grown. As we all know to our cost.'

'But all this *Un* stuff.' Karla frowned. 'Even her name –'

'That's *On*dine, actually. Although the Americans will probably change the spelling – they're good at that – so as not to confuse the readers. Keep it all of a piece, all *Uns* together.'

'You must have seen some of her titles.' Freddie took pity on Karla's bewilderment. '*Unspilt Blood . . . Unloving Thoughts . . .*'

'*Undying Enmity,*' Macho supplied. '*Unwitting Accomplice . . .*'

'*Unlit Candles . . .*' Even Lorinda was able to come up with the titles. '*Untruths . . .*'

'Clever of her,' Dorian said. 'It's easier to keep up a series with titles featuring the same prefix, rather than the same word, as so many of them do. Gives her a lot more flexibility.'

'Terrible woman, terrible!' Plantagenet Sutton had come up behind them bearing a tray of his experimental cocktails. 'Not even a proper crime writer. Three-quarters of her books are sloppy heavy-breathing romance. I'm surprised at you, Dorian, and not a little disappointed. What were you thinking of to allow her into our society?'

'She'll add a certain amount of lustre,' Dorian said. 'The locals and the Colonials will be impressed – and so will the Americans when she gets better known over there.'

'I agree with Plantagenet.' Rhylla had joined them and it was turning into an indignation meeting. 'We were all settled down quite well and now you're bringing in a disruptive personality like her to join us.'

'She's not that bad,' Dorian placated. 'Anyway, you know she spends most of her time out of the country. Now that she's trying to break into the American market, she'll be here even less. She'll really just use the flat as a base of operations.'

'What flat?' Freddie asked suspiciously.

'She's taking the last vacant flat in Coffers Court.' Dorian smiled uneasily as Gordie walked by him with a tray of canapés and a bitter glare. 'Opposite Professor Borley – *he'll* be glad to see her move in.'

'Hey, this is a party!' Jack interrupted. 'We can worry about this dame later. Let's all have another drink now and relax and enjoy ourselves. Pass them round, Plan.'

'Yes, yes.' The venomous glare should have told Jack that Plantagenet did not like his name being shortened, but Jack was oblivious, intent on mischief.

'We have concocted cocktails in honour of your characters, dear friends,' Plantagenet announced, distributing glasses of strangely coloured liquids that might have been the result of some ancient alchemist's failed experiments.

'A cider-based creation for our beloved Miss Petunia and her siblings –' He extended a glass to Lorinda.

'Thank you.' Lorinda took the poisonous yellow substance, smelling of sour lemon, with a wan smile and looked around for the nearest potted plant.

'And a suitably ghostly concoction –' The next glass went to Freddie. How had he managed to get that sickly grey colour? 'In homage to our dear Wraith.'

'Did you say ghastly?' Freddie accepted it absently, her gaze already straying towards a nearby poinsettia.

There was a hiss of breath indrawn in wicked anticipation

and a telling glitter in Jack's eyes as Plantagenet lifted another glass from the tray and turned to Macho.

'A really macho drink for' – his tone took on an exquisite irony – 'a really macho man.'

Recognizing mockery, suspecting worse in store, Macho kept both hands twisted around the glass he already held and stared with hostility at the murky green liquid being offered to him.

'Go on,' Jack urged, as Plantagenet held out the glass. 'We made it just for you. We thought we might call it' – he sniggered – 'the Tequila Torpedo.'

Macho stared at it in fascinated horror. Something lurked at the bottom of the glass, rolling lazily when Plantagenet jiggled the glass like an impatient nanny forcing medicine upon a reluctant charge. Macho's jaw tightened, he quivered as he fought to keep his self-control.

'You're gonna love it,' Jack insisted. 'Come on, we want to see you guzzle it like good old Macho Magee does: two or three long gulps, then crunch, crunch, crunch on the little critter at the bottom. ''Best part of the drink,'' he always –'

Macho snatched the glass from Plantagenet's hand and hurled the viscous green liquid over both men. Something small and round shot from the glass and bounced across the floor to slither under a chair.

'Ooh!' Gasps of astonishment came from the onlookers, while the attacked were momentarily too shocked to speak.

'Damn it all, man!' Plantagenet slammed the tray with its remaining drinks down on a side table and began dabbing at the sticky green mess on his shirt with his handkerchief.

'For God's sake!' Jack used his tie to mop his chin. 'It's only a Brussels sprout! Haven't you got a sense of humour?'

'No!' Macho shouted, turning and dashing for the door. 'No, I haven't!' The door slammed behind him with a force that rattled the glasses.

'You know he doesn't like tequila,' Freddie said reproachfully into the silence.

9

CHAPTER TWENTY

'How can Lord Soddemall bear to live surrounded by the very water in which his dear wife breathed her last?' Marigold shuddered as they crossed the drawbridge to Soddemall Castle. 'Surely, he ought to have drained the moat, if only for a few weeks, to show some proper respect.'

'Since he was responsible for her death,' Miss Petunia said, 'the question of the delicacy of his behaviour is beside the point.'

'Delicacy?' Lily hooted. '*Him?* He's moved the parlourmaid into the master bedroom – *and* they say she's four months preggers! Soddemall by name and Soddemall by nature!' She gave every syllable full value.

'It's pronounced "Small", dear,' Marigold corrected. 'All the guide books say so.'

'It will be pronounced "Felon" after we have given our proof of his guilt to the Nob Squad from Scotland Yard,' Miss Petunia said sternly. She raised the heavy iron door knocker and let it fall like the knell of doom.

'Don't know why we had to meet them here,' Lily grumbled.

'A confrontation,' Marigold said. 'At the very place where poor Lady Soddemall was discovered afloat in the moat.'

'Hello, you're right on time.' They had not expected Lord Soddemall himself to answer the door. In the background lurked a young woman whose apron bulged forward suggestively.

'We're all down in the dungeon. Do come in and join us.' He turned and pressed a concealed button, a panel swung inwards and they followed him through the secret door and down a narrow stairway. Sure enough, the Nob Squad were all there.

'I trust you have considered my letter.' Miss Petunia advanced upon Detective Inspector Lord Clandancing. 'And the inescapable conclusion to be drawn from it?'

'Eh?' Lord Clandancing said abstractedly. He reluctantly withdrew his attention from the delicious curve of Lady Briony Fitzmelon's ear as she bent to the task of lightly dusting fingerprint powder over the surface of an exhibit case. How had he so carelessly allowed her to slip away into the uncaring arms of Viscount Unabridged, brilliant pathologist though he was?

'The conclusion' – Miss Petunia saw no reason to beat about the bush – 'that Lord Ferdinand Soddemall murdered his wife!'

'No, no! Ferdie is a Lord,' Lord Clandancing said. 'A *Lord*,' he repeated slowly and distinctly. 'He could never do such a thing. Not a Lord!'

'Generations of fine breeding are behind Lord Soddemall.' Dear Lady Briony added her voice to his. 'He is above suspicion!'

'Oh, I say,' Lord Soddemall bleated. 'Thanks, awfully.'

'Only natural, Ferdie,' Lord Clandancing said with gentle reproof. 'We could never suspect *you*.'

'These outsiders just don't understand!' Sergeant the Hon. Jasmyn Monteryn, newest member of the Nob Squad, exclaimed.

They all turned and looked at her. There was an unpleasant silence.

'We ought to be able to sort this out in very short order,' Viscount Unabridged said. No one quite knew what a pathologist who had already performed his allotted tasks was doing on the scene of an ongoing investigation. Perhaps the way he was looking at Police Photographer Baroness Silvergate might provide a clue to the initiated. It was not so long ago that he had saved her life by an emergency tracheotomy after some miscreant who objected to being photographed had shoved her zoom lens down her throat. He had been unable to get the memory of the bubbling gasp of her cut-glass voice and the slow bright welling of oxygenated blood from the slit in her throat out of his thoughts ever since. *Oh, Sylvie . . .*

'We can prove it!' Miss Petunia pulled the sheet of paper containing her notes on the case from her handbag and waved it at them, trying to distract their attention from each other.

'Here now, what's all this?' Sergeant Sir Cuthbert detached the paper from her hand and perused it.

'They're trying to frame Lord Soddemall!' Sergeant the Hon. Jasmyn cried. 'How disgraceful!'

'Can't let 'em get away with that,' Sergeant Sir Cuthbert said. He looked to his superiors, but they were otherwise engaged.

'Briony, dearest Lady Briony,' Detective Inspector Lord Clandancing murmured brokenly. 'How can I explain? That mad night at Le Caprice with Lady Laetitia meant nothing. Nothing . . .'

'Unabridged,' Lady Briony implored, ignoring Lord Clandancing. 'Why did you never claim the last dance at the Hunt Ball . . . ?'

'Sylvie,' Viscount Unabridged whimpered. 'I swear I never intended to insult your mother. How could I have known whose riding boot was thumping into my coccyx . . . ?'

'Sir Cuthbert.' Baroness Silvergate turned to him. 'Although you rank below me, you fascinate me. No permanent alliance is possible, of course, but might we come to some temporary . . . ?'

'Lady Briony . . .' Sergeant Sir Cuthbert's frame quivered with emotion as he momentarily broke free of discipline. 'I know I am unworthy of an Earl's daughter, but my heart is as faithful as any . . .' He did not notice that Miss Petunia's piece of paper had slipped from his hand, nor that Sergeant the Hon. Jasmyn had swooped upon it.

'I say,' Lord Soddemall remarked brightly to Miss Petunia and her sisters. 'Now that you're here, would you like a proper tour of the dungeon?'

'Oh, yes, let's!' Marigold's eyes danced with excitement. 'Oh, thank you, Lord Soddemall.'

'Call me Ferdie,' he beamed.

'You two go ahead,' Miss Petunia said, watching Sergeant the Hon. Jasmyn, who was perusing the paper with the carefully presented case against Lord Soddemall set out clearly on it.

The pregnant parlourmaid followed Ferdie, Lily and Marigold, blocking them off from Miss Petunia's view.

'All working models . . .' She could hear Lord Soddemall explaining. 'Great-grandfather insisted on that when he inherited the title and estate and began restoring the Castle. "Must have a working dungeon," he said. "Never can tell when it will come in useful." Wise man, Great-grandfather . . .'

'This is incredible!' Sergeant the Hon. Jasmyn gasped. 'It almost seems possible!' She lowered the paper and regarded Miss Petunia earnestly. 'Detective Inspector Lord Clandancing must see this!'

'Genuine guillotine,' Lord Soddemall trumpeted. 'Straight from the French Revolution. Small provincial model, I'm afraid, but it did the work, all the same. We demonstrate it with cabbages . . .'

'Excuse me, sir.' Sergeant the Hon. Jasmyn approached her superior. 'But I think this might be important, sir. It sets out all the salient points in the case – '

'Case? Case?' Detective Inspector Lord Clandancing shifted his gaze from the soft beckoning curves of Lady Briony's cheeks, of Lady Briony's – dare he think it? – breasts. 'What case?'

'The case against Ferdie, sir.'

'Ferdie? There can't possibly be a case against Ferdie. I know you're new to the game, Sergeant, but surely you of all people should understand that. Ferdie is a Lord!'

'Yes, sir. Sorry, sir.' Sergeant the Hon. Jasmyn flinched under his disapproval.

'Quaint padded kneeling bench . . . really quite comfy, I'm told. If you'd like to try it . . .'

'Here!' The Hon. Jasmyn thrust the paper back at Miss Petunia. 'Take this! It's useless! We need evidence that someone is trying to frame Ferdie.'

'Some tourists try it . . . some don't. Superstitious about guillotines, I suppose . . . Ladies must be allowed their little squeamishnesses . . .'

'I'm no sissy!' Lily declared stoutly. 'I'll try it!'

'Lily!' Miss Petunia started towards her sisters. 'Lily, I don't think that's a very good ide—'

THUNK! A cabbage rolled across the dungeon floor. Only . . . it wasn't a cabbage . . . It was Lily's head.

'Damn!' Lord Soddemall said. 'Old Croakins has overoiled the mechanism again. How embarrassing. I say, I'm most terribly sorry.'

'Oh, Ferdie, bad luck!' Baroness Silvergate rushed over to console him. 'You must speak severely to Croakins.'

'Quite right.' Detective Inspector Lord Clandancing walked over more slowly, carefully avoiding getting blood on his handmade Leobb shoes. 'Accidents happen in the home – and it's carelessness like that that's responsible.'

'Better call the old quack, I suppose.' Lord Soddemall glanced at Lily's stricken sisters. 'I say, don't despair. They do marvellous things with microsurgery these days.'

'Oh, yes, of course.' Marigold brightened. 'They're always sewing arms and legs back on.' A faint doubt clouded her eyes. 'But . . . heads?'

'Umm, well . . .' Viscount Unabridged would not quite meet her eyes. 'We'll do our best. You never can tell.'

'It was murder!' Miss Petunia said. 'Cold-blooded deliberate murder! Just as Lady Soddemall's death was murder!'

'Now, now, mustn't talk like that,' Sergeant Sir Cuthbert frowned. 'That's slander – and a very serious offence. I expect His Lordship will make allowances as you're upset, but you mustn't repeat the offence.'

'Of course,' Lord Soddemall said magnanimously. 'Heat of the moment and all that, what? Why don't we ask Floribel to trot off and make you a nice cup of tea? You'll feel better then.' He patted the parlourmaid's rump as she moved off obligingly.

'Lovely girl, Ferdie,' Lord Clandancing said. 'Isn't there something familiar about her?'

'Ah, you noticed? She's Lord Dingdelling's youngest daughter – on the wrong side of the blanket, but breeding will out. I'm planning to make her Lady Soddemall next week. Hope you don't think that's too soon but, you see, we want the heir to be born in proper wedlock.'

'Ferdie! How marvellous!' . . . 'Well done, old man!' . . . They clustered around him, babbling congratulation. 'You *did* say heir?'

'It's a boy.' Ferdie blushed becomingly. 'Floribel had a scan. A son and heir. The future Lord Soddemall.'

So that was it! The motive for the disposal of the first Lady Soddemall, a woman who had borne no child, no heir. Miss Petunia's eyes narrowed. She looked at Marigold to make sure she had grasped the significance of what had just been revealed.

'Oh, Pet!' Marigold's eyes were misty. 'Isn't it romantic?'

'Don't drink the tea!' Miss Petunia whispered urgently as Floribel flounced back into the dungeon bearing a laden tray.

'Oh, but, Pet, that would be rude,' Marigold said. 'And after the future Lady Soddemall has gone to so much trouble.'

Floribel set the tray down on an exhibit case and turned to blow a kiss to Ferdie. An unspoken message seemed to pass between them as she did so.

'Poor you.' She turned to Marigold. 'I must say, you're looking a bit ragged. Would you like to freshen up?'

'Oh!' Marigold's hands flew up to hide her burning face. Did she look so terrible that everyone had noticed. 'Yes, I would.'

'You wait here, Marigold,' Miss Petunia ordered. 'I must speak to Lord Clandancing – and then I'll go with you.'

'No need to wait,' Floribel said easily. 'There's only room for one at a time in there anyway. You reach it through the Iron Maiden – there's a hinged door on the other side. Here, I'll show you. Just step inside . . .'

'Marigold!' Miss Petunia said warningly, spinning around just in time to see her sister step into the Iron Maiden.

'Oh, it's so dark in here!' Marigold gasped. 'I hate to seem stupid, but I'm afraid I can't seem to find the catch –'

'Keep looking,' Floribel said encouragingly. 'It's right under your fingers.'

Slowly, inexorably, the spiked door began to close.

'But where? I can't see . . . And it's getting darker . . . *Eeek!*'

'Marigold!' Miss Petunia tried to dash to her sister's side but, just as she passed Lord Soddemall, her feet went out from under her. He caught her as she fell and held her tightly. 'Easy does it. We don't want anything to happen to you.'

'Let me go!' Miss Petunia struggled with him.

'Help! Oh, help! Something's wrong with the mechanism!' Floribel clawed at the lid of the Iron Maiden, but seemed only to be hastening its closure, rather than preventing it.

'*EEEeeeeaaarrrgh . . . !*'

'Sergeant!' Lord Clandancing ordered. 'Do something!' Since he hadn't specified which sergeant, they both reached the Iron Maiden just as the lid rammed home with a decisive thud.

Marigold stopped screaming.

'Good Lord!' Viscount Unabridged said. 'It's just not your day, Ferdie!'

'Oh, dear!' Floribel burst into tears. 'I couldn't stop it!'

'Mustn't blame yourself, darling.' Lord Soddemall dropped Miss Petunia and raced to his beloved's side. 'These things happen.'

'They happen rather often, it seems, in Soddemall Castle.' Miss Petunia spoke through stiff lips.

'You're right.' Lord Soddemall frowned. 'I shall have to discipline Croakins. He's been much too free with the oiling can. Lucky this didn't happen on a day when the public are allowed in.'

'Croakins! That's it!' Lady Briony's eyes flared with inspiration. 'He's the one who's been trying to frame you, Ferdie!'

'I believe you're right.' Viscount Unabridged nodded. 'Over-oiling the mechanisms like that. He wanted accidents to happen – so that Ferdie would be blamed.'

'And he killed Lady Soddemall!' Lady Briony could see it all now. 'For years he had cherished a mad secret passion for her, as these peasants must when living in close proximity to the grace and breeding of their betters. At last, he could contain himself no longer. He followed her when she went for her nightly stroll around the battlements, declared himself and – and perhaps even dared to try to kiss her! And when she so rightly repulsed him – he threw her from the parapet to her death in the moat below.'

'That's the solution!' Detective Inspector Lord Clandancing agreed. 'Good work, Lady Briony! He won't escape us now. Ring for Croakins, Ferdie. We'll confront him with his villainy!'

'No, no,' Miss Petunia protested. 'You've got it all wrong. The true perpetrator of these hideous crimes is Lord Soddemall. Aided and abetted by his . . . his paramour!'

'Pardon me for a moment, Lady Briony,' Lord Clandancing said tenderly. 'I must reason with this poor deluded creature.'

'Noblesse oblige!' Lady Briony's eyes shone. 'Don't be too hard on her, my dear. These people don't know any better.'

'But,' Sergeant the Hon. Jasmyn said, 'she *has* collected some evid . . .' She faltered to a halt as they all turned and glared at her.

'What do you know about it?' Lady Briony demanded. 'You're the newest member of the team. You're here on sufferance, really.'

'*And* off to a bad start,' Lord Clandancing frowned. 'I've been meaning to have a word with you about it. You aren't really entitled to call yourself an Honourable, you know. You're only the daughter of a Life Peer.'

'Oh!' Sergeant Jasmyn was cut to the quick. 'How can you?' She pressed her hand to her heart and paled.

'I say.' Lord Soddemall was at Miss Petunia's side again. 'You're looking a bit peaky. Have a cup of tea.'

'Good thinking, Ferdie,' Baroness Silvergate said. 'We could all do with a cup of tea.'

'Not you,' Ferdie said quickly. 'Thought I'd break out the Napoleon brandy and champagne for us. A cup of tea will do the old dear nicely, then I'll have Croakins see her home. Get one last job out of him before he knows we've rumbled him.'

'Good-oh!' Viscount Unabridged said happily. 'I could do with a drop of the old Napoleon.'

'Come upstairs,' Floribel said. 'We'll be so much more comfortable.' She wrinkled her nose at the rivulets of blood on the floor. 'It's getting rather untidy down here.'

'That's right, my love,' Lord Soddemall said. 'Take our friends upstairs. I'll join you as soon as I've given this woman her tea.'

'No!' Miss Petunia tried to push away the hand bearing the cup to her lips. 'Not the tea!'

The cup crashed against her clenched teeth, the liquid spilled into her mouth and cascaded down her chin. She fought in vain against swallowing as the tide of tannin swept down her throat.

'Help!' Miss Petunia gurgled feebly. 'Help!'

'My instincts are as fine as any of yours!' Jasmyn insisted as they filed from the dungeon. 'I have even refused a man who dared offer me only mere wealth. "Marry you, a *stockbroker?*" I told him. "I may only be the daughter of a Life Peer, but I have *some* standards!" . . .'

'Help . . .' *Gulp, gulp.* 'Help . . .'

'Oh, well said!' Baroness Silvergate applauded. 'We may make something of you yet. A suitable marriage . . . A younger son, of course . . .'

'Help . . .' Miss Petunia could barely whisper now.

'Oh, thanks awfully,' Jasmyn said gratefully. She was the last to follow the others up the stairs, as befitted her lowly rank.

'Help . . .' The cry was barely audible, but there was only Lord Soddemall to hear her. Miss Petunia felt herself being lowered to the floor. The voices in the distance faded. There was no help from that quarter . . . if, indeed, there ever had been.

This was . . .

T

h

e

E

n

d

'Take *that!*' Lorinda said to the figments of her imagination, rolling the page out of her typewriter. Then, nervously, almost superstitiously, she hesitated and looked upwards. Just in case a thunderbolt was on its way.

She was getting to be a bundle of nerves. Not as bad as Macho, perhaps, as witness his performance the other night. Since then, he had been incommunicado, shutting himself away in his house, refusing to answer the doorbell or telephone. Even Roscoe hadn't been out and around.

For that matter, they had all pretty much kept themselves to themselves over the past few days. It was as though the party had drained away all the holiday spirit they might have had. Not a great deal, in any case.

Perhaps Dorian had had the right idea: escape to some foreign, warmer clime and leave the rest of the world behind. An airline limo had collected him shortly before the break of dawn this morning and he would be flown to some Caribbean port to connect with a cruise ship and spend the next fourteen days lazing in the sun.

On second thoughts, she was not so sure she would like it. While Dorian might escape the festivities ashore, he would be a captive audience for all the enforced holiday caperings aboard ship. The Christmas tree and crackers, paper hats and turkey dinner, games and merrymaking with strangers. In fact, it was most unlike Dorian to let himself in for such a series of events. He would have done better to shut himself away, like Macho, and let the holidays roll by without him. There also had to be the dark suspicion that, having gathered his friends and colleagues around him, Dorian was finding anything preferable to their company.

Tap-tap. . . tap-tap. . . A light clatter downstairs caught her attention. Not the catflap, a sharper more definite sound. *What on earth?* She rose to her feet and went downstairs.

The noise was coming from the other side of the front door. Not exactly someone knocking but . . . *tap-tap . . . tap-tap . . .* something was going on. She turned the knob and swung open the door.

'Oh, sorry. Didn't mean to disturb you.' Gordie stood there, a hammer upraised in his hand. 'It's supposed to be a surprise. Season's Greetings to you and the Pettifogg Sisters from Dorian and Field Marshal Sir Oliver Aldershot.'

145

An enormous Christmas wreath swung crookedly on the door. Pine branches twisted into a circle, dotted with silver-painted pine cones, red holly berries, plaited with red and silver ribbons, deliciously fragrant, but . . .

'How . . . kind of them,' Lorinda said coldly. She had not planned to have a wreath this year – or any year. She had learned her lesson about wreaths. The cats considered a wreath a cross between a personal challenge and a mini-gymnasium. They leaped for it, swung on it, dragged it to the ground and tore it apart, trying to eat the berries and playing knock-them-down-the-steps-and-chase-them with the pine cones.

'Dorian wanted everybody to feel that he was here with them in spirit,' Gordie said. Behind him, a wheelbarrow was heaped high with wreaths. She was evidently the first stop on his rounds.

'Yes, well . . .' *tap-tap. . . tap-tap. . .* 'I'll just finish up here and be on my way. Unless there's anything else you'd like me to do,' he added politely.

Lorinda watched in silence, shivering in the cold, as he finished securing the wreath to the front door. It was a good effort, but her money was on the cats.

'There!' He stepped back, admiring his handiwork since she obviously wasn't going to. Her silence seemed to unnerve him, as his expectant attitude always unnerved her. He seemed always to be waiting for pearls of wisdom to drop from her mouth, giving him the secret of being a successful writer. He did it with the others, too, she knew. It left them all feeling rather inadequate and unwilling to socialize with him as much as they might have otherwise.

'Well.' He gave a disappointed sigh. No secrets this time. 'I'll get on to the next place then. It will look really nice when they're all up. Like a Christmas-card village.'

'Yes,' Lorinda said. 'I can't wait to see what Dorian is going to do with us in the summer. Presumably, he intends to enter us in the Prettiest Village in England Competition.'

'Er, I wouldn't know about that.' Gordie slipped his hammer into a loop in his belt and returned to his wheelbarrow, tilted it up and trundled it off the premises.

Lorinda gazed at the wreath thoughtfully, but decided to let Nature red in tooth and claw take its course. What a shame

Dorian wouldn't be here to see what happened to his wreath. Perhaps Jack could take a picture of it.

She closed the door, chilled to the bone and not in a very good mood. She went into the kitchen to put the kettle on. Where *were* the cats? It was nearly lunch time and they were usually underfoot and nagging by this hour. She opened the refrigerator door, a sound guaranteed to bring them running if they were within earshot. Nothing happened.

She took a carton of fish chowder out of the freezer; that would do for all of them, and flipped on the radio for the midday news report. It was reassuring to discover that nothing of any great importance was happening anywhere in the world.

Flip-flop. . . flip-flop. . . Those were the sounds she had been waiting for. She turned to see Had-I and But-Known advance into the kitchen and head straight for her with little mewls of greeting.

'Just in time,' she said. 'Soup's on.'

Had-I lifted her nose, inhaled deeply and expressed loud approval. But-Known's response was equally enthusiastic, but muffled, her mouth was already full.

'Oh, no! What have you got there?' Lorinda crouched down to investigate. 'Come on, let me see.

But-Known backed away skittishly, ready for a game, but too proud of her prize to keep it up for long. She advanced again and allowed herself to be captured.

'Clever girl, let me see.' Lorinda reached for it without fear. In hunting matters, But-Known was a conscientious objector. Had-I was the one you had to watch. In any case, the worst was over; they had bagged Clarice's white rat. What further terrors could their scavenging hold?

'Macho's hair ribbon!' Whoops, how he would hate to hear it described like that. She wondered absently just what he called it. But the narrow black ribbon he tied back his ponytail with was definitely a hair ribbon.

It was also cold and soaking wet. How long had they been playing with it before they brought it home? Lorinda examined it suspiciously for teethmarks. No, no telltale little pinpoint holes, no ravelled threads. She could drape it over a chairback to dry and return it to Macho without too many apologies.

'Where did you get this?' she asked in mock reproof. 'Did

Macho lose it?' That would mean he had left his self-imposed imprisonment and was moving about the village again.

'Or . . .' Another thought occurred to her. 'Have you been in visiting Roscoe and decided to do a bit of pilfering while you were there?' That was quite possible. They had been missing Roscoe lately, he usually came over to play with them every day. It was quite typical of them to go out to find him. Macho, of course, would have had no objection to opening the door to them, whatever he was feeling about his human acquaintances these days.

But-Known purred and rubbed against her ankles. Had-I made a sharp remark and looked pointedly at the saucepan simmering on the electric coil and sending out delicious aromas.

'Quite right. I'm hungry, too. We can sort this out later.' Cheered on by the cats, she dished out the fish chowder.

They were just finishing it when there was a clatter at the back door. Macho slithered into the room just as Lorinda called out, 'Come in.' He clutched Roscoe in his arms and nudged the door closed with his foot, looking over his shoulder.

'You should never leave a door unlocked like that,' he said ungratefully. 'It isn't safe.'

'It's perfectly safe.' She didn't want to admit that she hadn't noticed the door was unlocked. Macho was nervous enough. 'What's the matter with you?'

'Matter? I'll tell you what's the matter! Someone's hung a wreath on my door! I'm not dead yet.' Roscoe gave a protesting yowl as the arms around him tightened uncomfortably. 'He hasn't got me yet!'

'Macho, it's a Christmas wreath. We've all got them. A little present from Dorian.' The import of his words hit her belatedly. '*Who* hasn't got you yet?'

'*Aaarrreeoow* . . .' Roscoe had had enough; he twisted from Macho's grip and dropped to the floor, immediately heading for the corner where Had-I and But-Known were hunched over their bowls. He made the mistake of trying to thrust his nose into Had-I's bowl and got a sharp clip across the ear. But-Known growled a warning and a brisk skirmish ensued. They didn't mind sharing the dry cat food with him, but luscious creamy fish chowder was something else again.

Macho recaptured Roscoe and murmured soothingly to him. They both sniffed the air wistfully.

'Have you had lunch?' Lorinda asked. Or even breakfast, she wondered. Macho was looking more haggard and unhappy than when she had last seen him.

'Er, no,' he admitted. 'I was going to, but I was distracted by the knocking at the front door. By the time I got there, I found the wreath hanging there and no one in sight. I got Roscoe and came over here to ... to ...' He seemed to have forgotten just why he had come.

'Sit down,' Lorinda said. 'I'll heat some more chowder, there's plenty in the freezer.' And, after Macho had eaten and was more relaxed, perhaps he might be willing to tell her why he was so upset.

Roscoe stretched forward to sniff at the bowl Lorinda placed before Macho and drew back with an injured look at discovering that it was empty.

'Don't worry,' she told him. 'It will be ready soon.' She placed an empty bowl for him on the floor. Had-I and But-Known promptly roamed over to check it. 'You can have some more, too, if you like,' she told them. 'There's plenty for everybody.'

The cats protested as she served Macho first, then settled down impatiently over their bowls waiting for the chowder to cool enough to eat. They probably envied Macho's ability to blow on each spoonful before ingesting it.

'By the way ...' Lorinda lifted the black ribbon from the back of Macho's chair and laid it beside his bowl. 'I'm afraid But-Known owes you an apology.'

'Little devil's been at it again, has she?' Macho said indulgently, his mood improving with every spoonful. He picked up the ribbon, then frowned.

'No apology due,' he said. 'That's not one of mine. I don't have any with silver threads running through them. Bit too excessive.'

'Then where – ? Oh, no!' She turned to But-Known in dismay. 'You *didn't* nick it from Plantagenet Sutton!'

'There goes a good review on your next book.' Macho was positively cheerful now.

'On the next five books,' Lorinda said dolefully.

'He doesn't like cats, anyway. Or dogs. Or children – although he may have a point where Clarice is concerned.' Macho brooded for a moment. 'Maybe he hasn't noticed it's missing. For God's sake, never admit the cat took it. If you take it back

149

to Coffers Court and drop it just inside the door, he may think it fell off.'

'It must have fallen off,' Lorinda said uneasily. 'Otherwise, how would But-Known have got it?'

They looked at the cats, who had finished their chowder and were slumped together in a contented heap, replete and purring. Roscoe, eyes closed and with an expression of bliss, was being groomed by Had-I, with But-Known nestled under one forearm, already asleep.

'I'm sure he thinks your girls are his personal harem.' Macho was bemused and perhaps a trifle envious. 'And sometimes they act as though they think so, too.'

'He's certainly sweet-natured. He doesn't even mind when they bully and tease him.' Lorinda suddenly noticed that they had slipped into a variation on the theme of how well the cats got along together, the argument Macho had put to her when asking her to take over Roscoe – if anything happened to him. Had this anything to do with the way Macho kept looking over his shoulder, and the curious remark, 'He hasn't got me . . . yet,' he made as he came through the door?

'Macho –' she began.

A sudden disturbing sound erupted into the silence. Distant, at first, but rapidly approaching, a siren warning everyone out of its way. Urgent, demanding . . . ominous – and all too familiar these days.

'Ambulance!' Macho was on his feet.

'No!' So was Lorinda. 'Now what?'

They rushed to the living room windows. Behind them, the cats were all asleep now, undisturbed by the wailing siren. Not an ear twitched, not a whisker stirred. It had nothing to do with them.

Lorinda pulled the curtains back just as the ambulance roared past and turned at the corner leading up to the Manor House. Another burst of sound heralded its approach. She had heard once that the paramedics sometimes turned on the siren from some distance away, just to reassure the injured that help was on its way.

'Dorian!' she gasped. 'He must have had an accident!' He should have been in mid-flight now – unless something had happened to him. If the airport limousine had called at the door and no one responded to the bell, they would probably have gone away again, cursing, but assuming some friend had volunteered to drive the passenger to the airport and no one had thought to cancel them.

'Get your coat!' Macho was already heading for the door. 'Come on!'

The blast of cold air struck her like a blow in the face as she stepped outside. Frost dusted the trees and bushes; they might have a white Christmas in store but, right now, it was too cold to snow. She pulled her coat more tightly around her and they joined the straggle of people who had suddenly appeared from nowhere and were following in the wake of the ambulance.

'What the hell is happening now?' Jack came up behind them, pulling on his gloves. Karla was beside him, pale and speechless as she stared at the braking ambulance. 'Dorian,' she whispered.

There was a deafening moment as a police car swept past them, siren blaring, after which no one spoke, they just walked faster. Nearly running, they reached the gate to the grounds of the Manor House where the two vehicles had pulled to a halt.

Doors slammed and uniformed people began piling out and along the grey stone wall to the gate. Gemma Duquette stood by the wrought-iron gate, dabbing at her face with a crumpled tissue. The dogs, strangely subdued, were sitting at her feet, but began to bark as the strangers ran past them.

'Gemma!' Betty Alvin dashed ahead of the others. 'Are you all right?'

'I . . . I found him,' Gemma choked. 'Rather, the dogs did. I . . . I was walking them and . . . they began pulling at their leads . . . they wanted to come in here. They must have known –' She broke off and wielded the tissue again.

Out of the corner of her eye, Lorinda saw Freddie slip past and through the gate. She followed quietly while the others were waiting for Gemma to resume her story.

At first, all she saw was legs: the legs lying flat on the ground, surrounded by the columns of other legs, upright legs, belonging to the emergency services rallying around him. Too late. He had been lying there a long time, probably all night. The frost outlined his form. A killing frost, literally. He would not get up – aided or unaided – and walk away.

Some of the legs moved aside as the paramedics shifted to crouch by the body. For a moment, there was a clear view.

He could have been sleeping, except that he looked far more

151

dishevelled than one could have imagined him in life. His Barbour jacket was awry, his tie askew and long untidy strands of limp grey hair straggled around his neck and spread out wildly behind his head.

'He –? He's dead?' Freddie wanted to be told it was all a mistake, that things weren't the way they looked, that the paramedics could load him into the ambulance, rush him off to the hospital and he would be bellowing for better service and claret in no time.

'I'm afraid so.' Lorinda felt numb and it was not just from the cold. It was all very well to write glibly about the discovery of bodies, state of the corpse, and sundry matters, but it was quite another thing when the corpse was someone you knew personally.

'I wonder if he got his last column in.' Freddie was recovering. 'And who they'll get to replace him?'

Lorinda shook her head weakly. These were questions she could not deal with at the moment. She stared at the grey locks, rimed with frost and straggling out over the sered grass.

Had But-Known raked them out like that as she clawed her ribbon trophy from his ponytail?

'It's Plantagenet Sutton, isn't it?' Betty Alvin had come up behind them. 'I knew I shouldn't have left him there.' Her voice rose, wavering out of control. 'I should have waited and walked him back to Coffers Court, no matter what Dorian said. He was in no condition to be left on his own.'

'You knew the deceased?' She had attracted the attention of the police. One of them detached himself from the group around the body and came over to them. 'Are you the person who made the telephone call to us?'

'No.' Betty quailed under his frown. 'No, that was Gemma. The lady with the dogs. She was walking them when she discovered –'

'Then perhaps you'll be good enough to clear the area.' He lost interest in her. 'All of you. Leave your names and addresses with the constable and we'll be around to talk to you later.' He waited patiently, expressionless, obviously determined to see them off the scene.

They turned reluctantly and walked back through the gateposts to join the others on the pavement outside.

'Is he really dead?' Jack asked, earning an indignant look

152

from Gemma, who had already told him so. 'What happened?'

'Doornail,' Freddie confirmed. 'Don't know. There wasn't a mark on him. Not,' she qualified cautiously, 'that I could see.'

'Yeah? Well, whatever happened to him, there'll be a lot of dancing in the streets when the word gets round.'

'Jack!' Karla's protest was automatic; she looked anxiously at the others to see how they were taking his remark.

'I thought you got along very well with him,' Macho said.

'Hey, listen, I liked him OK. Don't get the wrong idea. But that Brussels sprout was his idea, you know.' Jack paused thoughtfully. 'You know, down deep, he had a lot of hostility towards you people.'

'And vice versa,' someone muttered, too low and too quickly to be identified.

'I don't think it's smart to make cracks like that with all these cops around,' Karla said. 'We don't know what happened to him yet – and he wasn't the most popular guy around.'

'Now who's making stupid remarks?' Jack looked over her shoulder at an approaching constable. 'Considering the kind of books you people write, the last word in the world any of you should hint at is *you-know-what*. Oh, hello, Officer –' He gave a bright, nervous smile. 'We aren't blocking the way, are we?'

'Good afternoon, sir.' The words were unexceptional, the tone said, *clear off, you lot*. 'Madam.' He turned to Gemma, glancing down at the dogs, who were beginning to stir restively again. 'I understand you reported this, er, incident?'

'That's right,' Gemma said. 'We . . . the dogs and I . . . found the – Found him.'

Betty Alvin suddenly began to weep quietly.

'Perhaps we could speak to the rest of you later.' The constable was young enough to be uncomfortable. 'If any of you have any relevant information, that is.' His tone showed that he doubted it. They were just another crowd of bystanders trying to pretend they weren't just being nosy.

'Come on.' Impulsively, Karla threw an arm around Betty's shoulders. 'Let's go back to my place and have coffee. All of you,' she added. 'I baked cookies yesterday; wasn't that lucky?'

'Honey,' Jack protested in a warning tone. 'I'm not sure we have enough cups.'

'Then Freddie will help out, won't you, Freddie?'

'Sure,' Freddie agreed promptly, a gleam in her eye. 'No problem at all. What are neighbours for?'

'Gemma –' Karla called as they began walking away. 'You come and join us when they've finished with you.'

'Gemma –' Lorinda hung back. 'Would you like me to take the dogs? You can collect them at Karla's.'

'Oh, would you?' Gemma handed over the leashes gratefully. 'They've had their walk. I don't want them to stay outside too long, they might catch a chill.'

The dogs frisking in front of her, Lorinda did not catch up with the others until they reached the house.

'How charming,' she said, looking around as Jack tethered the pugs to the banister and took her coat.

'Karla likes it.' He shrugged. 'But I feel like I'm drowning in chintz. No, I mean it,' he answered her smile. 'Some nights I really dream I'm sinking down through waves of chintz, past chintz rocks into a deep undersea cavern all swathed in chintz. I wake up choking and trying to breathe.'

'How uncomfortable.' Lorinda had chintz curtains herself; there wasn't much she could say. 'Would you prefer leather?'

'What do you mean by that crack?' He glared at her suspiciously.

'Mean?' She raised an eyebrow and stared him down. 'What could I mean?'

'Sorry,' he muttered. 'My nerves are shot to hell these days. Accidents all over the place – and then people dropping dead. I wish we'd never come here.'

Lorinda was spared trying to answer that by a kicking at the base of the front door. Jack opened it to find Freddie, laden with a tray full of mugs, cups, saucers and glasses.

'You've got enough to supply an army there,' he said.

'Just wait,' Freddie predicted. 'We'll use them all.'

'Wait! Hold it!' Footsteps pounded down the path as Jack started to shut the door. Professor Borley appeared in the doorway. 'What's going on?'

'You see?' Freddie said meaningly, carrying her tray through into the kitchen.

Jack took a quick nervous look around outside before stepping back smartly and almost slamming the door shut.

'I was working,' Professor Borley explained earnestly to Lorinda, 'so I was only vaguely aware of all the commotion. By the time it registered and I went out to see what it was all about, there was nothing to see. That is, there probably was, but the police were putting up tapes to seal off the scene and trying to chase everybody away. They wouldn't answer any questions and told me, in the nicest possible way, of course, to get lost.'

'Oh, Abbey –' Betty Alvin advanced to meet him as they entered the living room. 'Abbey, it was terrible!' The ever-present tears spilled over again. 'And I'm so terribly afraid it was all my fault!'

'I hope to hell you're not going to talk like that in front of the cops,' Jack snapped. 'You'll give them the wrong idea.' He paused and stared at her stonily. 'I *hope* it's the wrong idea.'

'Now, just a minute –' Abbey Borley, one hand patting Betty's shoulder consolingly, glared at him. 'Can't you see she's upset?'

'Coffee's up!' Karla brought in a tray of steaming cups, then glanced uncertainly at Betty. 'Or something stronger, if you want.'

'Coffee will be fine.' Betty smiled bravely and reached for a cup. Professor Borley caught her hand.

'Something stronger,' he ordered. 'The strongest you've got.'

'Brandy?' Karla offered. 'Or the last of the full-strength duty-free Bourbon?'

'Bourbon sounds good to me,' Borley said.

'Well, perhaps a teeny splash of brandy in my coffee.' Betty dabbed at her eyes with her tissue and appeared to pull herself together a bit more. She remained within Abbey Borley's encircling arm.

'Right,' Jack said in answer to Karla's imperative glance. 'Coming right up.' He moved to the cluster of bottles on the sideboard, a reluctant host about to do his duty.

The doorbell rang. 'I'll get it,' he said, with the look of a reprieved prisoner, but Freddie was ahead of him, shouldering him aside as she dashed into the front hall.

'Gemma's here!' Freddie called out, although the yapping of Lionheart and Conqueror had left no one in doubt as to the identity of the latest arrival.

'They let you go then,' Jack said, somewhat tactlessly.

'Why shouldn't they?' Gemma glared at him, affronted.

'Sorry, sorry. I just meant . . .' He trailed off, as though unsure of just what he did mean.

'What did the police say?' Karla edged forward. 'What happened to him? Was it his heart?'

'Heart? What heart?' Gemma stared at her, bewildered.

'Well said,' Macho applauded.

'Hey, come on, now,' Jack protested. '*Nil-boni*-whatever-it-is. The guy's dead, after all.'

'And not before time,' Macho said. 'It's easy for you to talk, you only met him socially. You were never reviewed by him.'

'My books haven't been published in this country,' Karla snapped. The vagaries of international publishing were always a delicate subject, as was the fact that Jack had not actually written any books himself. 'They said no one would be interested in a couple of young American backpackers. They didn't think it would work, even if I turned them into Australians.' She brooded quietly. 'Not that I'd do that. There are so many differences –'

'Oh!' Betty gave a choked sob. 'How can –?' She broke off abruptly, but it wasn't hard to guess what she nearly said before recalling herself. Lorinda supposed that their preoccupation with their own characters and work must sound like untrammelled ego to other people.

'Take it easy. Here –' Jack thrust a glass into Betty's hand. 'Drink up and you'll feel better.'

'I think I need a drink more than she does.' Gemma spoke with some asperity. 'I was the one who found him, you know. *And* the police have been questioning me.'

'Coming right up.' Jack poured with a lavish hand, perhaps because he had some questions of his own. 'What did you tell them? I mean, what did they tell you? Do they know what happened? Will they have an inquest? An autopsy?' He looked suddenly queasy and turned away to pour and gulp at a large drink for himself before serving anyone else.

They all knew too much about the inner workings of a police investigation, Lorinda recognized sadly. It did not make for comfortable conversation or thoughts when those workings were being applied to someone they had actually known.

'They . . . they think he was there all night,' Gemma said slowly. Her reluctance was obviously because she did not wish to think about it herself, not because she was hesitant to share the information with them. 'He . . . he would have died of hypothermia. Exposure, we used to call it. It was the coldest night of the year so far.'

'I knew it! I knew it!' Betty began sobbing uncontrollably again. 'I shouldn't have left him! I shouldn't!'

'There, there.' Professor Borley patted her shoulder ineffectually, but she broke away from him and hurled herself into a corner of the sofa, wailing incoherently.

'Pull yourself together!' Freddie had dealt with hysterics before, as evinced by the expert way she yanked Betty upright and shook her. 'You are not responsible. You didn't go off and leave him lying on the ground, did you?'

'Of course not!' Betty was shocked into indignation. 'I'd never do a thing like that!'

'Then where did you leave him?' Lorinda had the feeling that she already knew the answer.

'With Dorian.' Betty hiccoughed and dabbed at her eyes. 'I – I'd been up there helping him pack . . .'

She'd been doing all the work, she meant. It was par for the course with Dorian; he'd use his part-time secretary as valet, waitress, chief cook and bottle-washer and anything else he happened to be in need of. The thought caught Lorinda unawares. *Anything* else? She blinked and looked at Betty with a sudden question in her mind.

'Mr Sutton . . . Plantagenet . . . had come up say *Bon voyage* to Dorian and . . . and he'd brought a bottle of champagne with him. They . . . *he* . . . gave me a glass,' she said defiantly, 'while I was packing. We all drank the champagne – but it wasn't the first drink Plantagenet had had that night, I could tell.' She sipped at her own drink again, as heads nodded in agreement.

'Then . . . then the packing was finished. Except for the last-minute bits – toothbrush, toothpaste, razor, you know – to be tossed in in the morning . . . and I was ready to leave. I expected Plantagenet to come with me – we were both going back to Coffers Court and Dorian had to get up at the crack of dawn, but . . . but . . .'

'But you left alone.' Lorinda had done her best to sound sympathetic, but Betty was looking for criticism.

'I *did* suggest . . . but I couldn't insist. And . . . and Dorian said he had this special bottle he wanted Plantagenet to sample . . . but that I didn't have the taste buds to appreciate it. And . . . and . . . he'd ring me in the morning to come up for last-minute instructions and . . . and to finish his packing. I knew they . . . *he* . . . didn't want me around any more . . . in case they had to be polite and share their precious bottle with me. Well . . .' For an instant, something indescribably ugly flashed in her face. 'It didn't do them any good, did it?'

She had been used and coldly dismissed until she was needed again. How typical of Dorian. And . . . how unfortunate for Plantagenet Sutton.

'But I should have waited outside –'

'Don't be silly, you'd have caught pneumonia,' Freddie said sensibly. 'They could have lingered over that bottle for a couple of hours – and there was no guarantee that they wouldn't have opened another one. There was nothing you could have done.'

'But – but that wasn't the worst,' Betty wailed. 'When I got home, I – I unplugged my telephone. So that Dorian couldn't call me at the crack of dawn –'

'Good for you!' Karla said.

'I was going to tell him the phone was out of order. But, don't you see? If I'd gone up to do all those last-minute things, I'd have found Plantagenet hours earlier than he was found. I – I might have been in time to save him.'

'No, you wouldn't.' Freddie was still being sensible. 'A couple of hours on that frozen ground would have been enough to finish him in last night's weather.'

'Sure. Once he hit the ground and didn't get up right away, he didn't have a chance.' Jack quietly topped up Betty's glass.

'And now Dorian will find out.' Betty's real terror spilled over. 'Dorian will know I did it deliberately. Unplugged the phone because I didn't want him to bother me. He – he'll sack me. I'll lose my job.'

'So what?' Jack was puzzled. 'He's not the only one paying you around here. The rest of us will still need you – and your hours will be a helluva lot better.'

'But I'll lose my little home, too. I won't be able to stay in Coffers Court. It – it's a sort of a tied cottage.' She began to cry again. 'Oh, I wish I'd never done it! But I was so tired . . . exhausted . . . I'd had all I could take. I couldn't stand even one morning more . . .'

'Don't worry,' Freddie said grimly. 'You'll stay in Coffers Court. The rest of us will see to that.'

'Anyway, Dorian will never know if you don't admit it,'

Macho pointed out. 'There's no need for you to tell all these details to the police. All that's relevant is that you finished your job and left. Plantagenet wanted to stay and keep on drinking. It isn't as if you arrived together in the first place. You couldn't be expected to leave together.'

'Will the police make Dorian come back, though? He'll be furious. And –' Betty would not be comforted. 'And he'll take it out on us . . . on me.'

'I doubt that the police will have any inquiries that can't be handled by a telephone call,' Lorinda said. 'Given the circumstances, the verdict is sure to be "Misadventure".'

'That's right,' Freddie agreed. 'Once they get a reading on the alcohol level in his blood, the only mystery will be how he managed to stagger as far as he did.'

10

CHAPTER TWENTY

'I fear that my patience is becoming exhausted.' Miss Petunia aimed the spray gun at the greenfly on the roses and wielded it violently.

'You, Petunia?' Lily was incredulous. 'But you're the one with all the patience. Got none myself, I know. And Marigold is too impetuous for her own good. You got the patience for all three of us. And the brains,' she acknowledged humbly. 'You *can't* run out of patience, it's practically your middle name.'

'Perhaps – but I can be pushed too far. I have warned that woman!' . . . *squirt* . . . 'I have given her every chance.' . . . *squirt* . . . 'I have bent over backwards –' . . . *squirt* . . .

'Oh, do be careful, Petunia.' Marigold turned worried blue eyes on her eldest sister. 'You're going to wrench that spray gun apart.'

'I'll wrench *her* apart!'

'Petunia!' Marigold was scandalized.

'Action,' Lily agreed. 'That's what we need. Been rusticating too long. Nothing to get our teeth into. No action except for –' She broke off and frowned, not wanting to admit the action they had been involved in, even to herself.

'Precisely!' Miss Petunia said.

'You mean . . .' Marigold quavered. 'That terrible dream . . . nightmare . . . I had last night? The rest of you had it, too?'

'Precisely!'

'It won't do,' Lily said. 'Can't go on like this. Never knowing when a perfectly innocent investigation is going to explode in our faces.'

'Precisely!' Miss Petunia took a deep breath and hurled the spray gun into the herbaceous border, something she had never done before. 'The ingratitude of it all! We have fed her, clothed her, bought her a house, supported her for all these years – and now she turns on us like this!'

'Not good enough,' Lily brooded.

'My whole body aches,' Marigold said piteously. 'And I'm afraid to look in the mirror for fear I'll discover I'm covered in . . . in blood.'

'Got a fearful pain in the neck,' Lily agreed.

Miss Petunia rubbed her stomach reflectively and said nothing; her expression was grim.

'I feel *so* peculiar,' Marigold said. 'As . . . as though . . . I'm fading away.'

'This cannot be allowed to go on,' Miss Petunia proclaimed.

'Quite right.' Lily nodded. 'Had enough.'

'But, Petunia . . .' Marigold quavered. 'What can we do? We've already tried to plead our case with her.'

'Fired a warning shot across her bows,' Lily corrected.

'Neither of which she heeded.' Miss Petunia faced them implacably.

'Perhaps we should try again,' Marigold said nervously. 'Surely, we can make her understand.'

'Waste of time,' Lily said.

'Quite right. The woman is obtuse!' Miss Petunia declared. 'Furthermore, she is completely self-obsessed. She does not care what happens to us.'

'Thinks only of herself,' Lily said. 'Bone-selfish.'

'We have established that, dear,' Miss Petunia said. 'Now we must decide what to do about it.'

'Chop!' Lily looked into the distance, her mouth pursed in a soundless whistle. Her hand came up to make a slashing motion across her throat. 'Give her the chop!'

'Oh, no!' Marigold gasped. 'No! That's too drastic!'

'She's trying to do it to us,' Lily reminded her.

'I fear dear Lily is right,' Miss Petunia said. 'The time has come for decisive action. Before it is too late.'

'Too late?' Marigold's eyes widened. 'Oh, Petunia, whatever can you mean? However could it be too late?'

'Only too easily, I fear,' Miss Petunia said. 'Just suppose that our ... our Chronicler –' She gave the word an unpleasant sneering twist. 'Our Author ... were to actually *use* one of those evil disgraceful chapters one day? Suppose that, either by accident or design, she ended the current book with it, sent it off to the publishers – and they published it?'

'Oh, Petunia!' Marigold reeled with dismay. 'Surely they wouldn't do that! They'd expostulate with her, make her rewrite the ending ... Wouldn't they?'

'They might,' Miss Petunia conceded. 'Then again, they might not. They might consider that the publicity she would achieve by killing us off might outweigh the disadvantages.'

'Barmy bunch, publishers,' Lily agreed. 'Never can tell with them.'

'But ... all those books ...' Marigold did look as though she were fading. 'All those years ...'

'Precisely,' Miss Petunia said. 'They might think we'd run our course.'

'Outstayed our welcome,' Lily said. 'Time for a change.'

'Precisely! Especially if Lorinda Lucas has an idea for a new series. The publicity attendant upon our demise would get it off to a flying start.'

'And she'd never look back,' Lily said.

'But ... but ... *we'd* be ... gone.' Marigold could not encompass the thought. 'Of course' – She brightened – 'there are still all those previous books.'

'Much good they'd do *us*,' Lily said. 'Oh, she could lean back and still collect royalties from them, but we'd be on the shelf. In our graves.'

'I fear dear Lily has put her finger on the nub of the matter.' Miss Petunia adjusted her pince-nez and gazed sadly at her sisters.

'But ...' Marigold was still unwilling to believe it. '*Has* Miss Lucas another series in mind? Surely, we'd know about it. I ... I haven't received any *intimations*. Have you?'

'That is why we must act now,' Miss Petunia said. 'Before she does. Her mind is a blank on other characters at the moment, but there are pernicious influences afoot. She is being unsettled by the company of her peers and all their dissatisfactions. Things have not been the same since the fateful day she moved to Brimful Coffers!'

'Then why don't we ask her to move away again?' Marigold suggested brightly. 'Then everything can be the way it was before.'

'No.' Miss Petunia shook her head gravely. Even Lily was shaking her head. 'The situation is too advanced. There can be no going back.'

'No going back . . .' Lily echoed grimly.

'But . . .' Marigold's mood veered, now she seemed on the verge of tears. 'But . . . what can we do?'

'Now, Marigold,' Miss Petunia said gently. 'We have discussed this before. You know the options.'

'But we can't!' Marigold wailed. 'It would be too brutal . . . too cruel . . .'

'Too soft-hearted for her own good,' Lily snorted.

'Any less brutal or less cruel than what she has been doing to us?' Miss Petunia asked bluntly.

'But . . . but we have always stood for law and order.' Marigold raised tear-drenched eyes. 'For justice! We . . . we're the *good* guys!'

'Do it right,' Lily muttered, 'and nobody will ever suspect it was us.'

'Quite right, dear,' Miss Petunia approved. 'As dear Marigold has pointed out, we are the "good guys". For that reason alone, no one would ever suspect us. Apart from other reasons . . .' She let the thought trail off delicately.

'What other reasons?' Marigold asked innocently.

'Well, dear, we are . . . after all . . .' Miss Petunia tried to think of a tactful way of phrasing it.

'Fictional.' Lily had no such compunction.

'Er, yes. We *do* exist . . . for the most part . . . on the printed page,' Miss Petunia admitted reluctantly.

'Then . . . then how are we going to *do* anything?'

'We will find a way,' Miss Petunia vowed.

'Oh . . .' Marigold brightened. 'You mean like "Love will find a way"?'

'Not exactly,' Miss Petunia said. 'In this case it's more like . . . hate.'

'No two ways about it,' Lily said. 'Only one thing to do.'

Marigold covered her face with her hands and sobbed as her sisters chorused in unison:

'Lorinda Lucas m
u
s
t
d
i
e.'

'I was shattered to get the news,' Dorian said, squinting into his champagne glass. 'Quite shattered. However, we can be thankful for one thing. He went the way he'd have wanted to go: drunk.'

There was no doubt that he relished the shocked gasps from some of his audience; those who knew him well wouldn't give him the satisfaction.

'That guy is beginning to get on my nerves,' Jack snarled quietly to Lorinda. 'It was nice and peaceful while he was away, now everybody's on edge again.'

Lorinda nodded, more in acknowledgement than agreement. So far as she had noticed, life had not been especially peaceful in the two weeks that Dorian had been on his cruise, and everyone had been on edge well before his return. Freddie and Macho in particular.

True, the holiday season had passed by quietly. Plantagenet's demise had put paid to any festive spirit that might have been stirring. Once the police had wrapped up their perfunctory (Plantagenet's reputation was well known; there were rumours the wine merchant was going to drape his windows in black) inquiries, those who could manage it escaped Brimful Coffers for their holidays. Rhylla Montague had picked up a last-minute reservation at a Country House Hotel and taken off for Devon with Clarice. Gemma Duquette and Betty Alvin had retreated to the respective family Christmases they had been congratulating themselves on avoiding before the prospect seemed an improvement on staying in a depleted Coffers Court. The Jackleys, in an excess of hospitality, or possibly because they couldn't face each other's unadulterated company, had invited Lorinda, Freddie, Macho and Professor Borley to Christmas dinner and they had all found it the line of least resistance to accept.

Everyone was relieved when the holiday season ended and life began to chug slowly back to normal. Except . . . except . . .

Lorinda tore her mind away from the thought of that new and menacing chapter she had discovered beside her typewriter. Her mind . . . her mind . . .

'Oh, I'm sorry –' She became aware that Jack was staring at her questioningly. She hadn't heard a word he'd been saying. 'I – I'm afraid I missed that. It's noisy in here, isn't it?'

'That's OK. I'm getting used to it with you people. Either you snap my head off when I make a little joke, like Freddie. Or you look right through me, like Macho. And even my own wife. And the excuse is always you're thinking about the new book.'

'I'm sorry.' Lorinda was beginning to feel guilty about Jack and resented it. 'But we are.'

'Not your fault.' His attention was on the group surrounding Dorian, where his wife was being breathlessly attentive. He gripped his new camera so tightly that he winced.

'Jeez!' he burst out. 'I'd like to nail that guy. I'd like to get a picture of him picking his nose, or something worse. I want him in pieces. I want him –'

Dead. The unsaid word hung in the air, resonating clearly. Jack darted a furtive look at her to see if she had heard it, too. She tried to keep her face blank and appear oblivious.

'Dorian's in great form.' Freddie came up to them. 'His cruise seems to have done him a world of good.'

'Maybe we should all try it,' Macho said, closing ranks on the other side. 'We need something. There are still a couple of months of damp and fog until spring. I'm not looking forward to February here – or March, either.'

'Why don't we just send Dorian away again?' Jack was bitter. 'That would improve the atmosphere one hundred per cent for me.'

'Shh!' Freddie said. 'He's coming this way.'

'I don't care,' Jack muttered, but he subsided.

'Ah, a cluster of colleagues.' Dorian was upon them, tanned, fit, the corners of his eyes crinkling with amusement. He glanced at Jack. 'Almost,' he added.

Jack responded by stepping back swiftly, raising the camera

and firing off a shot he obviously hoped would blind Dorian, but Dorian was too quick for him and shifted focus just in time. Jack lowered the camera and walked over to join his wife.

'Freddie, you've lost weight,' Dorian said. 'You're growing positively Wraith-like.' He chuckled at his own joke. No one else did.

'And Macho, how many blondes have you bedded and blasted while I've been away?' Again the joke fell flat.

'Lorinda, I won't try to equate you with any of your characters. You're still too pretty and too young . . . perhaps in a few more years . . .'

Lorinda stared at him as coldly as the others. The thought of tiptoeing into the sunset years with Dorian was chilling. How had they allowed themselves to be persuaded into this trap? On the other hand, Brimful Coffers was quite a pleasant village, most of the inhabitants were congenial . . . now that Plantagenet was no longer with them. It could be even pleasanter . . . without Dorian.

Dorian looked around with a vaguely dissatisfied air, probably wondering if there was anyone he hadn't insulted yet.

Lorinda saw Jack tense as Dorian looked his way then, with a dismissive smile to the rest of them, stroll in that direction. Karla's face lit up as she saw him coming; she, at least, was glad to see him. Jack raised his camera defensively, as though it were a shield.

'I don't know about Dorian,' Freddie said reflectively, 'but it definitely looks as though absence has made Karla's heart grow fonder.'

'Perhaps that was the idea,' Macho said. 'If there really *is* something going on between them, Karla may not have been moving fast enough to suit him.'

'*If* he wants her to move.' Freddie was still thoughtful. 'He may have been hoping she'd cool down a bit. I think the situation suits him just the way it is; he doesn't want to formalize it. What Karla wants is another story.'

'I don't see why she doesn't just get a divorce,' Lorinda said. 'She hasn't any religious scruples about it, has she?'

'Religion doesn't come into it.' Freddie gave her a pitying glance. 'Unless you count Mammon as a religion.'

'But she doesn't need to worry about alimony, does she?

I'd have thought her sales were good enough to support her comfortably.'

'Haven't you heard about Equal Rights?' Freddie raised an eyebrow. 'The trouble is, as a lot of women are finding out, that it works both ways. It's not just the man who pays any more. If they divorce and he can show, as I'm sure he can, that he supported her through the early years of struggle, then he's entitled to a half share in her copyrights.'

'Wha-at?' Macho squawked incredulously.

'That's obscene!' Lorinda felt the blood drain from her face.

'That's the law – and it's coming over here, too. Same principle as the Little Woman keeping house, raising the kids and providing a secure base while the Breadwinner goes out and builds up his business, in which she's entitled to share because of her contribution to the joint welfare.' Freddie shot Macho a sardonic look. 'Lucky you got your divorce when you did, you could really be taken to the cleaners nowadays.'

Macho took a deep gulp from his glass. For a moment he looked as though, if there had been a worm at the bottom of the glass, he would have crunched it.

'If you ask me,' Freddie went on, 'that's why Karla was so willing to take on the contract for the Miss Mudd books. There's no question of her holding any copyright in them and she can use them to mark time and provide some income while she decides what she wants to do about her situation. Either bite the bullet and divorce Jack or . . .' Freddie drained her own glass. 'Shoot the bullet into him – which would be a lot neater and cheaper than a divorce.'

'And Jack has already had one nasty "accident" that could have been fatal.' It was unreal, perhaps surreal, to be standing in the gracious drawing room calmly speculating on whether people they knew socially might turn out to be killer and victim, but Lorinda could not keep her professional instincts from kicking in.

'Accident would be the best way.' Macho narrowed his eyes. She was not the only one whose professionalism was showing.

They all surveyed the group across the room, coolly assessing the chances of real-life drama overtaking fiction.

'It's no use.' Macho was the first to look away. 'We're all too civilized. We only do it on paper.'

On paper. . . Lorinda gave an involuntary shudder. She could

167

push her own preoccupations to the back of her mind . . . her mind . . . but they came back to haunt her at a careless word.

'I wouldn't bet on that.' Freddie was still watching. 'But I might give you short odds on Jack launching a murderous attack on Dorian, if he thought he could get away with it.'

'That could hold true for a lot of people.' Macho's gaze swung around the room from group to group. Viewing people as potential suspects, it was suddenly unnerving to realize that everyone had a sinister side to them.

Lorinda shuddered again and looked up to welcome the distraction of Betty Alvin and Jennifer Lane approaching. Betty kept looking back over her shoulder as though to ensure that she was putting adequate space between herself and Dorian. Of course, he would not easily forgive her for her defection on the morning he left and had to do his own last-minute packing.

'Where's the guest of honour?' Jennifer asked. 'I thought she'd be here to greet us. Or is she planning a Grand Entrance?'

'What guest of honour?' Freddie looked affronted. 'I didn't hear anything about that. Did you?' She glared at the others.

'I thought this was just Dorian giving himself a Welcome Home party,' Lorinda said, refraining from adding: *Since no one else was likely to.*

'I thought it was just a belated New Year gathering,' Macho said.

'I think Dorian wanted it to be a surprise for everyone.' Betty hastened to spread oil on waters that were becoming troubled. 'Of course, he had to tell Jennifer so that she could put some books on display.'

'Hmmm,' Freddie said, echoing their thoughts. No one had failed to notice that the new window display had featured an interloper.

'So we're finally to be honoured by a visitation from Ondine van Zeet, are we?' Macho did not look pleased. According to local rumour, the lady had moved into Coffers Court, and then promptly gone back to London, with no indication of when – or if – she would return.

'Where's Rhylla?' Freddie looked around. 'Does she know about this?'

'She's in Dorian's study.' Macho had been keeping track. 'I think she's trying to convince Clarice of the delights of keeping tropical fish.'

'I wish her luck,' Freddie said. 'If you ask me, the kid is right. A Gila monster is just about her speed.'

'AAH!' It was as much a fanfare as a greeting. 'Ondine, my dear! How good of you to grace our little gathering!' Dorian swooped across the room to seize both her hands, somehow having disposed of his glass as he passed a side table. He raised both of her hands to his lips, in the manner of a monarch conferring favour, but it was easy to see who outranked whom in the pecking order.

'Dorian, dear boy.' Ondine van Zeet freed her hands and used one to pat his cheek as she stepped back from further intimacies. 'How sweet of you to invite me.'

'I think you know everyone here.' He led her forward. 'By reputation, if not personally.'

'I'm sure I must.' She glanced around without interest.

Dorian repossessed his glass and signalled Gordie to bring his tray over to Ondine. Eagerly, Gordie rushed to their sides.

Gordie. Lorinda was assailed by a fresh attack of guilt. What had Gordie done over the holidays? They had all forgotten about him – although he would have been the first person they called for if anything had broken down. She made a weak resolution to try to be nicer to him.

Ondine graciously accepted a glass of champagne from the tray with a mechanical smile and turned to survey the room. Was it Lorinda's imagination, or did several people shrink back, trying to make themselves smaller and inconspicuous?

This was in direct contrast to the very conspicuous Ondine, large and commanding in a shimmering iridescent silk kaftan, looking as though she were about to burst into an operatic aria. Lorinda remembered hearing, among other rumours, that Ondine van Zeet was one of those who had come to writing via an unsuccessful stage career – and she believed it. The other believable rumour was that, although the lady did not have the necessary talent for the stage, she certainly had the temperament. She stood there, radiating ego.

'Somehow,' Freddie muttered, 'I don't get the impression that she's going to make a valuable addition to our little community.'

'Don't look now,' Macho said, as Dorian began waving imperiously to them, 'but I think we're being summoned for an Audience.'

'Suddenly, I have another appointment.' Freddie began

169

edging backwards, slid behind a couple of Londoners and disappeared.

'We're going to have to meet her, sooner or later.' Lorinda took a firm grip on Macho's elbow before he could follow Freddie, and urged him forward.

When Lorinda escaped shortly afterwards, it was with a sense of relief that was disproportionate to the occasion. Nothing awful had actually happened. Ondine had been neither as insulting nor as outrageous as her reputation had led everyone to expect. Nevertheless, Lorinda had been conscious of the uneasy feeling that the Sword of Damocles had been poised above them all. She breathed more easily as she and Macho approached her front door.

'Coming in for a drink?'

'Thanks, not now.' He also seemed uneasy and glanced around with foreboding. 'I'll just collect my wandering boy and get back to my book, I think. I've been away from it all day.'

Roscoe was still sleeping and barely blinked as Macho gathered him up. Had-I and But-Known were more alert; they eyed Lorinda hopefully, trying to decide whether she had brought any treats for them.

'Don't open the fridge door until I've got Roscoe out of here,' Macho directed. He opened the back door, looked left and right as apprehensively as though he were about to step out on to a motorway, and left hurriedly.

Lorinda watched from the window until he reached his own house, sliding from shadow to shadow, acting like a fugitive and always looking back over his shoulder. Was he heading for a nervous breakdown? Or could there be some other explanation for his increasingly eccentric behaviour? Had his ex-wife surfaced again, possibly issuing some sort of writ he was trying to evade?

Had-I made an impatient remark, pacing back and forth in front of the fridge. But-Known sat quietly with a trusting look on her face. In deference to that trust, Lorinda gave them rather more tinned salmon than she had intended.

She had noticed the glow of the Message Waiting light on her answering machine earlier. With no sense of urgency, she strolled into the living room and proceeded to retrieve the message, hoping that there was one and that the light hadn't been lit by one of those technophobes who hung up on discovering that they were expected to converse with a machine.

For long moments, there was silence, then a voice spoke. It was a voice she had never heard before, but she recognized it instantly. It sounded just the way she had always thought it would.

'Oh, you *are* terrible!' it pouted. 'You must stop, you really must! They're getting so angry. I can't reason with them much longer. They want to . . . dispose of you . . . before you dispose of us. They mean it. They won't believe me when I tell them you'd never do such a thing . . .' The voice wavered. 'Would you? You wouldn't, would you? No, no, you couldn't! But they don't understand. They're plotting to finish you. Please, tell them you'll let us go on forever. Promise them you won't – '

'Marigold!' A sharp, autocratic, suspicious voice called imperiously in the background. Lorinda recognized that voice, too. 'Marigold, what are you doing?'

'Nothing, Petunia,' Marigold gasped guiltily. 'Nothing at all. *Please* –' she whispered urgently. '*Please* –' The dial tone buzzed abruptly. She was gone.

Lorinda stood frozen, staring down at the machine in horror. The cats strolled into the room, licking their chops, and paused to watch her, sensing something wrong.

Lorinda pushed the Rewind button, holding her breath as the message tape wound back into position. She took a deep breath and pushed the Play button.

Nothing happened.

The tape whirred quietly; no message emanated from the speaker. Lorinda let it run for a long time before pushing the Rewind and trying again.

Still there was no sound but the quiet whirr of tape.

She spent several frantic minutes stabbing the Rewind and Play buttons alternately, but she could not retrieve the message. She could not make Marigold speak again.

If Marigold had ever spoken in the first place.

She sank into the nearest chair, covering her face with her hands. The cats jumped into her lap anxiously, trying to comfort her. She clutched them to her, burying her face in their fur.

Her mind . . . her mind. . . she grieved quietly.

What would she do without it?

11

In the morning, Lorinda woke late and reluctantly. A new day seemed almost too much to bear. She pulled aside the curtains to discover blue skies and such an aggressively brilliant sun that she nearly closed them again and went back to bed. That wouldn't solve anything. She forced herself to dress and go downstairs; she could not force herself to glance in the direction of the answering machine. The Message Waiting light would always signal terror to her from now on.

The cats were not in the kitchen. On a day like this, they would be disporting themselves outside, or perhaps lying in a patch of sunlight, enjoying the weather before it changed. Which was more than she could do.

Tea and toast did not really interest her, but were the line of least resistance; she ate automatically, trying to keep her mind a blank. Her mind . . .

All last night's horrors rushed back into it. She got to her feet quickly and carried the dishes over to the sink. She *would* not think about it. Not now . . . not yet.

Keep busy, that was the thing. There was plenty to do. She could clean the house, do the shopping, work on the book – No! No, she could not bring herself to go near her study, and the thought of having to write about the loathsome Miss Petunia made her mind recoil. Her mind . . .

Flip-flop. . . flip-flop. . . The familiar sound brought her back to normality.

'There you are, my darlings.' She turned to smile down on them. And froze.

They advanced towards her trustingly, well pleased with themselves. Especially But-Known, who had something long and black trailing out of her mouth.

'What have you got there?' She had a terrible feeling she

172

already knew. 'Come here, let me see it.' She crouched down and tugged gently at one end. But-Known resisted playfully for a moment, then opened her mouth and let the ribbon slide over to Lorinda. Another ribbon . . .

'Where did you get this?' Having expected praise, But-Known started and backed away at Lorinda's tone. Had-I sat down and began washing her face, emphasizing that she had nothing to do with her sister's scavenging. She only brought home nice, sensible, edible offerings.

'Where – ?' Lorinda pulled herself together and straightened up, still clutching the black velvet ribbon. But-Known couldn't answer and she was only frightening the poor darling.

'I'm sorry. Good girl. Come on.' To make amends, she crossed to the fridge and distributed largesse.

She knew where But-Known must have got that ribbon. Only Macho wore such a ribbon now. The question was: what condition had he been in when she helped herself to it?

Lorinda looked down at the two sleek little heads bobbing over their saucers and poured some milk into their bowl, putting off the inevitable moment when she would have to do something.

She'd try it the easy way first. She went into the living room and dialled Macho's number. The phone rang just that couple of times too many before the click.

'BANG! Ya missed me, sucker! You don't get – '

She replaced the receiver. He wasn't going to answer the phone. Perhaps he couldn't answer the phone. She was going to have to find out the hard way.

But she didn't have to do it alone. She hoped. This time she tried Freddie's number.

'Hello?' Thank heavens Freddie was still answering the phone.

'Freddie . . . have you seen Macho this morning?'

'No. Why?' Freddie caught the uneasy note in her voice. 'What's wrong?'

'I don't know. It may be nothing. Only . . . But-Known has just dragged in one of her offerings. It's Macho's ponytail ribbon. The last time she brought home a ribbon . . .'

'Oh, no!' She didn't need to finish, she had already told Freddie about that. 'I'll meet you at Macho's. We'll break down the door, if we have to. Or climb in through the window. Or something.' Freddie hung up abruptly.

As a precaution, Lorinda immobilized the catflap before leaving. Doing so gave her a strange pang. Would she be bringing Pud – Roscoe – back with her to take up residence? What had Macho foreseen in his future to wrest that promise from her?

'Hurry up!' Freddie was waiting impatiently, her face pale and drawn, at Macho's front door. 'Let's get this over with.' She began pushing at the door.

'Why don't we try the bell first?' Lorinda pushed it. 'Just for form's sake.'

'Form!' Freddie snorted. 'At a time like this!'

They were both taken aback when the door swung open suddenly and a stranger stood there. Macho hadn't mentioned that he was expecting a guest. The man looked vaguely familiar, perhaps a relative . . .

'Macho!' Freddie recognized him first. 'You've cut your hair. And shaved. You *do* have a chin!'

'Come in.' Macho stepped back. 'And thank you for those kind words, Freddie. Of course I have a chin.'

'With that beard, who could tell?' Freddie shrugged. 'I thought you grew it because you were a chinless wonder.'

'Hmmph!' They had a fine view of the back of his head as they followed him into the living room where Roscoe, obviously roused from his nap by the doorbell, yawned and chirruped a greeting to them.

'Macho.' Lorinda eyed the uneven lengths of hair. He had clearly hacked it off himself, perhaps in a fit of temper. 'What did you do with your ribbon?'

'Oh.' He looked slightly abashed. 'I gave it to But-Known, she always fancied it and I have no use for it any more.'

'It's an improvement.' Freddie eyed him critically. 'At least, it will be when you get those ends tidied up.'

Neither of them quite dared ask him why he had made this sudden drastic decision. There was an awkward silence.

Roscoe stretched and gave them a bright-eyed appreciative look. He knew what guests meant: food, drink, hospitality. He ambled towards the kitchen.

'Coffee?' Macho offered, reminded of his responsibilities. 'Or . . . something else?' He seemed to listen to himself and added quickly. 'Sherry, I mean. Sherry? What time is it, anyway. I – I've lost track.'

'Coffee will be fine,' Lorinda said and Freddie nodded. 'It's about eleven.'

'Elevenses, of course.' Macho nodded and seemed to get a firmer grip on the situation. 'It will be instant, I'm afraid, but I do have some cream buns in the fridge.'

They all headed towards the kitchen. Lorinda and Freddie exchanged glances behind Macho's back. Something was wrong here. Was Macho going to tell them about it?

'Now then . . .' It appeared not. Macho began fussing pleasantly with cups, saucers, plates, putting the kettle on. He looked younger without so much facial adornment – he'd left the moustache – and yet . . . more careworn. The circles under his eyes were deeper and darker, his hands trembled slightly. Lorinda and Freddie exchanged another glance, this time with raised eyebrows, as he turned to the fridge.

'YAAAAAHHH!' A sudden cry of rage and despair brought them to their feet. Macho had opened the fridge door and a precariously balanced bottle had slid out and landed on his toe. He snatched it up and shook it with a violence disproportionate to the little accident. He could not have been seriously hurt.

'You filthy –' They gaped in awe as they were treated to a three-minute display of Elizabethan and Georgian obscenity. At least, Lorinda thought that was what it was, there were few words she even recognized.

'It isn't what you say,' Freddie observed as Macho slowed down, 'it's the way you say it.'

'Christ's blood!' They were the first intelligible words he had uttered. He shook the bottle savagely again, then took deliberate aim and hurled it at the window.

'You're through! Do you hear me?' he shouted. 'You're through! You're history! History –!' He slumped into a chair, leaned forward and buried his face in his arms on the table.

'Macho!' Freddie deftly caught the bottle just before it crashed through the window.

'What's wrong?' Lorinda asked. 'What is it?'

'It's –' Freddie squinted at the bottle. 'It's tequila! The stuff he always said he wouldn't have in the house.'

'I wouldn't!' Macho choked. 'I don't! Only . . . I keep finding

175

it. Hidden all over the place. Them – the bottles. And I never saw them before. I didn't buy them. I didn't!'

Roscoe padded over and stretched up, putting his forepaws on his master's knee with an anxious little mewl. Macho scooped him up and clutched him tightly.

'I'm starting a new series,' he told them defiantly. 'I'm going into historical mysteries. Listening to the rest of you talking about it set me thinking. History is my field. I'm ready to go back to it.'

'That sounds like a good idea,' Lorinda said cautiously. He seemed to have a precarious hold on his nerves now and she did not want to dislodge it. 'History mystery is very popular right now. What period?'

'Sixteenth century. Venice, that's popular, too. And –' He drew a deep breath. 'My private investigator will be Portia!'

'Portia?' Lorinda began to feel faintly giddy. 'Portia who?'

'I'll sort that out later.' Macho brushed the question aside. 'Will didn't specify.'

'Will –?'

'If you're going to steal.' Freddie was there ahead of her. 'Steal from the best.'

'Why not? He did.' Macho was still defiant. 'Only it's really borrowing . . . following on . . . continuing the story . . .'

'The story . . .' Lorinda said weakly.

'Yes. You see, Shylock was so impressed by her that, bearing no malice, he turns to her when he finds himself in fresh trouble. His dearly beloved daughter, Jessica, has disappeared. Dropped off the face of the earth. Lorenzo has been seen without her and claims they had a fight and she ran away from him and . . .'

Freddie set the bottle of tequila on the table in front of him with a decisive thud. He trailed off and stared at it unseeingly.

'I'll invent a new persona, too,' he said. 'For my author's biography, I'll be a lawyer turned journalist. You know how the media always hype books by one of their own, and lawyers buy like money is going out of fashion when one of *their* own has written a book. I suppose it's because both professions secretly think they could write bestsellers if they put their minds to it and it fuels their dreams when one of them succeeds . . .'

Freddie tapped impatient fingernails on the bottle and waited.

'There's another one under the sink,' he sighed, admitting

defeat. He rubbed his forehead against Roscoe's head and closed his eyes.

Lorinda opened the cupboard under the sink and retrieved a tequila bottle. It was half full. She placed it on the table beside the other one.

'I also found one at the back of the broom cupboard.' Macho spoke in a listless voice, as one not expecting to be believed. 'It isn't the way you think.'

There were two bottles in the broom cupboard, one in each far corner. Both had been opened and partly depleted. She placed them on the table beside the others.

'You might as well know the worst.' Macho sighed again and pushed back his chair. Still clutching Roscoe, he led them into his study and stopped by the desk. 'The bottom drawer,' he croaked.

Expressionless, Freddie pulled out the drawer. There were two bottles of tequila, one nearly finished, one unopened, and a glass with a tiny puddle of liquor at the bottom of it.

'That's new.' Macho stared down moodily into the drawer. 'He hasn't used a glass before.' He raised his head and bellowed suddenly into the air, 'Nice touch, you bastard!'

'Macho –' Lorinda started towards him. Roscoe twitched uneasily and looked thoughtfully towards the carpet.

'I never bought them,' Macho said desperately. 'I never drank any of it. I'd swear to it! And yet . . . if I didn't . . .' He glared at them, a cornered animal at bay. 'Who did? Only one person drinks tequila around here!' He slumped down into his desk chair and slammed the drawer shut.

Lorinda realized abruptly that Freddie hadn't tried to catch her eye in quite some time.

'Don't you see?' he pleaded. 'It *has* to be Macho Magee. He – He's come to life. He's stalking me. He – He's moving in!'

'That can't . . . really . . . be possible,' Freddie said slowly. She did not sound entirely convinced.

'I haven't seen him yet,' Macho said. 'But the bottles are everywhere. Those aren't the only ones. I've thrown a lot away. But I keep finding more. If I leave them in place, the level keeps going down, as though someone has been drinking from them. And I've never touched the stuff! At least . . . I don't think I have.'

Freddie opened the drawer again and took out the glass. She

177

raised it to her nose and sniffed. Then she opened the bottle and carefully poured a few drops into the palm of her hand. She touched them with her tongue and grimaced.

'No, it isn't water,' Macho said. 'I checked. I'm not a complete fool, you know. It's the real – imported from Mexico – stuff – and that brand sells for about twenty quid a bottle.'

'And we've found six bottles already,' Lorinda said.

'Which makes it a pretty expensive joke.' Freddie whistled soundlessly.

'There'll be more bottles around. They keep turning up everywhere. Places you can't imagine. I found one in the cistern. No one in their right mind would hide a bottle in a cistern – ' Macho paused and seemed to listen to himself.

'No one in their right mind,' he echoed. Roscoe gave a sudden indignant yowl and fought for freedom. Macho released him and watched him drop to the floor and walk some distance away before sitting down and beginning to wash his face.

'Remember – ' Macho met Lorinda's eyes with desperate entreaty. 'You said you'd take care of Roscoe if . . . if anything hap— . . . if they put me away. You promised you'd take him.'

'And I will,' Lorinda promised again. 'Unless they put me in the padded cell next door to you. It looks as though it might fall to Freddie to take care of all three cats.'

'Much as I'd like to oblige,' Freddie said, 'I wouldn't advise you to count on me. The way things are going, you'll find me in the padded cell on the other side.'

'What are you talking about?' Macho looked from one to the other with a faint puzzled hope beginning to dawn on his face.

'You find bottles.' Since she had started it, Lorinda accepted that she should go first. 'I found Miss Petunia's pince-nez, but they disappeared again and I keep finding chapters I haven't written.' There was no need at the moment to confess to the chapters she *had* written. 'And the latest wrinkle was a message from Marigold on my answering machine that disappeared when I tried to replay it.'

'Then it's not just me.' Macho quivered with relief. They both turned to look at Freddie.

'OK,' Freddie said. 'I can admit it now. Wraith O'Reilly has staked out the old graveyard. I keep seeing her there. Just glimpses, almost out of the corner of my eye, a flash of red hair, a flutter of the grey skirt. She's gone when I try to approach for a closer look. So far, she's confined herself to the graveyard, but I sometimes wonder for how much longer. It scares the hell out of me to think that I might turn around some day and find her in the house with me.'

'That's it exactly!' Macho said. 'Where is he? What is he doing? What does he want? There's no overt threat, but the feeling of menace is there underneath.'

'Actually,' Lorinda said, 'mine *are* threatening. Miss Petunia and Lily are definitely out to get me. Marigold is softer and kinder, but she always is. Of course,' she added apologetically, 'I'm afraid I've given them good reason to be annoyed with me.'

'Wait a minute,' Freddie said. 'Wait a minute. We're talking about fictional characters. These people are all figments of our imaginations. Let's all pull ourselves together and try to be sensible about this.'

'That's right.' Macho was looking better. 'We can't all be going mad. And in the same way. Can we?'

'Highly unlikely,' Freddie said. 'Someone has to be behind this.'

'A common enemy,' Lorinda said, feeling both relieved and frightened by the thought.

'Who do we know who hates us all?' Macho asked. 'One of us, perhaps. Possibly even two. But all three? And who would go to such lengths?'

'It's a rotten joke,' Lorinda said.

'It's too nasty to be a joke. There's genuine malice there,' Macho said.

'That's right,' Freddie agreed. 'Trying to make us think we're losing our sanity is hitting below the belt.' She grimaced. 'That didn't come out right, but you know what I mean.'

'What enemy do we have in common?' Macho was single-minded in his determination to track down the culprit. 'Think!'

'I wonder if there are any more,' Lorinda said. 'We each thought we were the only one it was happening to. Now that we've found we're not . . . how many more of us do you think there are?'

'Not Karla,' Freddie said, after a reflective moment. 'She spends all her spare time locked in mortal combat with Jack. An army of backpackers could march through that house and neither of them would even notice.'

179

'And Rhylla has Clarice living with her right now,' Lorinda contributed. 'She's completely caught up with trying to work and keep the child busy. Clarice also has sharp little eyes and an inquiring mind. No one could try any of these tricks with her around.'

'Whereas we live alone,' Macho said slowly. 'When we're working, two or three days can pass without our seeing anyone. We don't have any human contact until we run out of supplies and have to go shopping. That makes us . . . vulnerable . . . to someone who is trying to turn our own imaginations against us.'

'What about Dorian?' Lorinda had a sudden thought. 'He lives alone, too. Perhaps that's why he went off on that cruise so suddenly. Things have been happening to him, too, and he decided to get away – as far as he could go . . .' She trailed off; Freddie was shaking her head with a slightly condescending smile.

'Haven't you sussed that one out? Our Dorian went on that cruise because the cruise line were paying him to go. He was a guest lecturer on the English mystery and doubled as detective on one of those Murder Mystery Cruises they run every so often. He got a free trip, expenses and a small honorarium for a very pleasant job.'

'Trust Dorian!' Macho said bitterly.

'I'm sure,' Freddie added, 'he also sold a good many of his own books to the happy holidaymakers and got in plenty of publicity for the tours he's planning to run through here.'

'What a busy little beaver.' Lorinda was bitter, too.

'Right, but that also means he's too wrapped up in his own machinations to take time out to play games with us – or to notice anyone trying to play games with him.'

'Then who hates us that much?' Lorinda felt chilled. 'It keeps coming back to that.'

'There *is* one person . . .' Macho said slowly. 'Ask yourselves: who has always had it in for us? Who has jeered at and humili-ated us at every opportunity? Who has a cruel and vicious streak in him? And' – Macho was warming to his theme – 'who could very easily get his hands on a case of tequila – and probably at a discount?'

'Plantagenet Sutton!' Lorinda identified correctly.

'Good thinking, chums.' Freddie applauded silently. 'There's just one little flaw in it. Plantagenet Sutton is dead.'

'Yes . . .' Macho deflated slowly.

'And our problems are still going on,' Freddie pointed out. 'I take it that bottle of tequila wasn't in your refrigerator the last time you looked?'

'No,' he admitted. 'Of course it wasn't.'

'My latest episode happened after his death,' Lorinda agreed. 'Well after. But they started before.'

'That's right. So did mi—' Macho broke off abruptly, staring at Roscoe.

Roscoe had halted his ablutions, one hind leg still pointing skywards, and raised his head, ears cocked, listening intently to something they could not hear.

'What is it, boy?' Macho looked around the room, looked over his shoulder, looked back to Roscoe. 'What do you hear?'

After a moment, they heard it themselves. The all-too-familiar whoop of an approaching ambulance.

Roscoe scrambled for safety as they leaped out of their chairs and charged across the room.

'Whoa! Slow down!' Freddie recovered herself first. 'We're in the wrong business to be ambulance chasers.'

'It's stopped in front of Coffers Court.' Macho reached the High Street first and reported back to them as they came panting up to join him.

'Maybe Rhylla has finally snapped and murdered that kid,' Freddie suggested. Macho threw her an impatient look before turning and leading the way along the High Street.

They hurried towards Coffers Court, where a small cluster of onlookers had already materialized on the pavement outside. There was a buzz of excited speculation, fragments of which met their ears.

'Throat cut ear to ear . . .'

'No, burglary and they bludgeoned . . .'

'Gas fire exploded. Lucky the whole place didn't go up . . .'

The rumour factory was working well, Lorinda realized, but hard facts did not appear to be available.

'Isn't it awful?' Jennifer Lane greeted them.

'What happened?' Freddie asked.

'We're not quite sure yet.' Jennifer watched avidly as one of the medics carried a stretcher in. 'But something serious.'

'Used to be a nice quiet village,' someone muttered behind them. 'Before *that* lot moved in.'

'There's gratitude for you,' Freddie observed, adding unfairly, 'This place was a dead-and-alive hole before we moved in.'

'Now dead is winning,' the voice hit back.

'Who's . . . hurt?' Lorinda intervened, trying to recall Freddie to decorum. This was not the time to antagonize the villagers.

'Has Gemma been taken ill again?' Gemma had never really looked quite well since her mysterious gastric upset. Lorinda stepped back and scanned the windows, but the curtains defeated her. In the absence of a light in Gemma's living room, nothing of the inside could be seen.

To her embarrassment, the curtain was pulled back abruptly and Gemma was staring out at her over the window box. She said something Lorinda could not hear and Karla appeared in the window beside her. Gemma battled briefly to open the window. Karla gesticulated frantically and puzzlingly over Gemma's shoulder.

'What's going on?' Gemma won and leaned out of the window. 'Can you see? They won't let us out into the foyer.' From somewhere behind her, there came the sound of sobbing.

'Listen, don't let them shove you around like that!' Karla said, shoving Gemma aside to take her place at the open window. 'Come in here with us. Tell them you're visiting Gemma. And take a good look at what's going on as you come through the hall.'

It sounded worth a try. Macho was already shouldering his way through the crowd. Lorinda and Freddie fell in behind him. After a momentary hesitation, Jennifer Lane followed them. You couldn't blame her for trying, either.

The paramedic just inside the door was not happy about allowing them through, but realized his authority did not extend to barring visitors to residents, especially as Gemma was standing in her open doorway beckoning them on.

Macho stood back and gallantly waved the women ahead of him, thus ensuring that he had more time to take in the situation. In her brief glimpse, Lorinda saw that two of the medical team were standing at the opened doors of the lift, leaning into it and looking down. The stretcher-bearers, led by an anxious Gordie wringing his hands, were being ushered to the stairs leading down to his quarters, the boxrooms – and the bottom of the lift shaft.

Gemma let them into her flat, even Jennifer, then tried to bar the way to Macho. 'I'm sorry,' she said, 'but this is a private – Oh!'

'That's right,' Freddie turned back. 'You *do* know him. Macho's just changing his image.'

'Oh, of course. I'm sorry. Forgive me.' Thoroughly flustered, Gemma closed the door behind them and leaned against it, still staring incredulously at Macho. 'Uuuh, it's very effective.'

'So you gotta haircut,' Jack greeted him. 'About time. And the beard is gone, too. Good. Hey, you *do* have a chin!'

'Yes.' Macho ground his teeth, chin jutted forward.

'Gonna keep the old soup-strainer, are you?' No one could ever accuse Jack of being sensitive to the nuances of a situation. Lorinda became aware of another set of teeth grinding. They were Karla's.

'Do you have to be such an asshole?' she snarled at her husband.

Now that they were in the living room, Lorinda could trace the source of the sobbing. Rhylla clasped a shuddering, shaking Clarice to her bosom, rocking her, patting her back, murmuring soothing meaningless sounds.

'I'm afraid poor little Clarice discovered the body,' Professor Borley informed them in measured tones.

Betty Alvin was making no sound at all. She sat in a corner of the room, her back to the wall, her face whiter than the paint on the woodwork. A glass of dark-brown liquid was clasped in her hands, unnoticed, untouched. She appeared to be in deep shock.

'Perhaps you could talk to Betty,' Professor Borley said. 'I just can't seem to get through to her.'

'What's the matter with her?' Freddie asked. 'I thought it was Clarice who found the body.'

'Well, yes. But Betty was the last to see her alive.' He lowered his voice. 'I'm afraid Betty blames herself.'

Betty Alvin seemed to make a habit of blaming herself, Lorinda thought in faint irritation. That was probably why Dorian liked having her around. Betty was one of life's martyrs, always ready to be put-upon, always ready to take any blame that was going around. And Dorian was very good at apportioning blame.

Outside, another siren sounded briefly, but was quickly silenced, as though acknowledging that there was no reason to hurry any more. Lorinda glanced out of the window in time to see a Fire Rescue van pull up in front of the building. A police car was immediately behind it.

Macho had been looking around the room like the teacher he once was, taking roll call. Now he turned to Gemma and asked, 'Where's Ondine?'

The question brought a fresh paroxysm of tears from Clarice and a faint protesting moan from Betty. Rhylla hugged Clarice closer. Gemma bent to stroke the dogs at her feet. Professor Borley cleared his throat and looked thoughtful. No one seemed in any hurry to answer.

'Well, hell, they're gonna have to know,' Jack said. 'Thing is, she's at the bottom of the elevator shaft.'

'Wha-at?'

'Lift, you idiot!' Karla snapped. 'They don't say elevator. She's at the bottom of the lift shaft. Well, not exactly. The lift is at the bottom of the shaft, she fell on top of the lift.'

'Hey!' Ignoring her criticism, Jack had stalked over to the window. 'There's a Fire Rescue truck out there.'

'Sure, there is,' Karla said. 'It's going to take some doing to get her out of the lift shaft. The ambulance people can't do it all by themselves.'

'It's all my fault,' Betty Alvin moaned. 'All my fault.'

'Don't be silly, Betty,' Gemma said. 'You didn't push her . . . Did you?'

'No, but I fought with her.' Betty seemed to be recovering; she noticed the drink in her hand and took a swallow. 'That is, *she* fought with me. I was trying to be reasonable and explain that I couldn't take on her work at a moment's notice. I had too much else to do. It's all piled up and I'm trying to get through it as fast as I can. I told her I was working on your book –' She glanced at Rhylla. 'And Dorian brought stacks of notes back from that cruise and he wants them all sorted out. Then I'm in touch with Plantagenet Sutton's sister-in-law about clearing the flat. She wants me to do it – but I don't have the time, I really don't.'

'All right, all right,' Professor Borley soothed. 'Take it easy. We're on your side.'

'Yes, I know. Thank you, Abbey.' She smiled at him gratefully.

'Anyway, she kept trying to persuade me to drop Rhylla's work and do hers instead. When I wouldn't, she got angrier and angrier and . . . more abusive. She began saying perfectly awful things to me – and, of course, that didn't make me want to help her at all. I – I'm afraid I was rather sharp with her.'

'Quite right, too,' Rhylla said. 'Ondine was always a bully on any committee she sat on. And bad-tempered with it.'

'That's right,' Betty said. 'She lost her temper completely and, finally, she stormed out and I could hear her stamping down the stairs and the door at the foot of the stairs slammed. And . . . and that must have been when it happened, but I didn't hear anything because I went into the bathroom to take a couple of aspirins. She must have tried to get into the lift on the floor below – that's as far as it comes up – they didn't bother about the attic when they put it in. I suppose it was only used to store old records in those days and it never occurred to anyone that the place wouldn't be a bank forever and that people might be living here some day.

'Oh, I'm not complaining,' she added quickly. 'I quite like the privacy of having my own little staircase. It gives me a bit of warning if someone is coming up to see me – Oh, not that I mind people coming unannounced! No one must think they're intruding –' She broke off in confusion, realizing how much she was betraying and took another swallow.

Now that it was called to Lorinda's attention, she realized she had been guilty of such behaviour herself. In the comparatively short time she had been living here, there had been more than one occasion when she had mounted those attic stairs unannounced with a small sheaf of letters to be properly transcribed and dispatched. She could tell from the expressions on Freddie's and Macho's faces that she had not been alone in this transgression.

'So Ondine van Zeet went plunging down the stairs in a rage and that was the last you knew about it.' Professor Borley led Betty Alvin back to the subject gently.

'Yes . . . until I heard Clarice screaming. But that was some time later. I . . . I went downstairs to . . . to investigate. I . . . I found Clarice standing in front of the lift. The doors were open, but the lift wasn't there. I pulled Clarice back and leaned forward and looked down myself and . . . and . . . I saw her. Dimly. Sprawled on . . . on top of the lift.' Betty gave up the battle, groped for her handkerchief and allowed the tears to flow.

Clarice, on the other hand, had become calmer. Listening to the events as recounted by Betty, she nodded agreement and pushed herself free of Rhylla, who let her go with obvious relief, flexing her cramped arms.

'It sounds typical,' Rhylla said. 'I heard the door to the attic stairs slam. I didn't think it was Betty, but I wasn't interested enough to care who it was, which is just as well. Ondine would have been, literally, in a blind fury. She must have seen the lift doors were open and quite naturally thought the lift was standing there. She'd have hurled herself into it and –'

'But –' It was Karla who asked the salient question. 'Why were the lift doors open without the lift being there? That's dangerous. I know it's an ancient contraption, but I thought even in those days, they had safety rules. The doors shouldn't open unless the lift was at that floor.'

'Kids!' A new bitter voice said. 'You have kids around the place, you get them fooling around, messing up everything.' An exhausted, harassed Gordie stood in the doorway, glaring at Clarice.

'I didn't!' Clarice screamed. 'I never touched those doors! Why would I do a thing like that?'

'You're a kid,' Gordie said. 'Kids will do anything. You probably thought it would be funny if someone fell down the lift shaft.'

'No! I didn't! I didn't!' Clarice hurled herself back into her grandmother's arms, bursting into tears.

'All right, that's enough!' Rhylla snapped at Gordie. 'That's a serious accusation and you have no right to say such a thing. If you ever repeat it, I'll sue!'

'Gordie, what are you doing here?' Gemma was staring at him in some perplexity. 'How did you get in?'

'Oh, the door was ajar.' Gordie wrenched his baleful gaze away from Rhylla and Clarice, obviously struggling to bring his mind back to the more mundane subject. 'I knocked, but nobody seemed to hear me so . . .' He shrugged.

'The Rescue Services sent me.' His voice grew firmer as he cited a higher authority. 'They want me to make sure everybody stays put for the next few minutes. They don't want anyone straying out into the main hall. You see' – he looked at them with grim relish – 'they're bringing out the body now.'

12

As soon as the ambulance had driven away from Coffers Court with its grim burden, the gathering split up abruptly. In the marble hall, the yellow tapes sealing off the area around the lift were an uneasy reminder that the police would be investigating this incident.

Gordie stood irresolutely by Gemma's door for a few minutes, but only Clarice paid any attention to him, sticking her tongue out as she passed him. Rhylla had noticed, but made no comment; she held Clarice's hand tightly as they started up the two flights of stairs to her flat.

'I'd better get back to my workroom,' Gordie said, quite as though someone had invited him to stay. 'I expect the police will want to talk to me.' He sent a malevolent glance after Clarice. 'They'll want to know what could have happened with the lift doors and all that.' There was little doubt as to what he would tell them and who he would blame. It did not make anyone feel any more kindly disposed towards him and they allowed him to depart unhindered.

Professor Borley swept Betty Alvin and Jennifer Lane up to his flat for further refreshment. Gemma decided that it was a matter of urgency that she walk the dogs at once.

Lorinda wanted to check on the cats and Freddie and Macho had naturally gravitated towards the house with her. Somehow, Karla and Jack had tagged along, happily unaware that they were blocking the conversation that would otherwise have ensued.

Had-I was furious and complaining, But-Known was resigned. Had-I marched over to the catflap and bumped her head against it several times, demonstrating the extent of her captivity and her annoyance. But-Known, curled up on a kitchen chair, watched with one open eye, waiting to see what would result.

Lorinda sighed and went to the fridge. Had-I slowed her tirade and began to relent. Oh, well, if she was going to apologize properly . . .

But-Known yawned, stretched and slithered to the floor, sauntering over to join Had-I at the fridge. This was more like it . . .

Last night's leftovers were quite acceptable, thank you. They watched with approval and some surprise as she scraped out the casserole into their dishes. She hoped they weren't betraying the fact that, if she hadn't brought company back with her, she might have just put the casserole down and left it to their rough little tongues to do the scraping.

As it was, only Freddie had an amused smile. Karla and Jack obviously weren't attuned to feline attitudes and the cats' silent communication went over their heads. Macho was too bemused to notice.

With relief, Lorinda led everyone into the living room and dispensed drinks, but first she snapped on all the lamps against the encroaching darkness.

'If you ask me, there are a helluva lot of accidents here for one little village,' Jack said, rubbing his injured arm. 'Now, if all this had happened in one of your books . . .' He let the uncomfortable thought lie there.

'Jerk!' Karla said. 'Most of what happens in life is too unbelievable to put into a book. We all know that. We have to tone it down to make it seem real.'

'Coincidences abound in real life,' Macho agreed, but looked as though he might be having second thoughts about it. 'At least, we always assume they're coincidences.'

'*Aaaaarrreeeooow* . . .' The long plaintive wail rose outside the windows and Macho leapt to his feet.

'Roscoe!' He rushed to the window and threw it open. He was nearly knocked over as the large orange tom flew past him into the room.

'Roscoe . . .' He closed the window again and turned to stare at his pet, who was now sitting complacently at his feet. 'How did you get out?'

Because someone else got in? Lorinda wondered whether there was now another bottle of tequila lurking somewhere in Macho's house, waiting to be discovered. Or perhaps something worse. The fictional Macho Magee had an unfortunate disposition towards finding naked female corpses in various corners of his seedy office-cum-dwelling. It would be a natural progression of the harassment campaign being waged, but, if it had not occurred to him, she did not want to be the one to put it into his mind.

'That cat gets bigger every time I look at him,' Jack said. 'You got him on steroids, or something?'

'Don't be insulting,' Macho huffed. 'Some breeds are just naturally large.'

Roscoe blinked amiably at them both. When neither food nor affection was forthcoming, he got up and ambled towards the kitchen where the faint sound of bowls scraping along the linoleum could be heard.

Jack opened his mouth, perhaps to question Roscoe's pedigree, but the doorbell cut across him. Before anyone could move to answer, it rang again. And again. Someone without much patience was intent on entry.

'Hello, Dorian.' Lorinda opened the door, winning the mental bet with herself.

'Your telephone is out of order,' he said irritably. 'I've been trying to get you.'

'Oh?' This was not the moment to explain that she had unplugged it when she went out. The fear of coming back to find another sinister message waiting had been too much for her. 'Come in.'

'Where's Betty?' Dorian halted in the doorway and looked around the room with dissatisfaction. 'I thought she'd be here. I can't find her anywhere else.'

'She's with Professor Borley,' Karla said. 'At least, she was when we left.'

'I've tried Abbey. He isn't there.' Dorian looked at the glass of Scotch Lorinda had automatically given him and tasted it suspiciously. 'Or else he isn't answering the telephone.'

That was only too possible. Lorinda was in no hurry to plug hers back in.

'Perhaps they went out for a meal.' Karla shrugged. 'Or maybe they went back to the bookshop with Jennifer. She was there, too.'

'Why does everybody call him Abbey?' The question had evidently been bothering Jack for some time. 'I know his initials are A.B., which I'd pronounce Abie. So why the Abbey stuff?'

'Because his name is Borley,' Dorian said impatiently. 'Don't you see it?'

'See what?' It was clear he didn't.

'Borley Abbey,' Freddie elucidated. 'The most haunted place in Britain.' He still looked blank. 'It's a joke,' she explained.

'An English joke.' His voice was flat as he found the joke.

'That's right, dear.' With Dorian present, Karla cooed sweetly. 'It's over your head.'

'You didn't get it, either,' he snarled. 'And I'll give you odds Borley doesn't think it's funny.'

'On the contrary,' Dorian said. 'He was quite amused. Once I'd explained it to him.'

'I'll bet,' Jack said. 'The guy's got a proper name, hasn't he? Why the hell don't you let him use it?'

'Dorian –' Freddie broke into the dialogue. 'You *do* know, don't you?'

'Know?' He looked blank.

'About Ondine?'

'Oh, that. Yes. Gordie reported to me. That was why I was trying to get hold of Betty. We'll need to draft a press release. Notify her publishers, agent, relatives . . .' He faltered, perhaps sensing that he was not quite in accord with his audience. 'It's all very sad,' he said quickly. 'But she wasn't a young woman, nor, I suspect, a particularly well one. It's just very unfortunate that it happened here, when she'd just moved in an –'

The doorbell made them all jump. Lorinda hurried to answer it. She was conscious of a muted yapping as she approached, so it was no surprise when she opened the door.

'Hello, Gemma.' The pugs at Gemma's feet surged forward, then stopped and moved back uneasily.

Lorinda glanced over her shoulder to see Had-I and But-Known advancing with a territorial glint in their eyes. Roscoe followed behind them, bristled up to nearly twice his size, clearly ready to do battle for his females.

'Come in,' Lorinda invited, crossing her fingers and hoping for the best. Gemma looked even more upset than the last time she had seen her.

'Yes, thank you. Come on!' Gemma tugged at the leashes, but Conqueror and Lionheart had suddenly become reluctant to enter the hallway.

'Behave yourselves,' Lorinda said over her shoulder to the cats. They paused and waited in ominous docility.

'I beg your pardon?' Gemma was startled. 'Oh –' She looked beyond Lorinda. 'I see. Come on.' She tugged at the leashes again. 'They're not going to bother you.'

With faint apologetic whines and bellies low, Conqueror and Lionheart scurried past the cats, keeping close to Gemma's ankles for protection. The cats watched implacably.

'Stay there,' Lorinda said to them, firmly closing the door behind her.

'I'm sorry,' Gemma said. 'I just couldn't go home. I tried. I got there just as the light over the front entrance went on and – and I could see it! In big black letters! I couldn't walk under it. I couldn't go in.'

'See what?' Lorinda asked. Behind her, the doorknob rattled. She tried to ignore it.

'The graffiti.' Gemma looked frightened. 'Someone has crossed out the "ERS" of COFFERS and written "IN" over it, so that the name reads COFFIN COURT. I couldn't –'

'So now it's vandalism!' Dorian exploded, more upset by that than he had been by Ondine's death.

There was a decisive click and Lorinda felt a draught on the back of her legs. The cats marched past her purposefully and took up commanding positions in front of the fireplace. The pugs cringed closer to Gemma, who was watching Dorian and didn't notice.

'Vandals!' Dorian raged. 'They didn't chip off the bas-relief letters, did they?' he asked in sudden anxiety. 'That would cost a fortune to repair. It was just the black paint?'

'Feelings are running pretty high in this town,' Jack said. 'Next thing will be broken windows,' he added, as Dorian winced. He didn't appear to find anything strange in Dorian's attitude, but Lorinda was beginning to ask herself just why Dorian seemed to be taking it so personally.

'Just the paint,' Gemma said. 'I'm sure Gordie will be able to clean it up. It will be quite a job for him, though. He'll have to scrub for hours. It's very messy.'

'If Gordie had been doing his duty, it wouldn't have happened in the first place,' Dorian snapped. 'He should have been keeping watch at the door.'

'Gordie has had his hands full today,' Freddie pointed out.

'He must be exhausted. I wouldn't blame him if he went to bed for the rest of the week with the covers pulled over his head.'

'I'll go over there and speak to him now.' There wasn't much chance of that with Dorian around. 'If he starts on the graffiti now, he should have it cleaned up by morning.'

'You expect him to work all night?' Karla was scandalized.

'If he'd been doing his job properly, it wouldn't be necessary. He brought it on himself.'

'An awful lot of people around here seem to bring things on themselves,' Jack muttered. 'At least, that's what other people keep telling them.' He rubbed his arm and flexed his fingers experimentally. He looked from Dorian to his wife, suspicious and unforgiving.

But Dorian had been on the terrace when Jack fell – or was pushed – into the bonfire. Hadn't he? Lorinda realized suddenly that they knew the moment Jack had been found smouldering in the ashes, but there was no conveniently broken watch to register the moment he actually had been pushed.

'You'd better leave poor Gordie alone for a while.' There was a distinctly bossy note in Karla's voice, perhaps she'd forgotten it was not her husband she was addressing. 'Morning is time enough for him to worry about graffiti. He's going to have to clean up the top of the lift first, isn't he? Before it can be put back into service again.'

Although both true and practical, the pragmatic statement was too graphic for its hearers. There was an abrupt deep imbibing of drink in the silence that followed.

Inadvertently, Lorinda intercepted the look Dorian shot at Karla. It went through her like an electric shock. It was as embarrassing as finding you'd opened someone else's letter by mistake, as disturbing as though that letter had been a piece of hate mail.

Lorinda recalled abruptly that Jack and Karla had been dressed alike on Bonfire Night. In the darkness and excitement, it would have been quite easy for the wrong Jackley to receive that nearly fatal push.

'SSSsss . . .' . . . 'RRrrreeeeeooooow . . .' . . . 'Aarrfff . . .' The uneasy truce was over. Hostilities broke out.

'No! Stop!' Gemma tugged at the leashes, ignoring the fact that the dogs were already scuttling for shelter behind her.

'Had-I, But-Known – No!' Lorinda tried, although she could see it was useless.

'Roscoe!' Macho frowned, but the effect was lost because his tone sounded admiring rather than censorious.

Paying no attention to human protests, the cats advanced on their prey. Almost languidly, Had-I stretched out a paw and raked the air an inch from Conqueror's nose. He backed away, yelping as though the claws had connected with his tender nose. Lionheart wriggled forward a bit, but Roscoe gave a warning growl and he retreated again. Even But-Known had the light of battle in her eyes; no canine was going to infringe on her territory. She feinted wildly, with more enthusiasm than skill. Conqueror yelped and reared back so sharply he pulled the end of his leash out of Gemma's hand. She turned to go after him and Lionheart got away.

'Back!' Gemma flapped her hands at the inexorably advancing cats. 'Get back!'

But the only ones backing were the pugs. Not daring to take their eyes off the cats, they slunk backwards until their rumps collided with the wall and there was no escape.

'Had-I, that's enough! But-Known, stop it! You, too, Roscoe!' Lorinda might just as well have never spoken. She circled round behind the cats, waiting for her moment to swoop on Had-I, who was definitely the ringleader and bully-in-chief.

Gemma had abandoned her flapping motions and was making suggestive little movements of her feet.

Don't you dare! Lorinda shot her a look as menacing as any of the cats' and Gemma subsided into shuffling.

'I can't understand it,' Gemma complained. 'They all got on so well in my place the other day.'

Because they were the invaders. But this was not the moment to explain.

'Throw a bucket of water over them!' Jack and Karla had retreated to the far side of the room. It was clear that they were not going to get involved. Dorian had retreated just far enough to stay clear of the action, but not so far as to be suspected of opting out, although no one in their right mind ... mind ... would have looked for help from that quarter to begin with.

'Really, I think we'd better go now.' Gemma tried to recapture the leashes. 'Conqueror! Lionheart! Come along! Home!'

The dogs were more than willing, but the cats blocked their

way. With an anxious whine, Conqueror tried to sidle along the wall, but Had-I cut him off. Roscoe kept Lionheart paralysed with a baleful stare.

'Call off your cats.' Jack was full of bright suggestions. 'Let the poor dogs go.'

'Have you ever tried to call off a cat?' Freddie's question was rhetorical. Jack obviously knew nothing about feline characteristics.

Abruptly, the final onslaught erupted in a flurry of slashing, flashing paws, against high-pitched yelps and scurryings. Hisses, yowls and spitting imprecations filled the air.

Conqueror was the first to crack. He slithered down and rolled over, belly up, waving helpless paws in the air. Lionheart hesitated only a second longer, then Roscoe's paw caught him across the nose and he joined Conqueror in abject surrender, whining.

'Those dogs' – Dorian looked down at them with distaste – 'give an entirely new dimension to the expression pussy-whipped.'

The cats hovered menacingly over the pugs for a moment longer then, honour satisfied and no doubt as to the victors, they exchanged glances and strolled away.

'Come *along!*' Gemma had the leashes now and tugged the dogs to their feet.

'I'll walk you back,' Dorian said. 'I want to have that talk with Gordie.'

'I still think you should leave him alone for tonight,' Karla volunteered. 'I told you, he's had a rotten day.'

'And I think I'll go up to London for a few days tomorrow,' Dorian added reflectively.

'Again?' Karla was indignant. 'You're always going up to London. What's the big attraction up there?'

Dorian looked at her with almost as much distaste as he had shown for the cringing dogs. For a moment, Lorinda thought he might be going to tell her.

'Work.' He slid away from confrontation. 'There are several projects that require my attention.'

'Yeah?' Karla's tone was unpleasant. 'Did it ever occur to you that there might be a few projects around here that require your attention?'

Lorinda stooped and gathered up Had-I and But-Known, trying to pretend that the conversation was meaningless to her. It was so embarrassing when people thought that they were talking to each other in code, unaware that their listeners had long since cracked the code.

'I told you,' Dorian said, a trifle testily. 'I'll see to it that Gordie cleans up the building immediately. That's the main priority. Anything else can wait until I get back.'

'Don't be too sure of that.' Karla was glaring at him. Jack was glaring, too, but probably for a different reason. Even the most untalented can eventually crack a code when it becomes blatant enough.

Lorinda hoped Dorian was learning his lesson and that this would be the last time he got involved with impressionable women he met abroad. She wondered whether there might be a further influx from the contacts he had made on his cruise. Dorian, pouring on that Olde-English charm and those tropical nights at sea, would undoubtedly have proved a dangerous combination on a shipful of vulnerable ladies looking for romance.

She had a further disquieting thought: with the deaths of Plantagenet Sutton and Ondine van Zeet, there was now accommodation available again at Coffers Court.

'The sooner that disgraceful mess over the entrance is removed, the better!' Gemma sailed through the front door as Dorian opened it for her. 'And if you have to pay Gordie double for overtime, it will be worth it.'

The door slammed behind them with a vehemence that betrayed Dorian's opinion of that idea. Gordie would be lucky to be paid at all; he was more likely to get a lecture on his carelessness in allowing the graffiti artist to operate in the first place.

'We'd better go, too.' Jack had a firm grip on Karla's arm with his good hand. 'Maybe I oughta get down and take a picture of the defaced building before Gordie gets scrubbing and destroys the evidence.'

'Evidence? What are you talking about?' Karla was prepared to fight about anything. Luckily, they kept moving towards the door. 'What do you mean, evidence?'

'The way things are going around here, who can tell?' Jack opened the door.

'Yeah? Well, you'd better not let Dorian catch you taking any pictures. He wouldn't like it.'

'Yeah? Well, maybe I don't care what Dorian likes. Some

people around here may think he's God Almighty, but I sure as hell don't! He can –' The door slammed behind them.

The sudden silence was so peaceful no one wanted to disturb it. There were faint exhalations of relief and a few throbbing purrs as they sank limply into the nearest chairs and the cats found welcoming laps.

'Coffin Court . . .' Freddie mused aloud eventually. 'That will be Clarice's doing, I suspect.'

'She's the only one small enough and agile enough to scramble up over the arch and get at the lettering,' Lorinda agreed. 'Also, she has the best motive. Gordie insulted her and this will cause him maximum annoyance and extra work.'

'It's always a mistake to antagonize a clever child.' Macho spoke with the full weight of his schoolmastering experience behind him. 'It's better to have them with you than against you. They have ways of getting their own back that would never occur to unwary adults. Gordie will be lucky if she stops there.'

'I'm not sure I begrudge her a little revenge,' Freddie said. 'That was a very nasty accusation for Gordie to make.'

'And a highly unlikely one,' Macho added. 'Clarice has never appeared to be a child who was fascinated by machinery. Fooling about with the lift isn't Clarice's sort of game. She's far more interested in trying to manipulate poor Rhylla.'

'I've seen her with those black-felt marking pens,' Lorinda said. 'I hope Gordie hasn't noticed. Or that he doesn't put two and two together. He could give Clarice a very bad time.'

'And vice versa,' Macho said. 'He'd better be very careful about taking her on. She's younger, faster and, I suspect, a great deal smarter than he is. She could teach him a trick or two.'

'Tricks . . .' Freddie looked at them. 'Do you suppose Clarice could be behind what's been happening to us?'

'Not with tequila involved,' Macho pointed out. 'No wine merchant would risk losing his licence by selling spirits to an underaged child. It would mean prosecution. And where would she get that much money?'

'If an adult bought the tequila – a case of it, as you said before.' Freddie was reluctant to relinquish the idea. 'Clarice could slip into your house and plant the bottles, or pour drinks out of them down the sink and no one would notice.'

'All other considerations apart' – Macho gave her an old-fashioned look – 'if you were up to no good, would you choose Clarice for an accomplice?'

'Perhaps not,' Freddie admitted, after a moment's reflection. 'Not unless I were Rhylla – and I can't see her doing any of this.'

'No,' Lorinda agreed. 'It's too ... vicious.'

'The cap fits Plantagenet Sutton to perfection. Only ...' Macho hesitated. 'I suppose he *is* dead? It's not some kind of double bluff ... ?'

'Believe me,' Freddie said, 'he isn't going to jump out of the woodwork at the last minute, tearing off a false beard. This isn't a Hitchcock film or one of Dame Agatha's plots.'

'We saw the body.' Lorinda shuddered. 'He was dead, all right.'

'All wrong ...' Macho hesitated again before venturing a new theory. 'Of course, Dorian has a pretty warped sense of humour. Look at that dummy on top of the bonfire. I believe Dorian would have stood by and not said anything, even if someone risked their life trying to rescue it.'

There was a thoughtful silence. It was not a theory that could be refuted instantly.

'Dorian persuaded us all to move here,' Lorinda said.

'Straight into his clutches.' Macho nodded.

'But why should he hate us so much?' Freddie asked. 'It's not as though we were more successful than he is. We're all pretty much on a level pegging; doing well, nothing spectacular, but comfortably situated.'

'Who knows what might upset Dorian?' Macho was still look-ing on the dark side. 'He's been going for a long time now and readers can be fickle. Perhaps they're tiring of Field Marshal Sir Oliver Aldershot and turning to newer creations – like ours. Although,' he added plaintively, 'what with the political and the historical perspective changing, I suspect Macho Magee may have just about run his course, too. So why pick on me?'

'Perhaps because you're young enough to start a new series,' Freddie said. 'And he's out of ideas.'

'But Karla isn't,' Lorinda said quietly.

'Right!' Freddie glanced at her approvingly. 'The problem is that Karla still has Jack attached and in line for a half share of her copyrights in the event of a divorce. The bonfire ploy didn't finish him off but ...' She paused significantly. 'He was at Coffers Court when Ondine died. It's possible that the lift trap had been set for him, but Ondine fell into it – literally – before Karla had a chance to send Jack into it.'

'I'm not so sure that Dorian is all that keen to link up with Karla any more – if he ever was,' Lorinda objected. 'Now that he's had a chance to, um, see more of Karla, in action as it were.'

'He's gone off the boil!' Freddie said. 'Not that I could ever imagine Dorian *on* the boil. If he lived on the other side of the house, the way I do, he'd be sending Karla down the lift shaft.'

'And that's another possibility,' Macho said.

Roscoe sat up in his lap and gave a prodigious yawn.

'By the way' – that reminded Lorinda – 'I hope you're prepared to find another bottle of tequila when you go back.'

'Yes.' Macho stroked Roscoe's throat. 'I thought of that. He couldn't get out on his own. Someone let him out. If only you could talk, eh, old boy?'

Had-I decided to talk. She bounced off Lorinda's lap and launched into a short tirade to the effect that heroic cats who had fearlessly battled and seen off marauding canine invaders were entitled to some reward. And pretty quickly, thank you.

But-Known dropped to her side and agreed. Roscoe brightened and looked around hopefully. He'd done his share, too.

'Yes . . . yes.' Lorinda led the way to the kitchen. 'You've been very good. Very brave. Very clever.'

The others followed her. Roscoe, still in Macho's arms, was half singing, half purring encouragement. He stopped only to yawn again. Macho yawned with him.

'Sorry, it's been a long day,' Macho apologized. 'Very long. I think it's time we went home.'

'Let's sleep on it,' Freddie agreed, 'and meet for elevenses in the morning.'

'Come round to my place.' Macho stifled another yawn, while Roscoe uninhibitedly gave way to his.

'Have this for Roscoe.' Lorinda gave him a salmon-and-trout from the diminishing pile of gourmet cat food. 'I think it's his favourite.' She peeled the top off chicken-and-game for Had-I and But-Known.

'See you not too early in the morning then,' Freddie agreed, opening the back door.

Suddenly, capriciously, Had-I decided that freedom was even

more enticing than gourmet cat food. She darted between Freddie's feet, nearly knocking her down, and bolted into the night.

'Oh, no!' Lorinda slammed the door just before But-Known could follow.

'No, you don't!' Freddie helpfully caught up But-Known. 'You don't really want to go out. Stay here and eat.'

'Now I'll have to unfasten the catflap so that Had-I can get back in,' Lorinda said resignedly. 'And But-Known can get out. I was planning to leave it shut tonight, so I knew where they were.'

'You can't win,' Freddie said cheerfully. 'Not with cats.'

13

Macho took his responsibilities as a host seriously. He had been out early to the bakery and jam doughnuts, cherry muffins and Danish pastries were set out on the table. Macho filled the cream jug and placed it beside them, then looked around vaguely, still holding the cream jug.

'Roscoe's not back yet,' he muttered.

'Mine have been gone all morning,' Lorinda said.

'I know. Roscoe went out with me and I saw him link up with your girls. They went off together up the hill.'

Freddie helped herself to a Danish and munched on it moodily. Lorinda noticed that there were dark circles under her eyes, but supposed she didn't look too well herself. She had spent a lot of half-wakeful hours agonizing over what she might have done to incur Dorian's enmity. She could think of nothing. Nor could she imagine what Freddie and Macho might have done. Presumably, they had done their own soul-searching during the dark hours, they didn't look as though they had done any sleeping.

'Have you seen the facade at Coffers Court this morning?' Macho filled their cups and sat down.

'I've been working,' Freddie said.

Lorinda shook her head, hoping it would be assumed that she had been working, too. In fact, she was once again unable to bring herself to go into her study. She had pottered around, promising herself that she would get some work done in the afternoon.

'It's a mess.' Macho spoke with some relish. 'Gordie hasn't cleaned it up properly at all, he's just smeared the black paint into a great big blot. You can still read the graffiti and the bas-relief lettering is filthy, even the letters that hadn't been scribbled over before. Dorian will be furious.'

'Oh, good.' Freddie cheered up a bit. 'Anything that annoys Dorian is going to get my support. I must stroll past and admire it later.'

'Gordie will probably be up there doing more cleaning by then,' Macho said. 'It's my guess he only did that much last night with Dorian standing over him. As soon as Dorian left, he packed it in for the night and I, for one, don't blame him.'

'But Dorian will,' Lorinda said. 'Poor Gordie, he didn't know what he was getting into. It must have seemed like such a good job offer at the time.'

'Gordie and Betty both,' Freddie said. 'Although I'm happy to see that she's showing signs of rebellion.'

'Have another muffin,' Macho urged hospitably.

'I haven't finished this one yet,' Lorinda said. 'But I will have some more coffee. No, don't get up. I'll get it myself. Anyone else?'

'Well, while you're up . . .' Freddie held out her cup.

'Oh . . .' Something in the distance caught Lorinda's eye as she passed the window. 'Here come the cats now.'

'Just in time for food,' Freddie noted. 'You can always trust the little blighters for that.'

'They . . . they seem to have something in their mouths.' Lorinda strained her eyes to see what they were carrying. Had-I was in the lead, something pale and gossamer fluttering from both sides of her mouth. 'It looks as though they've been catching butterflies.'

'Butterflies? At this time of the year?' Lorinda heard the scrape of chairs being pushed back from the table, then Freddie and Macho were behind her.

'They've got something, all right – and probably something they shouldn't have.' Macho went to the back door and opened it. 'What have you got there, you little wretches?'

Roscoe bounded forward. It was his house and his human in the doorway. He carried the biggest butterfly of all in his mouth. Only . . . Freddie was right: it wasn't a butterfly.

'No . . .' Lorinda whispered faintly. 'Please . . . no.'

'Put it down, Roscoe.' Macho's voice shook. 'Let Daddy see what you have there.'

Had-I and But-Known brushed past Roscoe, rushing to Lorinda with high-pitched little sing-song cries of triumph. They laid their trophies at her feet.

'Oh, no!' She covered her eyes. 'Tell me it isn't true!'

'Sorry,' Freddie said. 'I'd like to be able to tell you they've raided the fishmonger's stall, but I'd be lying. The last time I saw fish like that, they were swimming around the aquarium in Dorian's study.'

'We're in trouble,' Macho said bleakly.

'You sure are,' Freddie agreed cheerfully.

'We might be able to save them!' Lorinda stoppered the sink and ran cold water into it. She scooped up the tiny bodies – over Had-I's indignant protests – and tossed them into the water, where they floated inert.

'It's worth a try.' Macho tossed in Roscoe's prize. For a moment, the wide graceful fins seemed to flutter and swoop . . . then it flipped over, belly up, and they realized it had been an illusion created by the ripples of the water.

'They're goners, I'm afraid.' Macho absently wiped his hands on the nearby dish towel.

'They felt . . . strange.' Lorinda looked around for something to dry her own hands on, then wincingly accepted the dish towel. 'I don't think they're . . . fresh kills.'

'How can you tell?' Freddie peered into the sink curiously. 'Do fish get rigor mortis?'

'I've never had occasion to research that,' Macho said with dignity. 'Fish have never figured in a Macho Magee story. However, in Venice, with all that water . . .' He joined her at the sink. 'Mmm . . . they do look a bit odd.'

'I'll tell you what else is odd.' Freddie had picked up But-Known and was cuddling her. 'The cats' paws aren't wet. Not the way they would be if they'd been dipping them in the tank trying to scoop out the fish.'

'You're right.' Macho bent and checked Roscoe's dry forelegs. 'Then how did they get hold of those fish?'

'I can't imagine how they got near them in the first place,' Lorinda said. 'It can only have been over Dorian's dead bod—'

They looked at each other, dropped the cats and charged for the door.

By the fourth time they had rung the bell, they had got their breath back after the dash up the hill. They rang again; still no one answered. They tried the door, but it was locked. They stepped back and surveyed the front of the house: the windows were all closed.

'No,' Freddie said. 'I never believed in all those locked-room mysteries. The cats got in and out. Let's try around back.'

The French windows leading from the drawing room to the terrace were ajar just about the width of a cat's body.

'There we are!' But, having been proved right, Freddie became oddly hesitant. She approached the window frame and rapped on it gingerly. 'Dorian – ?' she called. 'Dorian? Are you there?'

There was silence inside. They looked at each other uneasily.

'If we were the police,' Macho pointed out, 'we'd be quite justified in investigating. It isn't as though we're breaking in. The windows are open and the circumstances are suspicious. The law is on our side.'

'I'm not worried about the law,' Freddie said. 'I just don't want to confront Dorian in his dressing gown asking us what the hell we think we're doing trooping through his house.'

'He said he was going up to London today,' Lorinda remembered belatedly. 'He may have caught an early train.'

'That's right.' Freddie's sigh of relief was audible. 'So, the house is empty, the French window is open – and your cats have been helping themselves in the fish tank. Every reason in the world to check up on things. What are we waiting for? Let's go in and see what the damage is.'

'Perhaps we can replace the missing fish before Dorian returns.' Macho saw a ray of hope. 'Unless they ate a few others before they brought any home. I couldn't tell which ones are gone, though, could you?'

'Dorian – ?' Not dignifying that with an answer, Freddie advanced into the drawing room, still calling out – just in case. 'Yoo-hoo . . . Dorian . . . anyone home?'

The drawing room was silent and empty, looking like a stage set waiting for the actors to appear. On the far side of the room, the door to Dorian's study was ajar – again, just enough to allow an enterprising cat to go in and out.

'Dorian – ?' Freddie crossed the room and rapped on the door. 'Are you in there . . . ?' Silence. Lorinda and Macho came up behind her and waited.

'Oh, well,' Freddie said. 'In for a penny, in for a pound.' She pushed the door open and they started in.

Lorinda had the sudden unnerving sensation of stepping into a quagmire. The carpet gave way strangely under her foot and it had an odd spongy texture. She looked down to see tiny bubbles of water well up around her shoe.

'This carpet is soaking wet!' Macho discovered indignantly.

'I can't see a thing.' Freddie reached for the light switch on the wall, but Macho caught her hand.

'Don't touch an electric switch when you're standing in water!'

'Thanks, I wasn't thinking. I'll open the curtains instead.' Freddie started across the room. 'Uuggh! I've stepped on something!'

That was enough to discourage Lorinda from venturing further without light. She and Macho hovered just inside the doorway.

'There!' Freddie swept back the curtains and daylight flooded the room. They could now see the extent of the devastation. 'Oh, my God!'

The carpet was littered with tiny dead fish, sprayed out across it from the gaping jagged hole in the side of the glass tank. A few remaining fish – tiny Neons – darted about hysterically in the few inches of water at the bottom of the aquarium, dodging in and out around the glittering shards of glass that loomed like icebergs in their midst.

'Well . . .' Macho broke the stunned silence. 'He can't blame the cats for *that!*'

'It must have happened hours ago.' Lorinda began to recover. 'Perhaps during the night. The carpet couldn't have got so saturated in any shorter space of time.' She became aware that a steady trickle of water was still dribbling from the tank, emanating from the little device Dorian had installed to keep fresh water circulating for the fish. There was another faint background sound . . . she looked around for the source.

'Oh, God!' Freddie found it first. She stared at the other side of the room where Dorian's big desk skewed across a corner, where he could sit, back to the wall, commanding the room. He was slumped in his desk chair now, watching them through half-closed eyes.

'Dorian! We didn't realize you were here.' No, that didn't sound right. Lorinda corrected hastily, 'I mean, we thought you'd caught the early train to London –' No, that was worse. 'I mean –'

'Frightfully sorry, old boy,' Macho apologized. 'We wouldn't have dreamed of intruding had we known you were still . . .'

'Gug . . .' Dorian said faintly. He seemed to be trying to rise. 'G . . . g . . . gug . . .' He pitched forward, face down on the desk.

It was then that they could see the dark red smear congealing on the back of his head.

It was hours before they were able to return to their homes. First they had to wait for the ambulance and the police, carefully restraining themselves from touching anything – except for Freddie, who wiped the squashed fish off the sole of her shoe and threw it into the wastebasket. (Something which required explanation when a policeman looked into the wastebasket and thought he had discovered a clue.)

Darkness had fallen on Brimful Coffers by the time they returned. They had followed the ambulance in Freddie's car, waited at the hospital while Dorian underwent emergency surgery, notified his sister when he was safely settled in intensive care, snatched a meal they had neither tasted nor noticed, and now looked without favour at the dark empty shells of their respective homes.

'All I want is to collapse.' Freddie halted the car and rested her head on the steering wheel for a moment. 'I want to fall into bed and sleep for a week.'

'You do remember that you promised –' Macho began.

'I promised to meet Dorian's sister at the train station in the morning and drive her to the hospital,' Freddie said. 'I know. Me and my big mouth.'

'You'll feel stronger in the morning,' Lorinda encouraged, opening the car door. Collapse suddenly sounded like the best idea she had ever heard. She felt so exhausted she wondered if she'd have the energy to change into her nightgown.

'Don't bet on it.' Freddie pulled her keys from the ignition and opened her own door, shuddering as she looked at the encroaching mist. 'At least we got home before the worst of the fog sets in. It's going to be a filthy night.'

'I hope Dorian lasts through it.' Lorinda stepped out of the car and a movement beyond the mist drew her attention.

'He's pretty tough,' Macho said. 'And the doctor was what

I'd call cautiously optimistic. But it was lucky for him we found him when we did.'

'Thieving cats have their uses,' Freddie said dryly. 'If they hadn't filched those fish . . . and speaking of devils – '

Three little forms bounded towards them, scolding.

'Oh, darlings, have we gone away and left you all day?' Guiltily, Lorinda stooped and gathered up her two. There was always dry cat food left out for them to nibble, but they expected more than that in the course of a long day.

'Here, Roscoe. Come here, boy. What's the matter with you?' Each time Macho bent to pick up his cat, Roscoe evaded him, backing just out of reach, then returning when Macho straightened up. He was uttering plaintive little cries.

'That's odd,' Macho said. 'He usually only behaves this way when I'm going to take him to the vet.'

'Why aren't you in the nice warm house?' Lorinda asked Had-I and But-Known. She ruffled their fur and frowned. 'They're wet and cold. They didn't just run out to meet us – they must have been outside for some time.'

'Roscoe's wet, too.' Macho finally captured his skittish friend. 'He hates being wet or cold. Why isn't he inside?'

'You know' – Freddie closed her car door silently – 'I think I'm going to revise my scenario. Suddenly, collapse doesn't seem like a very good plan. Not until we know what's going on around here. When comfort-loving, spoiled-rotten little creatures like yours take to the great outdoors on a night like this, there's got to be something nasty in the woodshed . . . or in the house.'

They looked at the dark silent houses awaiting them.

'Roscoe?' Macho sniffed sharply, lowered his nose to Roscoe's head and sniffed again. 'Roscoe reeks of liquor.' He looked thoughtfully at his own house. 'Probably tequila.'

'I'm not going to sleep tonight,' Freddie said, 'until all our houses have been searched top to bottom.'

'We'll have to search them ourselves,' Lorinda said. 'I'm not keen on the thought of what the police might say if we call them in for something as vague as this. I'm afraid they have a fairly low opinion of us already.'

'In the best old tradition,' Macho said.

'And I wouldn't like to tell them that story about us being haunted by our own characters, either,' Freddie said. 'Here, let me take one of the cats, you can't manage them both.' She took

But-Known into her own arms. 'No, a story like that would be a one-way ticket to Colney Hatch.'

'Which is undoubtedly what was intended – and why we tried to hide what was happening to us.' Macho stared at the unresponsive facade of his cottage. 'At best, people would think we're harmless lunatics; at worst, they'd suspect we're so disturbed that we're behind all the death and destruction in Brimful Coffers.'

'Someone is.' Lorinda knew there could be no doubt about that now.

'Yes – and our best suspects are dead. Or dying.' Macho was grim. 'I think we can consider Dorian exonerated . . . the hard way. And Plantagenet has been dead for weeks.'

'Again in the best tradition.' Freddie shivered. 'Look, I'd rather be doing something other than standing here catching pneumonia. Suppose we start with Macho's house and see if there's anything . . . or anyone . . . to find.'

Roscoe twisted uneasily in Macho's arms and mewled distress as they entered the house. Macho snapped on the front hall light. Nothing happened.

'Of course, the bulb was there when I moved in,' Macho said. 'I suppose it *could* have burned out naturally.'

'Mmmm-hmmmm . . .' Lorinda said.

Freddie snorted.

There was nothing wrong with the living room lamp . . . or the room, either. Roscoe renewed his struggles as they headed for the kitchen. Macho walked more warily.

The kitchen light responded to the click of the switch, flooding the kitchen with a harsh bright glare. Too harsh and too bright. They glanced upwards instinctively.

The frosted globe that diffused the light had been shattered, only a few jagged remnants still curved out from the fixture. The rest of the globe lay in a trail of shards across the floor, ending at the far wall where a broken tequila bottle lay in a reeking puddle.

On the kitchen table, another tequila bottle, two-thirds empty, stood beside a glass with an inch of liquid still remaining in it. The chair lay on the floor, as though it had been pushed back so roughly it had tipped over.

'Ah, yes.' Macho took it in quietly. 'A very pretty picture. Macho Magee, drunk as usual, hurls bottle at the light, possibly

207

because pink elephants are lurking behind it, tips over chair and, presumably, staggers upstairs to bed. Through the pitch-black hallway.' Macho crossed to a cupboard and took down a small flashlight.

'Shall we go upstairs and see what was waiting for him?'

They didn't need to go upstairs. As Macho swept the beam of light up the staircase, something glimmered at the top that shouldn't have been there.

'Ah, yes.' Macho swung the light back to illuminate it. 'Very neat.' A transparent nylon cord stretched taut at ankle level across the top step.

'So drunken Macho stumbles at the top of the stairs and pitches backwards down them and, if the fall doesn't kill him, doubtless someone will be along to finish the job and remove the cord. Another tequila bottle will be found clutched in his hand, its contents liberally sprayed over and around him, as much as possible poured down his throat if he's in any condition to do any swallowing –'

'Don't!' Freddie choked.

'There's a certain symmetry about it you have to admire,' Macho said dispassionately. 'An echo of the Plantagenet Sutton demise, as another drunk falls – literally – prey to the bottle. And note the similarity of the violence of broken glass and spilled liquids in Dorian's study and Macho's kitchen. I wouldn't be surprised if a few clues surfaced to point to Macho, in one of his uncontrollable rages, as the killer.'

'Dorian isn't dead yet,' Lorinda pointed out. 'He's got a fighting chance, thanks to our finding him when we did.'

'Ah, yes. Someone's plans are going wildly awry – and all because the cats interfered in their own little way. No one could have foreseen that.' Macho started forward.

'No, please!' Lorinda pulled him back, nearly dropping Had-I as she did so. 'Don't go up there. You don't know what else might be booby-trapped. Let's wait until morning.'

'Morning?' Freddie looked at her with a strange expression. 'And how do we get through the night? I don't fancy being in my house alone – and you shouldn't, either. I think we ought to stick together for the rest of the night.'

'That's not a bad idea,' Lorinda said. 'Since I'm the only one with enough rooms, that makes it my place. I suggest you be my guests.'

'It's a bloody great idea,' Macho said. 'You're on!' He started for the door.

'Don't you want to collect your pyjamas or anything?'

'No, you're right – this is no time to go upstairs. Anyway, who's going to sleep?' Macho gave a lopsided grin. 'You two can, but I'm doing guard duty.'

'I'll just borrow something from you,' Freddie said. 'I'm not going near my place. I saw those next-door curtains twitch. The jackals are ready to pounce the instant I show up.'

They saw the fog had closed in with deadly intent as they crossed the lawns between the houses. Another hour or so and it would be so thick someone could get lost crossing that short distance.

Lorinda held her breath for a moment, but her hall light went on without a blink. Everything looked the way she had left it.

Only the cats gave the game away. Had-I's ears pricked, But-Known twisted uneasily in Freddie's arms. Roscoe gave a menacing growl.

'"Steady, the Light Brigade",' Macho said, stepping in front of the women. As one, the cats tensed and leaped from their arms to the floor. Roscoe was not the only one growling now.

'Who's there?' Lorinda called.

Silence. Deadly silence? They could not be sure. The cats might be reacting to something that had already happened. A trap already set and waiting to be sprung, while the murderer was somewhere else . . . establishing an alibi.

The lamps in the living room responded instantly when Lorinda flicked the wall switch. The room was empty . . . it appeared safe.

'In here . . .' She led the way. The cats brought up the rear, twitching and uneasy. They all looked around carefully.

Freddie peered behind every piece of furniture and even, with an apologetic grimace, under them. Lorinda looked behind the drapes, then drew them closed. If the menace were lurking outside, it was better not to give him a clear view.

Or her, she thought suddenly, unnervingly. *Lily could be as dangerous as any man.* Once there, the thought would not go away.

'Would you like a drink?' Lorinda tried to pretend it was the usual social gathering.

'Only from an unopened bottle,' Macho growled, bringing her back to reality.

'Shouldn't we search the house before we relax?' Freddie asked.

They looked at each other. Beyond the pools of comforting light thrown out by the lamps, the rest of the house loomed large and dark.

'Oh, well, perhaps not.' Freddie threw herself down on the sofa. 'Personally, I'm quite happy to spend the rest of the night right here. Who needs a bed?'

'Quite right.' Macho wandered over to the fireplace and picked up the poker, weighing it thoughtfully.

'The only unopened bottle is Scotch,' Lorinda said. 'Is that all right?' She began to break the seal.

'*Grrrrrr* . . .' All the hairs rose on Roscoe's back.

'*Sssss. . . haaaaah!*' Had-I spat, her suddenly bushy tail lashing.

But-Known's eyes seemed to grow to an enormous size as she stared at the doorway.

The cats were all watching the doorway and the shadows in the hall beyond it.

Lorinda took a tighter grip on the neck of the bottle. Freddie slid off the sofa, clutching a pillow defensively in front of her.

'You'd better come in,' Macho said loudly. 'We know you're out there!'

After a long hesitation, a female figure glided into view. She was wearing a long grey chiffon dress that seemed to float around her.

'Don't move,' she whispered huskily. She was levelling an evil-looking black gun at them. She had red hair.

'Wraith!' Freddie gasped. 'Wraith O'Reilly.'

'Marigold . . .' Lorinda said faintly.

'I think not.' Macho had taken a colder more dispassionate look at the figure, had seen past the wig and noted the bulge of the ever-present hammer at the waist beneath the flowing chiffon, the hammer that had already smashed a fish tank – and a skull.

'Gordie,' Macho said. 'Gug . . . g . . . g . . . Gordie. Dorian tried to tell us.'

'Very clever. No – don't move!' Incongruously, even though he had been recognized, Gordie kept to the husky pseudo-female whisper. 'Put down that poker.'

'Make up your mind,' Macho said. 'Do you want me not to move? Or do you want me to put down the poker?'

'Put it down! Slowly! . . . The bottle, too.' The gun moved to aim at Lorinda.

He was mad, of course. And he hated them. All of them. Even if they obeyed his every instruction, what chance did they have of surviving?

Slowly, Lorinda set the bottle down on the table. Out of the corner of her eye, she saw Macho replacing the poker.

'Sit down!' The gun moved to indicate the sofa. 'All of you. Together. Where –' He broke off, on guard as they moved towards the sofa.

Where I can keep an eye on you . . . Where you'll make a better target . . . The unspoken endings to his sentence hung in the air.

Lorinda and Freddie sat on the sofa. Macho tried to perch on the arm.

'Down!' He didn't get away with it. The gun gestured imperiously. 'On the cushions with the women.'

But, having got them where he wanted them, Gordie didn't seem to know what he wanted to do with them.

'There are too many of you,' he complained fretfully, brushing back a red lock. 'What are you all doing here? Why aren't you in your own houses?'

'We were invited here,' Freddie responded. 'Which is more than you can say.'

'That's right! You never invited me anywhere! Any of you!' It had been the wrong thing to say. It fuelled his grievance. 'I was nothing but good old Gordie. I could repair your typewriters, mend your fuses, fix your plumbing – but I wasn't good enough to mix with socially.'

'Oh, God! I've set him off.' Freddie shook her head. 'I'm sorry.'

'It's not your fault.' Macho patted her hand absently. 'Dorian's, perhaps . . . all those unrealistic promises . . .'

'Dorian!' Gordie snarled, his voice roughened. 'Dorian – the Great I-Am! I hope he rots in hell!'

'Well,' Macho said mildly. 'You did your best to send him there. I think I can understand . . . up to a point. What I don't understand is why . . .'

'Why *us?*' Freddie cut in. 'What did *we* ever do to you? All right, so we hadn't invited you anywhere. But it's early days yet. We haven't lived here all that long ourselves. We're still settling in. You might have given us a bit more time –'

The gun swung to point at her forehead, silencing her.

'I can write better than any of you!' He waited but, with the gun pointed in their direction, no one was going to give him an argument.

'I could write Wraith O'Reilly!' He pointed the gun at Freddie, then moved it on to Macho. 'I could write Macho Magee!' He aimed at Lorinda. 'And I can write Miss Petunia!'

'You certainly can,' Lorinda agreed. 'I couldn't be sure I hadn't done those chapters myself.'

'Yes, they were good, weren't they?' He preened. 'Wait till you see the suicide note I've written for you. Only ... you won't see it. No one will now.' His eyes shifted, as though he were listening to an inner voice.

'I can't do it that way now. You're all together.' His voice took on a note of complaint. 'You've ruined my plans.'

'That just about breaks my heart,' Freddie said.

'It will have to be a double murder and suicide.' Gordie looked at them assessingly and nodded. 'That will do.'

Lorinda felt soft fur brush her ankles from beneath the sofa where the cats had wisely retreated. It added to the unreality of the situation. How could this man be standing in front of them with a gun, calmly planning to kill them? And how long had he been planning it? He might be complaining now that they hadn't invited him into their lives, but that could not be the only reason. It was four months ago that he had taken her typewriter to do a minor repair and kept it longer than she had expected. He must have written the Miss Petunia chapters then. And the suicide note, too? They could have taken him to their bosoms and it wouldn't have made any difference, this had been cold-bloodedly plotted a long time before. But why? She remembered the argument for her death that had been voiced by his version of Miss Petunia.

'You cannot seriously imagine,' Lorinda said incredulously, 'that if you kill us, you'll be asked to take over writing our series?'

'Why not? I'm a good writer. I've just never been given a chance. Now I'll be right here on the spot when your publishers come down to sift through your literary estates and find out if you've left anything fit for publication. I'll be able to talk to them . . . show them examples of my work in your styles . . . Oh, I have no doubt we'll come to a satisfactory arrangement, all right.' He smiled into the future.

'You won't be able to write all three series,' Freddie objected. 'Our styles are all too different. And it would be a back-breaking schedule.'

'Oh, I expect I'll be able to take my choice,' he said casually. 'And you needn't talk to me about back-breaking. Anyone working for Dorian knows all about that.'

Yes, the last straw must have been when Dorian insisted that Gordie ought to work all night to clean up the graffiti. If it hadn't had such nightmare consequences, Lorinda might almost have felt some sympathy.

'But why kill Ondine?' Macho asked. 'She didn't have any series characters. Her gimmick was her *Un*-titles.'

'Rotten, arrogant bitch!' Gordie spat. 'She insulted me . . . treated me like dirt. She was *un*bearable, *un*civil, *un*kind, *un*charitable, *un*forgivable . . . and so' – he gave them a chilling smile – 'she was *un*done.'

Poor Ondine. Plunging down those attic stairs in a fury, bumping into Gordie, venting her wrath on him – and paying for it horribly. Lorinda shuddered.

'And Gemma had that odd, nearly fatal bout of food poisoning . . .' Freddie was following her own trail of thought.

'She rejected my short stories,' Gordie snarled. 'They were better than anything appearing in her miserable magazine, but she kept rejecting them. I didn't use enough poison,' he brooded. 'I didn't want it to be obvious and I undermeasured. She survived. Still' – he brightened – 'she has nothing to do with the magazine any more. She doesn't matter.'

'Plantagenet Sutton was pretty unbearable, too,' Macho said thoughtfully. 'If that's part of the criteria. Or did he criticize one of your unpublished manuscripts? The way he criticized, that would do it.'

'I thought he was my friend.' Gordie's eyes misted. 'He was the only one who ever asked me in for a drink and talked to me about writing. He was going to help me get started. He got the case of tequila for me, he thought the idea was really funny. Upsetting all you people, using your own characters against you, destabilizing you . . . He wanted to see what effect it would have on your books.'

'Yes,' Macho said. 'Plantagenet would think it was a howling great joke. I knew he was in it somewhere.'

'Only . . . he lost his sense of humour.' Gordie's eyes clouded. 'He said I could have killed Jack, pushing him into that bonfire. He didn't understand . . .'

'I suppose Jack had insulted you, too,' Freddie sighed. 'What a sensitive little flower you are.'

'Sutton said I was going too far . . . getting too dangerous,' Gordie complained. 'He was going to tell Dorian, but not until he got back from the cruise. I followed him up to the Manor House that night – I knew he'd drink too much. And, if he didn't, he could always be persuaded to have another. He was glad to see me when he rolled out of Dorian's. He thought I'd help him home. He didn't notice that I kept him in the cold, talking. When he did, I offered him a flask. It only took a couple of swallows before he passed out. Then I lowered him to the ground and walked away. Nature did the rest. It's lucky it was such a cold night.'

There was bemused silence at his idea of luck.

'It keeps coming back to Dorian,' Lorinda reflected. 'He found you, brought you here, installed you as Jack of all Trades and resident caretaker at Coffers Court . . .' Gordie, who could deal with anything mechanical or electrical – even to the extent of rigging false messages on an answering machine and then wiping them.

'I thought I was going to be his protégé,' Gordie said. 'But he only wanted a carpenter-mechanic who'd be on twenty-four-hour call.'

'Have you got that mess over the doorway cleaned up yet?' Macho had evidently decided to try to rattle Gordie. For a moment, he even sounded like Dorian.

'Yes. No. It's good enough.' Gordie looked at him with active hate. 'Dorian isn't going to care any more.'

'I don't see why Dorian cared so much in the first place,' Lorinda said.

'That's right,' Freddie agreed. 'Why was he so concerned? What was it to him?'

'You don't know?' Gordie was gratified at being able to tell them. 'Dorian owns . . . owned . . . Coffers Court. He bought it as an investment at the same time he bought the Manor House.

He also bought a controlling interest in the estate agent's. He had his fingers in every pie in Brimful Coffers.'

'Estate agent's! So that's why Dorian had the keys when he showed me the house,' Lorinda remembered. 'I thought he was just being very thoughtful. But he had a personal interest and . . .' She caught the smug expression crossing Gordie's face. 'You have those duplicate keys now – that's how you got in here. How you got in everywhere.'

'Who'd bother about good old Gordie roaming around doing his odd jobs? Not that anyone ever saw me going in and out. I made certain of that.'

'In your usual efficient way,' Freddie jibed.

'That's enough!' He swung the gun from one to the other of them. 'I know what you're doing. You're humouring me – playing for time. I've read this scene often enough in your books. But you could keep me talking all night and it wouldn't help you. No one's coming to save you. You know everything now and –'

'Just how do you propose to explain why three reasonably happy and successful people should wind up in this ridiculous murder-and-suicide situation you're trying to set up?' Macho still had traces of Dorian's cold disdain in his speech.

'Happens all the time,' Gordie said. 'The Eternal Triangle . . . a *crime passionnel* –'

Macho's guffaw cut him off. After a moment, Freddie joined in the scornful laughter.

'You'll never get away with that,' Macho said. 'It wouldn't stand up for ten minutes. If that's the best you can do, no wonder you never sold a book.'

'No, please –' Lorinda saw what he was doing. He was trying to draw Gordie's fire, hoping it would give them a chance to escape. 'Please, Lance—'

'Lance?' That threw Gordie into more confusion than Macho's needling.

'My name is Lancelot Dalrymple.' He met Gordie's eyes coldly. 'If you weren't so stupid, you'd know that no one could be named Macho Magee.'

'Don't call me stu—'

The doorbell rang suddenly. The cats dashed for the door, knocking Gordie off-balance. His finger tightened on the trigger and the first shot went wild.

'Hey!' Fists began hammering on the door. 'What's going on in there? Open up!'

Freddie threw a cushion at the gun and another shot went wide. Lorinda threw a cushion from the other side. Macho dived for the poker. There was a crash of breaking glass.

'Hey!' Jack Jackley thrust aside the drapes and stumbled into the room. 'What the hell is going on here?'

'Grab him!' Macho shouted, as Gordie tried to run for the window. He lashed out with the poker, knocking the gun from Gordie's hand.

'Got him!' Jack and Macho wrestled Gordie to the floor and sat on him. The doorbell pealed again.

'Would somebody like to let Karla in,' Jack said, 'and tell us what the hell is going on?'

14

'Oooohh, champagne!' Marigold gasped in excitement at the display in the centre of the tea table. 'And caviar! In Daddy's silver ice bucket! Oh, Petunia, have we got another case? Is it a special case?'

'We've got the rest of the case of champagne,' Lily said. 'I saw it when I was putting my bicycle on the back porch. Gift from a grateful client, was it?'

'No.' Miss Petunia drew a deep breath. 'I bought it myself.'

'Petunia!' Marigold said reproachfully. 'And you're the one who's always lecturing me about our budget!'

'We have no budget any more, my dears,' Miss Petunia said. 'We'll never have to pinch a penny again. We're rich!'

'Petunia! Whatever can you mean?'

'Great-great-grandpa's South Sea Bubble shares come good at last have they?' Lily frowned in thought. 'Or was it the Groundnut Scheme?'

'My dears.' Miss Petunia beamed upon her sisters. 'I am delighted to be able to tell you that the Blossom Cottage Syndicate has won the Lottery!'

'The Lottery, eh?' Lily took it calmly. 'I thought some of those numbers sounded familiar the other night.'

'Did they?' Marigold wrinkled her brow. 'Oh, dear, I just have no head for figures at all.'

'I didn't want to draw your attention to it until I was absolutely certain, but now I have had confirmation.' Miss Petunia adjusted her pince-nez and took a deep breath. There were still moments when she felt slightly giddy. 'There is no doubt about it. We have won ten million pounds!'

'Ten?' Marigold's eyes grew huge. 'Ten millioooooh . . .'

'Catch her, Lily,' Miss Petunia said.

After Marigold revived, they opened the champagne and began making plans.

'Won't have to move, will we?' Lily asked anxiously. 'Rather like the old cottage. Used to it.'

'Oh, no!' Marigold cried. 'I couldn't bear to live anywhere else!'

'No, no,' Miss Petunia reassured them – she had been giving the matter some thought. 'Of course we'll stay here. We might, however, add on to it a bit. Or buy some of the vacant land behind the cottage and build a studio for Marigold to paint in and a gymnasium for you, Lily.'

'Oh, and a lovely laboratory for you, Petunia!' Marigold's eyes glowed. 'Just what you need to help you solve the awful crimes we stumble over.'

'*Are* we going to keep on solving crimes now?' Lily asked. 'We won't need to, you know. Not if we're rich. Are we going to retire?'

'It *would* be rather nice not to have to go to Saints Etheldreda and Dowsabel *every* day,' Marigold said wistfully.

'Mmmm, yes, but I'd rather miss the old place. Wouldn't like to break all the ties.' Lily brightened. 'Perhaps we could cut down to two or three days a week.'

'I'm sure you can do better than that,' Miss Petunia said. 'When they hear about our stroke of luck, I wouldn't be at all surprised if they allowed you to take early retirement and then invited you to serve on the Board of Governors.'

'Oh, what fun! We could give out the prizes at Prize Day!' Marigold clapped her hands. 'Oh – and we could even donate some of the prizes!'

'Steady on, old girl,' Lily said. 'Don't want to go too far. Must say, though, can't wait to see Old Gumboots's face when she hears the news.'

'We can make all these decisions later,' Miss Petunia said. 'Before that, I think we should give ourselves a glorious holiday. What would you say to a round-the-world cruise?'

'Oh, yes! Yes!' Marigold began dancing around the room in her excitement. 'What a wonderful idea!' Her eyes grew dreamy. 'Just think of those tropical nights, with all those handsome ship's officers, and a full moon, and a romantic port, and . . .'

'Have to keep a sharp eye out for fortune hunters now.' Lily gave her sisters a sharp look.

'I'm aware of that, dear,' Miss Petunia said. 'You needn't worry, we won't let anything separate us.'

'What about staterooms? Only take two people, don't they?'

'We shall reserve the penthouse suite . . . with its own balcony.' Miss Petunia gave a happy sigh. 'Expense is no longer a consideration. We'll have a wonderful time.'

'They have a gym on board, haven't they? And deck games . . . tours of the engine room . . . the bridge . . .' Lily began to get enthusiastic.

'Shopping on shore excursions,' Marigold said. 'And we won't have to worry about how much things cost. Then there'll be cocktails with the Captain. Oh! – and we might even sit at his table.'

'With ten million pounds, I should think we might.' Miss Petunia bestowed a fond smile on her sisters. It would be a very pleasant trip. There would be a library on board, guest lecturers, the latest films, craft courses, talks for hobbyists . . .

Yes, and who knew? There might even be a mystery or two to solve. Many people travelled . . . and for many different reasons. It was not beyond the realm of possibility.

'Fill the glasses again, Lily, dear,' Miss Petunia said. 'And we will drink a toast to the future. This isn't the end of our little adventures. It is –

the beginning

Lorinda pulled the page from the typewriter and looked over her shoulder. Nothing moved in the shadows of the room as she snapped on her desk lamp. The only sound in the study was Had-I's contented purr from the corner of the desk where she lay curled. But-Known sat at her feet, looking hopeful. The finality with which Lorinda had torn the page from the machine had told her that the day's stint was over and food was imminent.

'Just wait a minute,' Lorinda told her. 'I just want to do one more thing before I go out . . .'

Freddie was giving a Farewell Party for the Jackleys, who were leaving for the Continent in the morning. It would be a small party, comprising of those who were left. Rhylla had already taken Clarice and departed for the States, considering a trip to Disneyland a small price to pay for the relief of delivering Clarice back to her reluctant parents. Dorian would not be there, either; his sister had taken him home with her to complete his convalescence. Somehow, in relating this to Karla, Freddie had made it sound as though Dorian would never fully recover and would require nursing for the rest of his life.

It was amazing how quickly Karla's ardour had cooled. It seemed like only the next day that she and Jack had decided that they ought to visit the mainland of Europe, since they were so close to it – and it would make for a better travel book than a rather parochial story of a year in a sleepy English village. Later, perhaps, they might make more of their stay in Brimful Coffers but, with Gordie likely to be judged unfit to plead, the excitement and publicity surrounding the recent events was already dying down.

Lorinda looked over her shoulder again. Nothing. She listened, but heard only Had-I's purr. It was silly of her, of course – it had all been Gordie's doing. The Spinster Sibling Sleuths would not return to wreak vengeance on her – now or ever. But it was better to be safe . . .

After a long pause, she rolled a fresh sheet of paper into the typewriter and began.

CHAPTER ONE

The sun sparkled in a bright blue sky and a spanking new carriage waited outside the front door. It was a splendid morning for a new enterprise.

All was in readiness and the woman smiled to herself as she fitted the newly engraved cards into her card case. In her mind was the list of the houses where she would call to leave her card. Someone in each house would have good reason to be interested.

A sweet and thrilling excitement rose in her, sweeping away the doubts to which she had been prey. Alas for the ingratitude of humankind; she had been snatched back from the depths, she had been lifted to a position of respectability and honour and . . . Bah! she had been bored.

If all went well from this day onwards, however, she need never know tedium again. She gazed fondly at the black copperplate engraving on the top card before she closed the lid of her card case. It read:

Becky Sharp
Discreet Inquiries Undertaken